STEPPING STONES

BY

M. GUMBLE

Published in 2023 by FeedARead.com Publishing

First Edition

A CIP catalogue record for this title is available from the British
Library.

STEPPING

STONES

BY

M. GUMBLE

CHAPTER ONE

FROM

SATIN TO SERGE

R uth shook her head and sighed when she saw pinned to a news seller's stand in large letters a sheet reading;

CALL GIRL CONVICTED OF DOUBLE MURDER IN
PORN FILM SCANDAL

Handcuffed between two uniformed officers, she waited while they unlocked the entrance to the reception hall. Groups of women saw their approach; a subdued murmur swelled into a sinister growl. As the escort party ushered her through, several inmates blocked their progress. Concealing all three from the duty warders' view. The hairs on Ruth's neck stood on end as they closed in.

The senior officer had to keep control and assert her authority. "Come on, you lot, move aside!" She pushed against the encirclement of bodies and ordered: "out of the way... Do as I say; I'm telling you for the last time, let us pass."

A burly inmate held an arm around the officer's neck and jerked her backwards, "Or you'll do what, crap face?"

She kept her tight around her throat; until her victims' knees buckled, and she collapsed to the floor, gasping for breath. Almost taking Ruth and her colleague with her.

With rasping gasps, she drew in gulps of reviving air, staggered to her feet, rubbed her bruised throat, and tried rational persuasion, "Come on now, this is lunacy. None of us wants trouble. The governor will deal with Page. I guarantee we won't say a word." She threw her free arm across Ruth's chest to protect her charge.

With rasping gasps, she drew in gulps of reviving air, staggered to her feet, rubbed her bruised throat, and tried rational persuasion, "Come on now, this is lunacy. None of us wants trouble. The governor will deal with Page. I guarantee we won't say a word." She threw her free arm across Ruth's chest to protect her charge.

Her colleague, hoping to cool the situation, gritted her teeth and implored, "Girls, don't be foolish. Page isn't worth more time or loss of privileges. We understand how you feel, but acting like this will bring you nothing but trouble. Just step aside, and we'll forget about this."

An inmate stepped forward and pushed the officer's restraining arm away. "Yes, right, like hell, you will. There's only one way to deal with this piece of shit." Her fist landed a stunning blow to Ruth's face.

The shackled trio disappeared beneath a storm of fists and feet in a split second. The commotion alerted duty warders, who dashed over to restore order.

Ruth remained in solitary confinement until her court appearance. Because of public outrage against her and hostile press coverage, her request to attend Lucy's burial was refused.

On arrival at the Old Bailey, a crowd lining the pavements hurled missiles and abuse at the van. Ruth couldn't fail to hear them but felt no emotion. No one could despise her as much as she loathed herself; her heart had died along with Lucy.

In the packed courtroom, the rumbling antagonism of spectators persisted. The judge pounded his gavel and roared to restore calm, but loud, aggressive voices ignored him. He retired to his chambers, returning only when the court officials cleared the most vociferous protesters' gallery.

Asked by the court clerk to respond to the charge of Rego's murder, Ruth turned to face the jury. Her face, animated in savage defiance, hissed, "Yes, guilty. I meant to kill that beast and do it again and again."

The clerk insisted on a single response to the charge.

Ruth fixed cold hard eyes on him and, with a sardonic sneer, replied

"Guilty as charged."

The clerk followed with the secondary charge of Lucy's murder.

Her bowed head shot up, both hands grabbed the dock rail, his words like a dagger pierced through her heart, white-knuckled, trembling to her core. Ruth screeched, "No. Never! Never!"

Overcome with anguish, she crumpled in the dock. Her sobs were met by shouts of ridicule from the gallery. When she regained her composure, the clerk asked once more for an answer to the charge. Ruth whispered, "Not Guilty," then retreated into her safe blanket of denial, stony-faced and silent.

During the long weeks that followed, Ruth paid no heed to the evidence given against her. Apart from reacting to her father's tirade in the witness box, she remained silent. Despite the repeated urging from her inexperienced young barrister, Ruth gave him nothing he could use in her favour. He maintained that Ruth's mind had been unstable at the point of Rego's murder.

He urged the jury to consider reducing the charge to manslaughter.

The jury returned to their places; the foreman rose.

The concluding formalities followed.

"Have you arrived at a unanimous verdict?" the clerk of the court asked.

"Yes."

"On the charge of the murder of Reginald Calvo, how do you find the prisoner guilty or not guilty?"

"Not guilty of premeditated murder but guilty of manslaughter."

An excited hum ran around the court.

"On the charge of implication by negligence in the death of Lucy Page, how do you find the prisoner guilty or not guilty?"

"Guilty."

The verdicts received loud cheers and foot-stamping approval from the public gallery. The judge called for order and warned that anyone causing further disturbances would follow those in the cells below. In due course, the court became silent, waiting...

Satisfied, the steely-faced Judge spoke. "Ruth Page, this jury has found you guilty of the manslaughter of Reginald Calvo. Also, by gross negligence involved in the death of your daughter, Lucy Page."

He paused for a moment to issue a further warning to the public gallery as the muttered jeering of approval intensified.

He turned his attention back to Ruth, standing with her head bowed and motionless in the dock. His tone was firm and even. "You will return to this court to answer additional warrants for arson and murder standing against you. Your legal representative will advise you of the hearing dates later." The gallery spectator's voices were silenced at this revelation. The Judge adjusted his robes and fixed his gaze on Ruth. "Until psychiatric evaluations are completed, you will remain in a secure facility. Be assured that at this stage, you will face a custodial sentence. You have shown no remorse for these offences; do you want to say anything now?"

Ruth's thoughts still tortured her with the last image of her daughter, motionless and pale in her arms. She stood silent, unaware of the officer's firm grip on her arms as they led her away.

While waiting for transport, her barrister informed her of the procedure to deal with outstanding charges. Ruth stared at the stark walls and ignored his droning voice.

. It was late afternoon when they ushered Ruth out of a side entrance to a waiting van with her head covered by a blanket.

Two officers struggled through the jostling hordes lining the pavement. A brick caught Ruth's upraised forearm. Eggs and stones hurled at her found their target. After a brief tussle, the officers pushed her into a cubicle of the prison van. With press bulbs flashing through the blackened windows, it sped away.

On arrival, all the prisoners were marshalled to a reception building. Ordered to wait in line while the officers filled out forms to record their personal details. Afterwards, they were taken to the shower cubicles for individual internal body checks for any concealments. Each new inmate was handed a clothing bundle and plastic eating essentials. They deliberately left Ruth to the last. Two warders held her bent over while the third performed the body examination.

The woman was too rough. "Ouch!" Ruth yelled as she twisted in protest. "Take it easy bitch; having a cheap thrill, are you?"

"Close your dirty mouth!" the woman thrust harder.

"That's enough," Ruth cried with pain.

"Hold still, just doing our job," came a brusque reply.

"What's your problem, don't like whores?"

"Oh, no, lady, we got lots of working girls in here, nicked for soliciting and such like." With one final hard, unnecessary push, the examination finished.

Ruth, inflamed by their conduct, lunged across the shower room, her fists flying, shrieking abuse. But she was no match for them.

They pushed her away. She stumbled on the wet floor and scrambled to her feet, full of indignation, "Great fat pigs. You can't treat me like this; I have rights. I'll report to you."

"As if anybody's going to believe the likes of you. Got too much mouth. You'll learn to respect your betters," one roared. Each one took hold of a saturated towel and used it to strike her bare body. When they'd had enough, they left her sprawled on the floor with snarled instructions to get dressed.

Racked with pain, Ruth dried herself and slipped into the drab garment. Fingered her soft, expensive lingerie and breathed an involuntary sigh. *It will be a long time before I'll have silk close to my skin again.* When she returned to the waiting area, all the other inmates had moved on to their assigned cells. She then handed over her possessions through the hatch as instructed to be recorded before storage.

"This suit needs to be cleaned before storage," the officer barked. "The cost will come from your work allowance, understand?"

Ruth nodded in response.

"Right then, check this record; sign at the bottom," ordered the gruff woman.

11

In a side room with an unobstructed reception view, Ruth waited for the prison doctor to look at the cut on her arm. Two prisoners carrying mops and buckets passed the room.

Through the glass sides, they caught sight of the solitary woman. One nudged her companion. Ruth's sharp ears picked up their conversation.

"Stef, it's her, Ruth Page. You know, the brass we've read about. Wasted her kid for cash. Love to get my hands on that bitch."

"You'll be lucky, Jean; they won't put her on our wing. They're bound to stick her in solitary, so no one can get to her."

"Now is the only chance we'll be in spitting distance. This is too good to miss."Jean pushed her companion forward

"In your dreams, Jean, best forget it; she's not worth the hassle. We'll cop it if we touch her," Stef protested, glancing at the warders behind the reception desk.

"So, what?! Be worth it, are you with me?"

Too afraid for Jean to say no, she nodded in agreement. The reception officers glanced over as the two inmates slipped into the room, ignored the pair, and continued their paperwork.

Ruth gritted her teeth, drew a sharp breath, and clutched her stomach with cold, sweaty hands as it churned and rumbled. She then swallowed back the vomit that rose in her gullet. Gripped with fear, she called out to attract the officer's attention, but the reception hatch slammed shut. The officers had no intention of helping her.

"Sweet Jesus! " Ruth groaned out loud. "You're on your own, girl. Deal with it." she squeezed the sides of the bench and waited for the inevitable.

Jean shuffled over, her intent clear, leaned down, broad lips curled and snarled; her foul breath made Ruth gag. "You're Ruth Page, ain't yer?" narrow, spiteful pig-eyes glared into Ruth's ashen face.

Ruth looked up at her adversary; she had to bluff her way through this. So, she swallowed hard and sneered in response. "What's it to you?"

"Bastard," Jean exploded, "I'll show you what!" She lashed out with her fist and brought it down onto Ruth's upturned face, rocking her sideways.

Ruth sprang to her feet, her mouth parched with fear and tried to speak, but the words caught in her throat. She wiped away warm blood trickling down her chin. Sick to her stomach with dread, Ruth clenched her hands, ignoring the pain as her nails sank deep into both palms. Jean lifted her fist again, expecting Ruth to shy away. But she stepped nearer, her unflinching green eyes parallel with Jeans.

With her last ounce of courage, she sneered, "You know nothing about me. Why don't you take your fat, lard arse out of here?"

Both women **stared** at her in total astonishment. This was not the response Jean was used to. Ruth, standing steady, demanded, "Go on, clear off. Mind your own damn business."

Indignant with fury, Jean grabbed her windpipe with broad, powerful fingers. Forced her backwards, pounded Ruth's head against the wall, "We read all about you, whoring bitch. Did you expect news stays outside these walls? Most women here would give their eyes and teeth just to catch sight of their kids?" She leaned her scowling face close to Ruth's and spat, "Sold yours for dirty fucking money. Bastard slag."

Steph jumped up and down excitedly and yelled, "Go on, Jean, give it to her."

The pressure on Ruth's throat intensified. Unable to breathe, Ruth brought up her knee in desperation and thrust it into Jean's groin. Bent double, Jean cried out in agony and stumbled back. "Useless piece of piss, you'll pay for that." She reached down, picked up her bucket, and rushed at Ruth.

Ruth sidestepped, locked her hands together and struck the back of Jeans' head with all her might. Jean staggered to her feet, steadied herself, and glared with murderous intent at Ruth.

Ruth struggled to fend off the pulsating terror that threatened to consume her. Her previous courage was abandoned, but with difficulty, she hung on to her nerve. Trembling from head to toe forced scorn to flash from wide, reckless eyes as she stood her ground. "Satisfied? Get back under the stone you slid from." Ruth tossed back her head and challenged, "Well, just going to stand there!"

Surprised by her companion's unaccustomed hesitation, Stef sniggered. Jean turned, glowered at her subordinate, who shrank back, then lowered her eyes in submission.

Jean roared, "Baby killer!" sprang at Ruth, delivering a ferocious headbutt and a savage punch to her stomach.

Ruth recoiled with the force of the impact and toppled against the bench. It crashed to the stone-tiled floor. Any desire for caution was forgotten; both women used their feet and fists to strike her. The reception desk officers had slyly witnessed the attack but made no move to interfere. By chance, other officers going by overheard the commotion and charged in to restrain Jean and Stef. They rushed Ruth to the infirmary wing, pursued by a flood of curses from the unrepentant women.

Several days later, two officers accompanied her to the governor's office. As the party entered the room, a woman with mousey brown, grey-streaked cropped hair stood before a glass bookcase, studying Ruth's reflection. Their eyes met; like twin lightning bolts, the older woman's eyes flashed with venomous scorn. Ruth stared insolently back, shaken to her core by such oblivious loathing. *What the hell's up with her?*

The Guv'nor bit down on her lips to halt the words of condemnation that threatened to burst out. Eased back her shoulders and gulped hard to compose herself.

The officers steered Ruth towards a large paper-strewn desk, then positioned themselves behind her.

"Prisoner Page, ma'am, here for her interview."

Head held high, Ruth waited. The older woman crossed the room, sat poker straight in her chair, and rearranged the documents on her desk. Peered over tiny, rimless glasses, cold, sunken eyes studied Ruth; her expression showed revulsion as if she shouted the words in her head.

At last, she spoke. "My name is Miss Carter. I'm in charge of this establishment. You will address me as ma'am. You will be here, Page, until the duration of your sentence is decided."

Ruth interrupted, "I want to make a formal complaint against the treatment I received from your officers. I have my rights, and I consider they acted incorrectly."

Miss Carter waved her hand in dismissal of the accusations. "I have a complete report of the incident here. It states it was you who attacked my officers; they restrained you without unnecessary force."

Ruth indignantly pointed to her bruised arms and legs. "Oh, really?" she scoffed. "What about all the marks I have on my body? Did the fairies put them there? I demanded you reprimand them and take my complaint seriously."

"I listen to all valid complaints; according to this document, the injuries you have are the direct consequence of other inmates attacking you, and that is all." She snapped shut the file. "The matter is closed."

The Guvnor shuffled loose papers on her desk. She dropped the file back on her desk, "Due to your crimes, I am placing you in C block, our top-security wing. Exercise and meals will be taken alone to protect you and my officers." Took off her glasses and stated. "You won't be here long, Page, provided you follow the rules. I should have no cause to see you again." A curt wave indicated the interview had ended.

Stung by the woman's caustic tone and manner, a surge of adrenaline pumped through Ruth's veins. She wasn't about to leave without having her say.

"Suits me fine not yearning for your company either, ugly old hag." Ruth wagged a slender finger in her direction, "Miss Carter, is it? I'm not surprised. The word 'Miss' says it all," Ruth, with a flourish, waved her hand. "I've had days you'll never experience and nights with hot-blooded men in my bed far beyond your wildest sexual fantasies," Now, in full stride, she dashed towards the desk. "What's more-" The officers dragged her back and pushed her to the floor.

Flabbergasted, Miss Carter slammed both fists down on the desk in disbelief. A prisoner had never spoken to her in such a manner. The blood rushed to her head, and the veins in her temples visibly pulsated. Her sunken face flushed with suppressed indignation.

She marched over to where Ruth lay sprawled on the floor. "Still weak, Page? On your feet, woman, I'll give you one piece of advice you'll follow: learn to curtail that vicious mouth. You'll gain no friends here in or out of uniform," She regained control, straightened up, smoothed back her sparse hair, and drew in a breath. "While you're here, I must ensure your safety, but there are no guarantees." Steel-grey eyes bore into Ruth's as she mocked. "As for appearance, old age comes to us all. Looks fade rapidly in a place like this. Be prepared to have grey hair and a lined face before you're set free."

Ruth opened her mouth to respond, but Guvnor's harsh tone stopped her. "Enough! You had your say." She gestured to the officers with a brusque wave, "Get that rubbish out of here."

C block an old part of the original prison, needed complete modernisation. Dismal, gloomy landings with waist-high railings ran around the building, connected by steel lattice stairways separated by solid iron doors at each level.

On the third level, the officers stopped. One opened a cupboard, passed Ruth a wash bag and a rough towel, and then took her to a cell. It contained a paint-peeled, black metal bed. A faded

18

mattress, one thin pillow, and a single wool blanket. A tiny sink in a corner of the cell sat beneath a narrow shelf. Rolling out the thin mattress tucked inside, she found a single, off-white sheet. *Hum! A home from home, Ruth mused.*

Alone for the first time since her capture. Out of reach from the glare of flashbulbs and the loud, aggressive reporters. Ruth had hungered for so long for this solitude. Stretched out on the narrow bed, thankful for the privacy of this quiet cell. Hot, salty tears of relief burnt trails down her bruised face. Angry at this weakness, she brushed them aside, got off the bed and paced around the sparse cell, striving to fend off the emotions that threatened to overwhelm her.

Ruth opened the wash bag and removed a small bar of unscented soap and a rough hand towel. Turning on the tap at the tiny sink, she cupped her hands to catch the ice cold water. Splashed it on her face and throat. She pulled aside her thick, auburn hair and let more water trickle down her back. Refreshed and back in control, she twisted the now damp dress into place. *Been in worse situations than this; at least these cells are warm and dry. I don't have to see a single soul unless I choose. What can harm me now?* Ruth arched her back as a spider scuttled up the wall and across the ceiling. "Yes, run away, little creature," she advised dryly. The spider disappeared through a crack in the ceiling. "Smart move, spider. Her mouth twisted into a wry smile, she shrugged her shoulders and mumbled: "Who needs friends?" she frowned at her absurdity, "God's sake, talking to a blasted spider now?"

Ruth glanced down at the shapeless dress and hauled it close to her body. She passed one hand over firm breasts down to a slender waist. Gathering up the coarse material as her fingers roamed over narrow hips. "Absolutely not Haute couture," she reflected, " I'll only be in my forties when I get out. Huh! wrinkles indeed. Stupid old cow, if I take care of myself, I'll still look good." Smiling with satisfaction, she tossed her head and ran her fingers through her luxurious hair.

A band of dust swirled in a ray of evening sunlight as it passed through the narrow-barred window. Ruth flopped down onto the bed, and all elation vanished. She mumbled, "Forty. Christ. What a fool. The old bag was right; I'll be old and haggard. My life used up in this hole." Ruth pressed her aching head against the metal bed rail and groaned. "Oh, God! All the clues were there." As weariness overcame her, a feeble moan escaped, "Why didn't I take heed?" She woke with a start; the sun had just caressed the horizon, its bright rays heralding another day. *There'll be hundreds of dawns before I'm free; I must deal with that. I mustn't think of Lucy, but I feel her scramble under the sheets and tiny fingers pulling at my hair to wake me and hear **her** infectious giggle*

Ruth clasped her hand to her mouth to suppress a scream of misery; *oh God, what's to become of me*? She crossed over to the washbasin and disapproved at the pallid image. "Come on, Ruth, my girl, pull yourself together; you'll be piling years on your face wallowing in this self-pity." Swiftly turned to straighten her bed, but her resolve faltered, and she dropped back onto the bed. She buried her face in the pillow, her mind crowded with images of her dark future. *Lucy would still be alive if I hadn't gone to the studio that day. I let myself be taken in along a fairy tale path by a mother's vanity and stupid pride.* Stark reality forced her to accept the role she played in Lucy's death. *How can I endure living without her? There's no one else to blame. I could have, should have, protected her.*

Tears of remorse drenched her cheeks. She clutched her chest to escape the searing agony that bit into a hurting soul. Dropped to her knees, curled her arms around her body and swayed back and forth in absolute desolation. Her head pounded like a thousand drums beat into her brain, a sharp rhythm until ready to spurt out. She couldn't shut out the disturbing nightmare vision of Lucy, lying throughout the endless hours of that torturous night like a shattered doll in her arms. Unable to accept her sweet baby was dead. She deluded herself into thinking that if love can perform miracles, perhaps Lucy may have returned to her. Why had she allowed that woman to take her? The news vendor's headlines flashed like a neon sign against the brick wall.

MOTHER CONVICTED OF DOUBLE MURDER IN CHILD PORN SCANDAL.

A scream of denial sprang from her tormented soul; Ruth covered her ears to block out the sound. Each wail and scream twisted on, shriller and louder, blood-curdling echoes tearing through the empty corridors of the silent prison. A pair of powerful arms lifted and dragged her away, then a sharp pain before swallowed by a welcoming void of darkness.

CHAPTER TWO

A LOST CHILDHOOD

When Ruth regained consciousness, leather restraints were holding down her arms. Others crossed her body. After a frenetic, futile struggle, she remained still, her mind in turmoil. She recalled how her father demanded that his sinful daughter be shut away from the witness box for the rest of her life.

He claimed, "We always did our best, gave the child every advantage. No parents could have done more; how did she repay us? By running away, but not before she stole our life savings. She never gave a moment's thought to the misery and anxiety she caused. We've had nightmares for years, not knowing if our only child was dead or alive." His tone, thick and cracked with emotion, he whimpered, "See what she did!" He turned to the jury and pointed to a long, ragged scar on his face. "I chastised her for shoplifting, a mild correction." His voice dropped to a hoarse whisper, "Without warning or reason, she attacked me with a knife." Taking out a handkerchief as if to wipe tears away. "Though with the Lord's help, I could have guided her back from self-destruction and excused all her crimes."

He raised water-filled eyes to the gallery. "As responsible parents, we sought to explain right from wrong, but she led a lifestyle of depravity." As he left the witness box, he called, "May God forgive me! I urge you to lock her away where she can do no further harm. It grieves me to say this, but my daughter is a depraved, insane, dangerous, vile woman who crushed a loving mother's heart."

The following day, the prison doctor examined her and ordered the restraints removed and confirmed she could return to C block the following day.

Alone in her cell, images flashed across her mind, reliving the events that led to this moment in her turbulent life.

She shuddered, recalling her terror as when just six years old, her father stood over her bed late at night, turned back the blankets, and raised her nightdress. Feeling still the chilling waves of horror as his hands moved little by little along her young naked body, fondling her while she remained still, traumatised by his menace.

Employed as a solicitor's clerk, William Page discovered her mother, Priscilla, had recently inherited a considerable fortune. With a prosperous business in the capital and a splendid country house, he determined to marry her and live a comfortable life. Tall and handsome, he was able to take his pick of eager village girls. Fifteen years his senior, Priscilla couldn't believe her luck and welcomed his unexpected proposal as a reprieve from the empty years ahead. She soon regretted her decision; her husband was a brutal, aggressive man with no tenderness. Early in the marriage, she learnt his temper was fiery and out of control, as his thick red hair.

Priscilla became pregnant but flatly refused to go near the child. Instantly ordered the waiting wet nurse to take the creature away.

They hired a woman from the village to take care of the baby's essential needs. The nurse had no affection for her charge and used her time gossiping downstairs with her mother. Often leaving Ruth in her room, wet and hungry. Ruth's mother tolerated her husband's brutal advances until he was tired of the passive creature she became. The young housemaids were more than willing to satisfy his demands. She couldn't tolerate the humiliation of his infidelities and found an excuse to dismiss them. She replaced all staff with older, unattractive women. He had to go into town and pay for his pleasure. Neither parent had ever held her or shown any affection. Ignored and neglected in her early years, Ruth grew up unloved and unwanted.

Each Sunday evening, her father led a prayer meeting in the lounge. Ruth had to sit still and silent in the corner. Forced to endure the tuneless singing and relentless sermons. A dour-faced tutor called each day at her father's insistence on an excellent education. Any mistakes corrected by a ruler brought down on the back of Ruth's hands. Apart from shopping for clothes and compulsory trips to the Sunday church service, she saw no one.

Ruth lingered as parents collected their children from the nursery school with welcoming smiles and hugs; she wondered why she wasn't loved in the same way. While eavesdropping on the stairs, she heard her mother complain to the housekeeper about how the pregnancy had ruined her figure.

Her voice hushed, confided, "I never wanted a child. I tried all the old wives' tales to get rid of it, but nothing worked. Then he found out I was pregnant, and that was an end to it." She drew in a shuddering gasp, "He would have killed me if he found out I tried to abort. The religious bigot calls it a sin and murder, but they don't carry them." She described the long and painful confinement in detail and how she couldn't bear to hold or touch the wailing creature. Concluded smugly, "When the registrar handed me the birth certificate, I screwed it up and flung it into a corner; I've never entered that room again."

Ruth ran back to her room; the shock of rejection seared her heart, and for the last time in her young life, she grieved for a mother's love. When all the child's tears had dried, it sowed the

26

seeds of lifelong hatred. Friendless and isolated, the empty years passed. Ruth cultivated her secret world where laughter, love, and happiness were all hers. Mother, always busy with her church duties, neither knew nor cared where Ruth was. Her father left early each day and drove into town most evenings. With this upbringing, she became an expert in deception and learnt to lie convincingly.

Every weekend Ruth sneaked out of the house and watched teenagers dressed in up-to-date fashions enjoy dancing to the latest music through the village hall windows. Full of envy, she yearned to join in but was afraid some busybody would be sure to tell her parents.

The lady who ran the village post office often showed her the colourful stamps from faraway places before her husband delivered the letters. Enchanted, Ruth promised herself she would see them all one day. From the parish board, she yanked off posters of local events. In her daydreams, she pretended she was there, having fun with people her age. Discarded magazines often left behind in the bus shelter offered her the ultimate pleasure. Ruth searched every page, fascinated by the photographs of the glamorous models. Ruth read all the articles with keen interest and saved the most attractive. She took them home and stuffed them away from prying eyes behind her wardrobe. Each night in her prayers, she vowed to find the means and courage to run away. *I'll go to London; even being homeless must be better than this.*

Ruth had peeked unseen through a crack in the door at her father putting money away in his desk. *"I'll need money for the train to get out. He's got plenty more,"* she wrestled in her mind trying to balance the risk against the pleasure of success. *"Would I dare take some? If he catches me, it will be just another belting. I already get plenty of those."*

Her mother often told the staff many keys fitted other doors to not bother her and just use another key if one got lost. Ruth had secretly tried her room key in the study door, and it worked. The more she considered this dangerous plot, the more the prospect of running away and finding happiness appealed, despite the risk. Searched through her belongings and found a pair of small scissors, a thin knitting needle, and long hairpins. Ruth lay back on her bed, fingering these items, and muttered, "One might open that lock. I'm going to try." A thrill of excitement shot through her, visualising this bold action breathed, "He'll never guess I'd have the nerve to rob him".

Ruth had her chance when both parents were out, hearing only the servants chatting in the kitchen as they never bothered her whereabouts. Ruth's hand trembled as she turned the cold metal doorknob. The clock ticked loudly in the corridor, like a steady heartbeat. Nervously ran her tongue over her dry mouth and tightened her fingers around the doorknob. She pushed it open. It creaked slightly but sounded like a clap of thunder to Ruth. She dropped her lock, picking tools; they clattered on the rugless floor. As she waited, she tried to quieten her breathing. Ruth hesitated briefly, straining to listen if anyone was coming. Her heart pounded; she bit down on her lips in dread, waiting and listening.

No one came; she picked up the items and crossed on tiptoe to the desk. Through trial and error, she learnt how to open the desk's lock with scissors without damage. The drawer slid open inside, she found a large tin cash box. Her heart sank in dismay; it was locked. Ruth persevered first with the hairpin but stamped her foot in expiration when it snapped in half. Her hands trembled with nerve tingling excitement, tried again with the steel needle. The lock popped open; Ruth pressed her hand over her mouth to stifle a squeal of delight and looked at the tightly packed notes inside. She gleefully patted the pile. "Hurrah, my ticket out of here," she giggled. The cash box lock was easy to secure again. "He won't notice for ages," and quietly slipped back to her room.

Ruth listened with pleasure when her father eventually realised some of his cash was missing and howled at his wife, blaming her for taking his money. Ruth became bolder and wiser over the next few weeks to avoid her father realising she took just a few notes each time from the cash box. Then hid her loot safely underneath the base of her drawer.

Sent to the chemist to collect sleeping pills for her mother, Ruth waited at the counter next to a display of lipsticks. Slyly, she dropped her handkerchief over the shelf, removed three and slipped them into her pocket. The assistant caught her and called the manager. They ushered Ruth into a back room, searched and recovered the lipsticks. As he stood over, the quivering, frightened child, gasping through her tears, pleaded,

"Please don't tell my parents; my father will take his belt to me. I'll never do it again. Honestly, I won't, I promise. I'm very sorry."

Her tearful claims disturbed the chemist. However, the girl had to understand that shoplifting was a crime.

The shop owner decided not to prosecute on that occasion. Ruth received only a severe reprimand and was taken home to face the wrath of her parents. Later punished, as she predicted, with her father's belt.

It was well past midnight when he stealthfully entered her room. Aware of his rasping breath, Ruth woke and sat bolt upright. His shadowy form hovered over her as he forced her back on the bed. He lay down beside her and, for the first time, pushed his fingers inside her. On that horrific night, her father subjected his child to the vilest abuse that Ruth was never to forget or forgive.

He whispered, "Ruth, listen to me. You are now twelve, almost a woman. I only punish you so you'll understand right from wrong because your mother demands it. Believe me, I get no pleasure in beating you. You are my only child, and I care for you. If you want to use little lipstick, that's fine by me. You should look nice; that's natural because you're growing up. We can do extraordinary things and share special times, just the two of us." Kissing her on the forehead, he swung from the bed and purred, "I'll come tomorrow with a lovely present for you. We will be great friends now."

Nature gave her a slight reprieve from his advances. The following morning, she entered the kitchen while her parents were having breakfast. With her head lowered, Ruth paused in the doorway and asked her mother to talk to her privately.

"What's the matter, Ruth?" her father inquired, his tone gentle. "We're here to help with any problem." His lips smiled, but his eyes carried a warning plain to understand. Agitated by her request, tiny beads of sweat formed on his brow as he clenched his fists. "What is it, girl, you can tell us? "Speak up, Ruth; how can we help?" His face paled as he watched her, "Come on, sit here," He guided her to the table, grasping her thin arm in a vice-like grip. "I am certain there's nothing we can't discuss together, is there?"

"What's so important that you disturbed us at breakfast? Quick, out with it," her mother shuffled in her chair, confused by her husband's conciliatory manner.

Ruth grappled for words. Her cheeks flushed red. "I noticed bloodstains on my sheets. I think I may have started my periods."

As he wiped his brow in relief, her father got up and collected his coat. "Is that all? Right, I'm leaving. This is woman's talk." He nodded to his wife. "you deal with it."

Her mother crossed her short, plump arms across her chest, told Ruth to sit down, and spoke in a low, hushed voice. "In a short while, your body will change as you approach womanhood. Your breast will grow, and hair will appear on your private parts."

With the thought of being grown up, a grin of pleasure filtered across Ruth's face.

Her mother snapped, "Nothing to grin at, my girl. It's a nasty, dirty time. Over the next year, you'll have regular monthly periods. As you grow into an adult, these will last for years. Not called the curse for nothing. A woman's world isn't pleasant at the beck and call of men." With her daughter's full attention, her fleshy lips curled, she sneered, "They use you to do unnatural things to satisfy their lust."

In excessive detail, Ruth cringed as her vulgar mother described how hideous an intimate experience and a pregnancy would be if she didn't keep herself decent. All this was too much for Ruth. She rushed out into the yard violently, sick with her mother's unpleasant laughter ringing in her ears.

After her vile mother's words, Ruth's nerves were at breaking point dreaded her father's next visit to her bed. She prepared her escape; there was no time to waste now; it had to be soon. In the attic, Ruth found a small case for her treasures. Stretched her arm behind the wardrobe to drag them out. She extended her arm as far as possible to reach one magazine stuck. A spider crawled up her arm with a start; she jerked back. Reluctant to put her hand in again, she used a wire coat hanger to drag it forward and pull it out with the tip of her fingers. With it came an old, yellowed, creased paper covered in cobwebs; it was the birth certificate her mother had thrown away. The information was now barely legible. Ruth smoothed it flat and lay it between the magazines, ready to leave the house empty the next time.

In the meantime, for protection, she sneaked a sharp knife from the kitchen and hid it under her pillow, determined that he would never hurt her again. From his desk, Ruth, her fingers quivering, picked up two handfuls of notes. When her father discovered the loss, pandemonium erupted. His furious roar resonated through the house. Ruth crept out of her room and squatted on the stairs to listen.

"Thieving bitch! You've been on my desk again." Her father thundered, "This will be the last time if you value your life." The constant whack of the belt resounded through the house.

"I haven't, I swear!" screeched Pricilla. "Must have been one of the servants, or maybe it's Ruth, the chemist caught her stealing. Why not ask her?"

"The servants are your responsibility. You question them, but I don't believe you." As for blaming the child who doesn't have the wit or ability to open a locked drawer, what could she possibly want money for? You should be ashamed to blame an innocent girl."

"It must have been robbers then," she squealed, trying to defend herself.

"Robbers, is it now? Tell me, woman, would they just pick up a few pounds and leave the rest? Stupid bitch, don't insult my intelligence."

Ruth heard the door slam as he stormed out.

She tiptoed downstairs and peeked into the room where her mother lay on the couch like a beached whale, her ponderous breasts heaved with sobs. Unconcerned, Ruth ran back to her room. A small part of her held a twinge of regret for the inert women downstairs being blamed. But memories of how her mother treated her soon removed it.

Later that night, he returned drunk and lurched into her bedroom, making no attempt to be silent. His stance was unsteady; he undressed, the foul reek of whisky and tobacco filling the air. Fumbled with his clothes as he wobbled from side to side, practically losing his balance.

"I'm having nothing more to do with that thieving old cow," he grunted, beaming at the mortified girl. "Good times are coming for you. It will be just you and me now, Ruth." The sight of her father naked paralysed her with fear. Despite her well-rehearsed plans, Ruth couldn't move. He got into bed beside her and turned her over onto her stomach. "Don't be frightened, Ruth. Trust me, this is natural for fathers and daughters. We'll go shopping and buy whatever you want. Forget about that thieving old trollop. You're the lady of the house now. Don't worry; I promise you won't get pregnant."

Ruth knew this was wrong from the messages in the agony aunts' column in her magazines; it was far from normal, but she was too petrified to protest. Her body trembled with fear as he straddled her.

"The first time is always the worst," he cajoled. "Don't be so tense; calm down, and it won't hurt." He manoeuvred a little for a better grip.

Ruth reached under her pillow as he released his hold, grabbed the knife, and dug it into his arm. In disbelief and shock, he fell off the bed, clutching the wound.

Ruth rolled away and stood against the far wall, brandishing the knife before her. "You come near me; I'll kill you," she waved the weapon wildly.

He roared, "Little bitch, how dare you threaten me? I'll teach you respect."

Ruth dashed about the room to escape. He lunged forward, caught the hem of her nightdress, and flung her across the bed.

"This should have been so simple. Never mind, we'll do it your way." He advanced to finish what he had started.

Ruth jumped to face him, slashing the sharp blade across his cheek. He stumbled back as blood poured through his fingers and reeled from the room.

"You'll pay for this, my girl," he sputtered

Afraid of what he'd do on his return, Ruth dressed rapidly and packed her few belongings. Collecting the hidden money held her breath as she sidled downstairs. Praying her father wouldn't hear the stairs creak under her feet, she heard him still cursing her in the bathroom as she slipped out the front door.

CHAPTER THREE

FREEDOM TASTES WONDERFUL

Unable to sleep, Ruth watched the intermittent flicker of bright stars as the wispy moonlit clouds floated past. She loved the peace of the night; it always seemed a long time until morning.

As the hours drifted, Ruth remembered her carefree days. Summoned up once more the sweet wine of happy memories. Her reminisces recaptured the giddy joy of a twelve-year-old running off with her few precious treasures. Held tight in one hand, a thick roll of father's money. Chuckled at the memory of the fifty pounds held tight in her hand. The thought of his rage, when he realised who had dared to rob him, made her smile. With stomach-churning excitement blended with quivering trepidation and fear, she waited for the morning train to London.

Soon Ruth was on her way, all misery behind her forever. At last, she was free, but what lay ahead?

Ruth arrived during the rush hour. The jostling crowds unnerved her, so she took refuge in a platform café. She placed herself by the window, scrutinised each face, and savoured the kaleidoscope of colours and shapes. Sad, happy, wealthy, penniless, all mingled intent on their destinations.

Sometime later, a short, well-dressed man sat opposite her. Removed his trilby hat and dropped it on the table. Smoothed back his thin, grey hair. He smiled at her as he lit a slim cigar. The smoke seeped through his gold-capped teeth; the pungent smell made her gasp.

He spoke in a subdued, refined tone. "Hello, my dear; why is a young lady like you doing alone?" He leant towards her, his brown, watery eyes fixed on her face. Ruth turned aside, determined to ignore him. "I have been watching you for quite a while," his manner was gentle and inquiring. "Had trouble at home? Needed to get far away, did you, dear?" fingering a wispy little beard, continued, "Such a big, dangerous place London is." He reached into his jacket and drew out a wallet full of money. "Do you need anything, sweetie? I would like you to take this." He handed over a note.

Ruth pushed it away. "Got my own money."

He grabbed her hand and tried to press the note into it. "Take it; you can never have enough," he persisted before putting it on the table.

"Go away, let me finish my drink in peace," she spat, realising that being polite would not stop this unwanted attention.

"Don't be like that," he **winced**, "Look here, how about we start again. My name's Henry, won't you tell me yours? I promise I won't harm you. Perhaps I can help you."

Exasperated, Ruth gritted her teeth and snarled, "Go away. Are you deaf? Go away now."

Unperturbed, he reached out under the table and squeezed Ruth's knee. "I know a safe place with no questions asked." Henry ran a manicured finger along her cheek. "Wouldn't you like me to arrange that? A young girl in this city alone is unsafe. Almost anything might happen. Come on, what do you say?" He pressed her knee again.

Ruth pushed his hand away. "Keep your grubby hands to yourself," she demanded. Tired of his unwanted advances, she got up to leave.

Henry rose, pushed her back in the chair, and reached for her case. His manner altered from wheedling to abrupt. He gripped her arm and yanked her out of the chair. "Come on, be a sensible girl; we'll be there in a few minutes," he snarled. "Make a sound, and I'll break your arm." Holding on tight, he marched her out of the café, elbowing past grumbling passengers with the squirming child.

Henry half-dragged Ruth along the platform, a porter pushing a trolley barged into them. Ruth kicked Henry's leg as they stumbled, but he grabbed her again and slapped her hard.

"Steady on, mate, no need for that!" the porter grabbed Henry's jacket.

Henry growled. "Mind your own damn business; she needs a good wallop. The little cow just kicked me, blasted brat, be the death of her mum and me, always running off, she is."

"Maybe so," snapped the porter. "You hit that kid again, and I'll give you a smack in the gob."

Ruth wriggled to get loose from the man's grasp as they exchanged words. She pleaded, "Help me, please; I don't know this man; he's hurting me."

Her captor screeched, "Shut up, you are lying, little bitch; I warned you for the last time." He grumbled to the infuriated porter. "Makes nothing but trouble to her mother. Just a disrespectful brat, always mouthing off."

Ruth sank her teeth into Henry's arm. Enraged, he lashed out, knocking her to the ground.

Incensed, the porter leapt forward. "Bastard git! I told you to leave the kid alone."

"Stay out of it; this is a family matter; she has to learn," Henry roared. Took hold of Ruth's coat collar and shook her until her teeth rattled. "Look at the trouble you cause. Just wait till I get you home!"

"Right, you asked for it," the porter punched Henry and sent him reeling.

Henry cowered down on the platform, too afraid to rise; his voice trembled, "This has nothing to do with you."

"Stop there, or I'll flatten ya," The porter shook his fist at Henry. He glanced down at the stunned girl and hoisted her to her feet. "Don't know what's going on. You run off home to your mum. I'll keep this little squirt here for a while."

Ruth snatched her case and took off. She continued running until, feeling safe, she came to a breathless halt.

Ruth strolled past the maze of shops, admiring the elegant window displays with no trace of her pursuer. *Such beautiful dresses. "I'll have all this one day,"* she mused, mimicking the mannequins' odd stances and giggling at her image in the polished windows. A shop assistant glared and gestured her to go away. To the women's disgust, Ruth stepped in and headed straight to the costume jewellery. She tried on rings, strings of necklaces and other glittering objects. Ruth picked up a pair of gaudy earrings and put them on using the counter mirror. She admired her reflection when she spotted a man moving fast towards her. Her stomach churned as she tried to think. The chemist's assistant had caught her taking the lipsticks and sent for the police.

I can't have that happen again. My parents must have reported me missing by now. Ruth dreaded to think about what they would do once back in their clutches. *I won't; can't be sent back.* Her fear of them had a stronger effect than the stern expression on the man's face as he approached. Her mind raced to form a plan before it was too late. She whirled around to confront him; she raised her foot and kicked his shin as hard as possible. While he screeched in pain, Ruth ducked past and sprinted towards the exit. He hobbled after her but was no match for the speed of youth.

Tight in her hand, she held her prize and murmured," I'll keep these earrings forever."

 Ruth bought her first brassiere in a street market and a pack of three skimpy briefs. A bright pink transparent nightdress, nylons, makeup, and a comb set. Fell in love with a shiny, vivid yellow dress. She picked out a handbag and a pair of high-heeled shoes to match. Passing another stall, Ruth couldn't resist the extravagance of a small transistor radio. The drab, pleated skirt was removed in a public toilet, hated twinset, short white socks, and brown brogues. She released her red hair from its pigtails and rearranged it to fall to one side to show off her new jewellery. She stuffed a wad of toilet paper inside the brassiere to give her a bust. Applied makeup as she studied the magazines.

Slipped on the shoes and wobbled around to get used to the height. Once satisfied that she had mastered her walk, Ruth shoved her old clothes into the waste bin. Took a long hard look in the mirror, pleased with the reflection. Ruth inherited her father's striking looks and was tall for her age. Straight away, she appeared much older. Transformation complete, the little frumpy country mouse had flown forever. Replaced by a flashy modern teenager.

She scanned advertising boards outside shops and cafes, seeking work. Towards evening, after many rejections, footsore and tired, Ruth noticed a bed-and-breakfast sign. With a cigarette dangling from her mouth, a woman looked Ruth up and down with apparent distaste and sniffed, "It's two bob a night in advance."

Her husband came from behind the desk. "Business a little slow tonight, dear?" He inquired with a smirk. He pulled on a threadbare cardigan. "Gets chilly up there; your thin dress won't keep you warm. " he sniggered. "I'm sure you'll soon find other ways."

"None of that," the woman curled her fleshy lips. "This is a respectable house. No men callers allowed, or you're out." Long spent ash fell from the cigarette onto the register. She flicked it off and grunted, "What's it to be, just the bed or with breakfast at eight sharp?"

"Just bed will be fine," Ruth stared at the smear of ash on the register; she'd already regretted choosing this place.

"Right then, that's two bob in advance now," blowing her smoke in Ruth's face, held out her hand for payment, then stuffed the coins into her filthy apron pocket. Pushed the register across and growled, "Sign here. Fred, show her to room eight, and don't be all day." As they moved up the stairs, the woman called out after them. "No funny business either!"

Fred looked back at Ruth, winked, and whispered. "Take no notice of the old hag. She doesn't want single girls here, but I do." He opened the room door a crack, so Ruth had to squeeze past him. Lingering in the doorway, his red-rimmed eyes watered in anticipation; gazing intently at Ruth, he slurred. "Give you a refund for a quick wank if you like."

Ruth gasped in contempt and snapped, "Fine, ok by me, but shouldn't we ask your wife first?"

Shaken by her reply, he stepped backwards. Ruth banged the door shut and crammed an armchair up against the handle. The dingy, sparse room had a single bed, a dilapidated armchair, and a single wardrobe. Under tattered net curtains and cracked window hung a dirt-encrusted sink. Ruth drew back the foul-smelling single bed cover. The sheets were grey, stained and threadbare. She spent the night curled up in the armchair. Early the following day, Ruth resumed her search for work, determined never to spend another night in that disgusting boarding house.

Late that afternoon, she spotted a sign in the window of a hotel. (Chambermaid wanted, live in position). The receptionist glanced up from her typewriter.

"I've come to apply for the chambermaid's job," Ruth shuffled her feet nervously.

"The housekeeper engages the staff, but she's unavailable right now," she replied. "Wait here. I'll see if the manageress is free." She smoothed down her uniform and remarked with a wry smile, "All this sitting play havoc with my hips." The receptionist returned and led Ruth along the hall, past the housekeeper's office's open door in a short while. She ushered her into the main office suite. "This is Ruth, Mrs Wallace, here for the chambermaid's position." Pushed Ruth forward, turned and left, leaving the door wide open.

A well-dressed woman whose light ash brown hair framed her friendly face held out a slim hand.

Ruth's heart sank as she picked up the receptionist's sniggering remarks to the housekeeper. "Did you see that one? All that makeup, and who poured her into that dress?"

"You should have called me."the woman glanced through the open door. "I would have quickly given that sort short shift.

Look at the state of her! A dirty little prostitute, I bet." the housekeeper sneered.

"No, Miss Allan, I don't think so; I'm sure that's not true", the receptionist disagreed. "Just a kid with no dress sense yet. She speaks well; I thought she was sweet."

"Sweet, is it?" hissed the housekeeper. "You're young and got a lot to learn. I tell you, I know exactly what she is. If you ask me, the Wallaces will never take on that sort; you'll realise I'm right when she's shown the door. Now return to your duties, stupid girl," Miss Allan snapped.

Mrs Wallace told Ruth to shut the door and invited her to sit. Ruth extended her hand in greeting. "Thank you so much for agreeing to see me; I appreciate how busy you must be."

Mrs Wallace sat back and listened. Ruth had practised her speech many times, well-acquainted in deception. She smiled, settled in the chair and began, "I am fifteen; I completed my education last term. My ambition is to manage a hotel as clean and pleasant as this one. Until I find employment, I'm living in London with my aunt."

"Oh, my dear, there is a lot more to hotel management that you would need to learn. You must be able to relate to people, use discretion and diplomacy, manage personnel and have a good business head." Mrs Wallace chuckled at her enthusiasm. "All right, my dear, complete this form with your details. Does a month's trial suit? We'll see how it goes, and then we'll talk again," She smiled

Ruth gave a massive sigh of relief and filled in the form.

Ruth couldn't believe it had been so easy and wished she hadn't given her actual name, but it was too late to change that now. However, the rest she made up. Writing a year of birth to disguise her actual age. Filled in the name of a street, she passed as the address of her fictitious aunt. Until she came across a question requesting her national insurance number. Ruth cursed. *I forgot I'd need one of those to work.*, She blurted out she'd left it behind at home, but her aunt would send for it and post it on. Mrs Wallace assured her that could be dealt with later. She tactfully suggested that less makeup would be appropriate while on duty. Then pressed a bell on her desk to summon the housekeeper.

Miss Allan entered the office and told Ruth she was on a month's trial. In a flustered tone, she requested a private word with Mrs Wallace.

Ruth waited in the reception area; after a while, Miss Allan emerged with a face like thunder, declaring, "Well, I am sorry you won't take my advice, madam. I believe you've made a poor decision; that type won't fit in here." She ordered the receptionist, "Show this person a staff room". Glaring at Ruth, she added, "Step out of line once, my girl, and you'll be gone," She stormed into her office, slamming the door behind her.

Ruth glanced around the neat, pleasant room and arranged her night dress on the bed. Slipping off her shoes, rubbed the soles of her aching feet, opened the window wide, and gazed out. She had new clothes, a new home, a job, and thirty pounds of her father's money still in her purse, all settled in one day. But one troublesome thought continued. *The national insurance card problem she had to solve or her time in this place will be brief.* Spread out on the soft bed, turning on her radio, extended each leg, loving the luxurious feel of the nylons, and sighed with pleasure. *Soon I will wear nothing except pure silk next to my skin,* she promised herself. Everything had been simple. Freedom was just as she dreamt it would be.

CHAPTER FOUR

LIVING THE DREAM

Ruth scraped away most of the number seven on the crumpled birth certificate with her fingernail and changed it to a five. The following day, she made her way to the crowded, local busy labour exchange on her lunch break.

A harassed clerk peered at the crumpled certificate, tried to smooth it out, and heaved a sigh, "This is in a right state! Where'd you keep it, under the floorboards?" she slammed a file on her desk. The frazzled woman filled in the required forms and passed over a temporary card. Then stiffly informed Ruth they would send her an official one in the post. No further questions were asked.

The evenings flew by, chatting and laughing with two sisters, Jenny, and Betty, who lived out. Ruth had the life she craved for so long. Mrs Wallace and her husband George made considerable efforts to teach her hotel protocol. Ruth proved to be a keen student. She liked Mr Wallace, a friendly man, short and stout without a hair on his head. He reminded her of a small Easter egg. Ruth soon made friends among the younger staff members. With them, she enjoyed going to dances and the cinema. The only person who made life difficult was the housekeeper, Miss Allen, who frequently criticised her work. Still smarting that the management employed such an obviously unsuitable girl, despite her warnings. To please Mrs Wallace, Ruth toned down her dress and applied less makeup to enhance her natural beauty. Some male guests were over generous with tips. She quickly learnt how to tactfully deal with the most flirtatious without causing offence. She made sure bedroom doors remained wide open while she worked. They promoted Ruth to trainee receptionist within three months, with a significant wage increase and regular free time. She gained a complete wardrobe of fashionable outfits and various delicate figurines to brighten her room from the markets. As time passed, Ruth could think of her mother in a different light and grudgingly excuse the unkind treatment she had suffered at her mother's hands. Married to such a domineering man would make anyone bitter. Her skin still crawled whenever she thought of what her father had done to her. Ruth decided to pay off her debt and make her peace with them, working extra hours to earn the balance needed to repay the stolen money. In due course, she had almost the right amount tucked away in her bedside cupboard.

On late duty, with nothing to do, Ruth spent the quiet hours chatting to the old night porter, Dave, about her plans. He always entertained her with stories of long-ago days. Chucked outrageously at his own jokes, using both hands to control his capacious juggling stomach, he panted for breath.

"Oh, Ruth, pet, don't make me laugh; I'll get a stitch." Ruth smiled; he looked so comical, leaning back in his chair, swinging his short legs three inches short of the floor. He dabbed his bald head with his handkerchief, "Phew, I'm knackered now, child. How about you make me a cuppa?"

Ruth obliged. Out of the blue, as they were drinking, he inquired about her home life. Ruth told him about running away and stealing from her father's desk and came upon this work by lying about her age. Ruth immediately regretted her confession and added quickly she was saving to pay back what she had taken.

Dave held out his hand and gently clasped hers, his kind blue eyes full of sympathy, "I find it hard to believe you would do such a terrible thing. However, knowing you as I do, you must have had a good reason. Don't fret; I won't breathe a word of this conversation." Dave promised to keep her secrets, wished her luck, and agreed that paying back the money was right. The doorbell sounded, and Ruth got up to answer.

Back in the hallway, she saw Miss Allan standing by her open office door with a self-satisfied smirk. Ruth wondered if the vicious woman had heard. With that thought in mind, she tossed and turned throughout the night. Her nerves are on razor edge, and physically sick to her stomach. She looked out the window at the people on their way to work. Slammed her fists down on the ledge and muttered: "This is the life I graved. I won't give this freedom now, but what can I do? They might try to send me back home? Well, I won't go, no one can make me either.". Ruth contemplated her situation. "What on earth was I thinking of telling Dave? Bless him, he won't say anything, but that old cow will. If she overheard, the nasty old bitch certainly wouldn't keep such a valuable weapon to herself. If she tells Wallace, what will happen to me? "

Unwilling to wait, Ruth decided to leave before dealing with such a crisis. She collected her possessions into a bag. As she snicked down the stairs, Miss Allan approached a broad smile on her spiteful face. The housekeeper snatched the bag away and grabbed Ruth's arm,

"I'll take that; you're wanted in the office; look sharp." Held fast in the older woman's firm grip, Ruth had no choice but to obey.

As Miss Allen threw open the office and pushed Ruth forward, the stern expression of her employer told her the housekeeper had repeated the overheard conversation. Mrs Wallace instructed Ruth to sit down. Her voice was devoid of its usual warmth,

"Ruth, Miss Allan reported disturbing information about you this morning. She assures me you lied about your age and had taken money from your parents when you arrived here. Is that so?"

As there was no point in denial, Ruth answered, her cheeks on fire, "Yes, that's all true, and I am sorry and ashamed."

Mrs Wallace cried, her chest heaving in annoyance. "You made an absolute fool of me. I can't tell you how often Miss Allan said you were unsuitable." In despair, she put her hands to her head and declared, "Damn, blind fool, I should have listened to her."

In utter misery, Ruth felt her time there had ended. A lump of despair rose in her throat; she stammered, "I tried to find the courage to tell you. The right time or opportunity never came."

"Would there ever be a right time?" her employer asked.

Ruth shook her head.

"Just so," Mrs Wallace responded. "I should have known from our first meeting. The way you dressed and your vague answers. Against my better judgement, I offered you an opportunity." Exasperated, she slumped down in her chair. "Well, it will never happen again. What a stupid woman I am! How can I be certain you haven't stolen from us?"

With all hope for a reprieve lost, Ruth protested in indignation, "I never stole from you! I wouldn't. I know stealing my parent's money was wrong, but I have saved almost enough in my room to repay them." Ruth buried her face in her hands and sobbed, embarrassed that these good people now knew her past. In a firm tone, she drew a deep breath and announced, "I'm glad all that is out in the open. I'll never go back home; you don't know how miserable my life was." She gathered what remained of her dignity. "If you allow me a day or two to find accommodation somewhere, I'd be grateful. Unless you prefer that I pack up my belongings and leave immediately."

Mrs Wallace calmed herself. "Ruth, I am certain there's more you're not telling me. Your reason for robbing your parents, I don't consider justified." She shook her head in disbelief. "I am so disappointed in you. You're not the girl, I thought. It's not just a matter of firing you. The laws for using underage workers are strict. Before deciding, I must discuss this matter with Mr Wallace and repeat what I learnt. You are relieved of all duties until we tell you what action we decide. Please remain in your room; do not leave the hotel."

Ruth spent a terrible day looking out the bedroom window, dreading what might be in store. Staff members brought meals to her room, all instructed by Miss Allan not to talk to her. Tossing and turning all night, unable to sleep, wretched and sick at heart, convinced her days at the hotel were ending.

After breakfast the following day, a smug Miss Allan called her to the reception. "I hope you have spent your time packing; it will be back home for you, and good riddance to bad rubbish." The internal telephone rang with a smirk on her malevolent face, replacing the receiver. Grinned with pleasure, "Now, you're getting the push. Not before time, I say." Then ushered Ruth into the office.

Mrs Wallace sat at the desk, strained and pale. Mr Wallace, standing beside her, motioned Ruth to a chair. He was always pleasant and kind; now, he scowled at her with cold, hostile eyes. He stepped forward, arms folded across his chest, his voice scathing when he demanded: "Now then, Ruth, is your surname Page?"

Ruth nodded.

"How old are you?"

"Fourteen," she muttered.

"What?!" George bellowed. "Did you say fourteen?"

"Yes," Ruth stammered in response.

Both adults made an audible gasp at this revelation. George bent down his face level with hers and barked, "You've been here nearly two years." Ruth jerked backwards in fright. "Which means you were only twelve when you arrived. Correct?"

Ruth nodded in misery.

George sucked in his cheeks. "Do you realise we may be in serious trouble?"

"Oh, my Lord," exclaimed Mrs Wallace. "I took you at face value. How could you be so deceptive?"

"I'm so sorry. I needed to find somewhere to live," Ruth sniffed as tears tumbled from her eyes.

"Much too late for tears," George grunted as he paced around the room. "The damage is done, my girl. I checked with a police friend that there is no record of you as a missing person. What parents wouldn't report their missing child?" He strode back to Ruth, shaking his head in disbelief. "No, Ruth, I don't believe you. I'm convinced there is more to this than you're telling us. What are you covering up?" he demanded. "Give me one solid reason we shouldn't report you. Come on, the truth, no more lies," he thundered.

Ruth bowed her head and stared at the carpet. Her hands locked together in her lap, unable to meet his cold eyes, afraid of the anger in his voice.

Nervous between sobs, Ruth related the entire truth about her life at home, including the abuse suffered at her father's hands. Gasping with emotion, Ruth ended with defiance, "I will never go back, never!"

Mrs Wallace rose. "No, we won't send you back to that life." Turning to her husband, she burst into tears, full of compassion, and moved towards Ruth, intending to comfort the distraught girl. George restrained her.

"No, Grace. I'm aware of how attached you are to her. Remember, Ruth was only thirteen when she arrived here. We must do what's right. Our reputation is already compromised."

He stroked his chin while he thought. "Perhaps we should tell the authorities. We've been harbouring a runaway child. I'm not sure we can afford not to report this."

Mrs Wallace rushed to his side and held onto his sleeve; her voice trembled with emotion. "No! George! The police will send her back home. I'm positive she never set out to take advantage of us but had to get away from a terrible situation." Tears fell as Grace pleaded Ruth's case.

George led his sobbing wife back to her chair. "Grace, please don't cry. I must think this through. I can't see how we can stay quiet about her. Whatever her motivations, we are hiding a thief and a runaway child. This is serious. We can't sweep it under the carpet. I am sorry, Grace; we must inform the authorities."

Mrs Wallace covered her tear-drenched face with her hands and wailed in despair.

Ruth sprang to her feet, "If you believe for one second, I'm going to sit here while you send for the police; you're sadly mistaken." She saw the look on Mrs Wallace's ashen face and regretted her harsh outburst. "I am sorry I misled you, but I'll leave now." She made for the door.

Mrs Wallace ran to stop her, caught Ruth's hands, and led her back to the chair.

Ruth sighed glumly, "What's the point? He won't change his mind."

Mrs Wallace pushed her into the chair and whispered, "He will, dear. He will. Just wait a few minutes more."

Although full of doubt, Ruth sat back down.

Mrs Wallace crossed over to George to make a last plea. Tugged at his jacket sleeve, she urged, "But George, Ruth's suffered so much; would you sleep easy if we turned her out? Where will she go from here?" she cried out. "Back to abusive parents? Out on the street, homeless and alone? I can't, can you?"

Indignant, George replied, "No! I'm not a monster, Grace. How can you imply that? Think about all these past lies. I'm concerned about how easily she deceived and hoodwinked us." Agitated, he wrung his hands together. "What are we to do? She can't remain here."

"Why not?" Grace asked.

"Be reasonable, Grace." Almost inaudibly, he moaned, "How can we harbour a runaway child?"

Grace, sensing victory, babbled, "I am confident she'll be honest from now on, George. I could never rest if we turned her away."

At last, badgered into submission, with a weary sigh, George accepted defeat. Glancing at his wife's face etched in misery, he asked, "What do you suggest we do, Grace?"

Breathless, with eager anticipation, Grace replied, "We can let her live here. Move her into our private quarters. No one need know she's not a family member." Her mind running ahead with plans continued. "We can't send her to school. They would ask too many questions. We could hire a private tutor to complete her education."

George's jaw dropped in disbelief. "Grace, think about what you're saying. Do you want to fool everyone and break the law? What about the staff? They'll know by now, thanks to that spiteful housekeeper."

She retorted dryly, "George, I don't see why we'd have to account for our actions to the staff. We wouldn't be lying; just not telling. We could empty and decorate the box room for her. Look at the miserable little soul. Terrified, we will send her back to those monsters. She'll be better off remaining here with us."

George groaned in resignation. "As usual, Grace, have it your way, my dear. I hate to see you become so upset. I hope she's come clean now. So, I'll trust your judgement, but pray you don't live to regret your good nature." Turning to Ruth, he warned, "As for you, young lady, I hope you understand our risk. If you let us down again, I won't hesitate to call the police, do you understand? Now I want your proper home address." Ruth opened her mouth to refuse. He held up a hand to silence her. "We will keep it in our confidential files."

Overwhelmed by this unexpected decision, Ruth had no words to convey her appreciation. She hugged Mrs Wallace and walked out of the office on wings. And bumped into Miss Allan, waiting impatiently outside the door.

Ruth darted back to her room, the housekeeper chasing after her retreating figure. Barged past Ruth into the room, her eyes narrow slits, her thin lips drew back over gritted teeth, and she sneered, "So you think you got away with it? Well, girl, you're not as clever as you think. I know more about you than you realise. I'll have my day, you'll see." She stored out.

CHAPTER FIVE

VENGEANCE AND RETRIBUTION

The Wallaces were out at a function and left Miss Allen in charge. The box room was ready; she'd be moving into the owner's quarters tomorrow. Ruth stuck her head around the staffroom door and wished the occupants a cheery good night. Then bounded up the stairs taking two at a time,

As she opened her bedroom door, she recoiled in shock. Her clothes were all ripped to shreds and thrown around the room. Each drawer and cupboard were wide open, the contents all scattered. Her treasured figurines lay broken on the floor. Amid the devastation stood her parents with Miss Allan. Her father seized her by the neck and sent her sailing to the opposite side of the room. She crashed into the wall and rebounded onto the floor. In his hand, he held her envelope of saved banknotes. Grabbed a handful of hair, pulled her up, and thrust the notes hard to her face.

"My money, dirty, little thief. How did you earn it? You can never pay back the evil you have done. The anxiety and shame you caused your mother and me! You'll pay back more than money for the rest of your worthless life."

Miss Allan stood motionless, excitedly biting her knuckles as the spectacle unfolded. The girl who had been a thorn in her side was now cringing in fear.

Her father raged. "If it were not for this good woman's letter, we'd never have come across you. You should go on your knees and bow down to her for delivering you from a life of debauchery."

Miss Allan's eyes flashed bright with eager anticipation. She positioned herself at the door, locking it to prevent escape, scowling at the frightened girl. "You tricked the Wallaces all right, but not me. From the first moment I saw you, I was sure something wasn't right. I found your home address in the office file and wrote to your parents. I, for one, will be happy to see the back of you."

Ruth ran to the window with the blood spurting from her mouth and her face crimson from the blows. "No, I never took that money! I've worked hard for it. I'll never go back with you. I'll run away again and again; you can't make me stay." Turning to her mother, she begged for help. "It was wrong to steal, and I am sorry. You can't force me back home. I won't go." Ruth pleaded. "That woman is lying. She despises me, don't listen to her."

"Believe you!" scoffed her mother. "With all that muck on your face. We've seen the undergarments you wear. No decent girl would have such things. Dirty slut is what you are. We know full well what you've been doing. You were always vain and willful." She yelled, "No one will help you, revolting, contemptible creature! Your father will beat the evil from you. Then you are coming home, where we can keep an eye on you."

The two women forced Ruth to the floor and held her there. Her father removed his belt and often brought it down on her back and legs. Ruth screamed for him to stop as the thick leather cut deep into her flesh. To avoid the swinging belt, the women placed themselves against the door. They stood in silence, absorbed and hypnotised by the violence. The commotion and Ruth's pitiful screams had woken up the entire hotel. The residents smashed open the door, sending the vindictive pair flying. They hesitated, frozen by the spectacle that met their eyes. Ruth pressed into a corner as her father, unaware of the intrusion, continued to use his belt. Another piercing shriek from Ruth geared the shocked group into action. Three men wrestled her deranged father to the floor and held him there.

Ruth struggled to her feet and rushed headlong towards the open door. Out of her mind with pain, she fought off people trying to help her and tumbled down the stairs in haste to escape. Wrenched open the front door and blundered out into the street. Half running, half falling, fear drove her on. Concerned passers-by attempted to stop her. She dodged past and ran for her life; in her mind, imagining her father close behind her. At last, near to collapse, she staggered down the nearest basement steps in a street of derelict houses, opened the coal cellar door, and crumpled, exhausted in the darkest corner.

CHAPTER SIX

SAFE HAVEN

In the morning half-light, she was aware of a sharp draft as the cellar door opened. A large, stocky man in his late forties peered into the gloom. He knelt beside her. "What's all this? Ain't no place safe? Got a squatter, 'ave we? You can stick around, but not out 'ere in the cold. Come on, littl'en, up ya come." As he reached out to help her, his broad stubby fingers paused as he felt a sticky substance. He pulled her out to the light and stared in disbelief. Her legs and arms were a mass of yellow and black bruises through the remains of the shredded, bloodstained clothing. Wounds covered her lifeless body. Few features remained visible on the battered, bloated face. "Christ's sake! What wicked, spiteful bastard did this?" Still cursing, he eased her into his arms and carried her into the basement, picked his way through sleeping vagrants and made his way to a large settee. He levered its grumbling occupant onto the floor with his foot, laid Ruth down, and covered her frozen body with old coats. He stretched out beside her and held her close to his warmth.

Through many pain-filled, half-conscious days, Ruth tossed and twisted. She was agitated as someone kept disturbing her. A cold, slimy substance was applied to her protesting body. A gruff voice cursed. Large, rough, clumsy hands turned her from side to side. Hazy inquisitive faces swam into her blurred vision and melted away. Hot sweet liquids were forced down her throat. Most of all, she had a pleasant sensation of heat and safety. Ruth groaned and opened her eyes. Every bone in her body screamed with pain as she eased herself up and looked around the cellar. An assortment of broken armchairs and threadbare battered settees were scattered around. The stone floor was cluttered with empty beer and wine bottles, rusting old cans and other debris. The solitary window, part boarded up, let in narrow shafts of illumination. On the brick walls hung an assortment of torn posters and street signs. Ruth massaged her throbbing temples and hauled herself to a sitting position. She appeared to be alone. A massive open fire gave the cellar its remaining light and suffocating heat. She pushed aside the ragged covers and tried to stand, but her legs gave way. A low growl broke the silence. Ruth caught her breath, waiting for the sound again.

"Wotcha, lazybones. Feeling betta' are we?"

"Who's that? Where am I?" Ruth swallowed nervously. Ruth attempted to rise, relieved she wasn't alone. Once on her feet, realised she was stark naked except for an oversized grubby old shirt. Ruth focused on forcing her trembling legs to obey, eager to reach her companion.

"You're safe here, dearie. Don't be afeared; come by the fire. Talk to old Violet for a while. Come on now, shift your arse," the odd scratchy voice encouraged. "Good gal, keep going, just a little more. Can't help, mate, my old legs don't work proper these days, 'ave a job getting to the bog most days," the crackling voice urged, "Come on dearie, your doing fine; keep going."

In due course, Ruth's erratic path took her near just to make out in the fire's glow a woman cradling a little dog. Ruth gazed; she was the oldest, ugliest woman in the world. Her old face creased and cracked with age, encrusted with years of grime. Slate grey matted hair tumbled over her hunched shoulders. On a tattered rug slung over her legs lay a small, emaciated dog who stared at Ruth with moist brown eyes. The woman leant over to reach a dented, scorched black teapot on the grate. She threw the remains of the liquid from a chipped mug into the fire; as it spat and sizzled, she refilled it with the steaming black tea. Ruth screwed up her nose and forced her eyes away. The woman held out the grimy, cracked mug full to the brim with the earth-brown liquid.

"Ave, a swallow of that, dearie, make yer hair curl, so it will. I'm Violet, this dump's home, ain't much, but the roof don't leak."

As Violet handed her the mug, the old woman wrapped long bony fingers around Ruth's arm, forcing Ruth to look straight at her. The woman's thin lips parted in a smile as their eyes met. Her entire face altered; the ugliness rolled away, replaced by a gentleness Ruth could feel. Violet patted her arm and loosened her hold.

"There, there, my lovely. I ain't no oil painting, but if yer takes a gander now, I reckon ya' be over the worst. It ain't the cover ya' go by. It's how big the 'art is. I'll never 'arm yer; don't be afird of me 'cause I'm an ugly old bent. Drink up that tea, do ya' the world of good. Sit next to me by the fire. We can 'ave a good old gab afore the others come back." Ruth relaxed as Violet prattled on in a course, thin voice. She told Ruth that Eddie had found her lying like a whipped pup in the coal cellar. "We never 'fought you'd make it. Eddie was too afird to call a quack cause we didn't know if you were on the run. So, he cared for you 'em self. That's Eddies best shirt you're wearing. Washed ya all over from top to tail, he did. Use up all the dripping on your sores. Still, must say ya mended right well." Violet chuckled when Ruth blushed bright red. Settled in front of Violet's chair near the fire, she finished the drink and put more wood on the fire.

They chatted away the hours. In response to Ruth's questions, Violet told her the other fleeting faces belonged to curious young vagrants Eddie picked up in his travels around London. "Can't bear the youngens living rough. Great soft lump." She beamed. "Not alf a brain in the soft lumps 'ead, but a big 'art. I don't complain; I enjoy having youngens about the place. When they can, they leave in a bob or two. There's always somefing in the stewpot to share. Most don't stick around long. Others keep coming back. They're safe wiv us 'cos we ain't got nuffink to do with them nosey parker, do-gooders." Violet told Ruth how she'd been crippled during the Blitz. Her husband, Albert, was killed by a bomb blast soon after. Unable to pay rent, they'd been forced out. Eddie carried her around in an old barrow till he found the cellar.

Violet sniffed, "So 'ere I've been since. All I got now is my boy, Eddie. Don't know wot I do without 'em."Her voice lowered as if somebody might hear. "Eddie was born with a twisted leg, always a big soft lad. Let other kids get away with pushing him around and calling out nasty names at school." She stopped to re-adjust the thin dog on her lap. "Just cos he walks funny and got raggedy clothes. The poor little bugger came back 'ome in tears. My boy could easily have bashed 'em, but it ain't Eddie's way. The little sod wouldn't go to school." Smugly, Violet declared, "I didn't make 'em either. So, without teaching, he never learnt to read or write." Violet violently shook her fist, "I tell you, Ruth, if my legs worked properly, I'd gone round that flipping school and give 'em what for."

Violet told Ruth with such little education, Eddie could not get work. Too proud to go to welfare for money, he brought in a little by busking. Violet bragged, "My Eddie's a top scavenger, often charms the butchers, misses out of cheap meat scraps."

She chattered on, telling hilarious tales of her youth. Ruth knew most were pure fiction, but she had been waiting for this fascinating old woman all her life. Without hesitation or prompting, she told Violet her story. Violet sat without a sound

69

while Ruth poured out all her past misery. Tears of compassion ran down her hollow cheeks as she stroked the head, leaning against her legs, and looked at the waning fire until Ruth had revealed all.

When the girl finished, Violet whispered, "Oh my Gawd, poor little sod. I swear on me Albert's grave, no one will ever 'arm you again. Not while I got breath in this useless old body. You stay 'ere as long as you want."

Into this intimate scene came Eddie. An enormous man, the battered violin case strung around his neck, seemed out of place with the image he presented. "Well, now, wot a beautiful sight!" he exclaimed. "Gasbagging again, Violet. While others do the work." He rubbed his hands together, hunched down before the fire. "It's bleeding freezing out there, and ya let this fire burn out again." He emptied a sack of mixed vegetables, odd bits of bread, and other sundries onto the floor. He added more wood to the grate, then turned his head to glance at Ruth. "Better now, mate?"

She nodded her reply.

"What's up, cat got yer tongue?"

Ruth blushed once more.

"Well! This ain't no good. I think she's a shy girl. Ma, where's yer manners? Introduce your favourite son to the lovely lady. Better still, I'll do it me self." He bowed exaggeratedly. "Mr Edward

Stanley Harris, busker and vagabond at yer service, known as Eddie to my friends. who am I addressin'?" Nodding to Violet, he grinned. "'Er don't talk to us low life, Ma."

Ruth, giggling, told him her name.

"Ruth," he echoed, nodding in approval. "Ah! Yes, I like that, nice and simple. Not all posh like Madam Violet." He pointed his finger in Violet's direction. "Thinks she's a proper lady, 'er do. Fancy, my dear girl with a handle like that." He winked and grinned at Ruth as he ended his performance.

"I wish she were my mother," Ruth cried.

Violet pulled her close. "So, I will child be right proud to call ya my daughter."

"Well, fancy that! Found me a sister, 'arter all these years." He pointed a finger in mock indignation at Violet. "Whatcha been up to, Ma, while I've been away, yer wicked old rascal?" Eddie lifted Ruth, levelled with his eyes, and studied her face; as he lowered her gently back to the floor, he caught her hands in his. In a low, gruff voice, said, "Ruth love, I ain't going to ask what brought ya to this state. You've been through the mill. Put it all behind ya now, try to forget and no more tears. You warmed me, old girl's heart, and I'll never want more than that. We're a family now, Rough and coarse, which I know you ain't used to. But honest in our love for each other. You don't need money for that. Now earn yur keep, kid." Pointing to a bag in the corner, he

71

ordered, "Grab them meat scraps, bung 'em in the stew pot, and peel a few spuds. We'll have a good gut bash tonight." With pleasure, Ruth obeyed.

CHAPTER SEVEN

A LEARNING CURVE

They always found scraps of food, but actual money was scarce. However, Violet ensured that sixpence went into the Co-operative funeral insurance fund each week. Saying. "Me and my boy ain't gonna rest in a pauper's grave. Both of us will rest next to my Eddie. All done and paid for, proper like."

Although rough and uneducated, through Eddie's eyes, Ruth saw the beating heart of London. He said the bridges along the embankment were the city's guardians. Dockland he named as

London's busy housewife. Covent Garden, its merchant son. The magnificent parks, free from the rumbling traffic, Eddie called next year's promise. The River Thames meandering past the many bomb sites, its muted conscience reminding all that death takes no sides.

Elderly and young children drew his warmth and time, prostitutes, drug addicts, and the homeless his compassion.

Pimps and drug pushers, he cursed. "Bastards, everyone, the scum of the earth. Never mix with that muck," he advised. "They'll bang nails in yor coffin and still expect to collect their dues. Never go near 'em, Ruth. Promise to mind me on this."

No matter how often Ruth assured him she would remain clear of all such people, he mumbled, "I couldn't bear it. Couldn't deal with it. What would I tell me?"

Together, they scrounged the cast-off clothing from the wealthier houses and sold them to second-hand stallholders. They'd search the market stands for dropped vegetables or damaged fruit. Impressed by her efforts, Eddie claimed she was the best little scavenger in London; Ruth soon became used to their desperate poverty.

She once asked why he didn't go to one of the charities or state agencies to help find a decent home. Eddie yelled at her. "Do yer fink I can't be fucking look 'arter ya and Violet? Those nosey bastards would whip Violet in an old folk's 'ome as quick as a wink. Piss off if yer life with us ain't good nuff. Sell yourself on the street if that suits ya flog better. Go on, flog yor mutton. Live with the other no-hopers, meths drinkers," he bellowed. "Don't show up at my door. Hear me!".

Ruth backed away like a startled rabbit. When he saw her shocked face, he immediately relented and drew her to him, patting her back to reassure her. "Oh! Come on, little mate, don't look like that; I didn't mean it. God knows I never want to lose ya. Sorry, I yelled; I've seen it all before, so I know." Pulling his jacket tighter against the biting wind, he grumbled, "Old girls like Ma dumped in those places and forgotten. No one goes to visit them. Left alone with their faded memories. Robbed of all dignity, surviving on handouts, they give up and die." He bit his lip to control the building emotions these words forced out;

 Eddie reached out and held her close."Don't understand? How can ya? I had plenty of that. Dragged out of me Ma's arms, those bastards took no notice of both of us howling. No one cared when I sobbed my little heart out in the council's kids 'ome. I bolted out of a window the first chance I had and raced back to Ma's. In the end, they got tired of me running off and gave up. It comes 'ard to think soap, water, and pound notes count afore a family." Eddie released Ruth, bent to pick up their day's takings, and, shaking his head, declared, "This is a miserable, brutal world, Ruth. I won't claim all those old folks' places all the same. I suppose they ain't."

Pointing towards a group of children huddled closely, sheltering from the cold. "Maybe those poor, little sods would be better off. Look at them shivering outside the pubs for hours, hoping for food tonight. All they 'av is good clout at closing time from blind drunk parents. Others have fathers who spend the little they have on ale then stagger home to beat the shit out of their mothers."

He slung the violin case around his neck, shuddering in the chill wind, and buttoned up Ruth's coat for her. "Winter's coming soon. What about old ones freezing in their homes, with never a visit from their kids. Left to die and rot away alone and neglected. Rejected by them wot' should care for them? For as long as I can get around on my twisted old leg, we'll manage, 'elping each other. Come on, we've wasted enough time." Eddie's education had been sparse, but his father had taught him how to play the violin. From this talent as a busker, he scraped a meagre existence. He refused to allow Ruth to look for other work. Worried whoever hurt her might discover her alone without his protection, he insisted he was the breadwinner. Not wanting to hurt his dignity, Ruth agreed. Did whatever she could to earn her keep, though. Eddie would often say that one day he would discover a sack of cash. He might take Violet to the slipper baths. He roared loudly at this notion.

Many of London's buildings were destroyed during the Blitz. Greedy landlords hiked up rents that only the middle classes could afford. Leaving hundreds sleeping wherever they could.

Unable to meet the increased rent after Eddies father's death, the pair roamed the streets for days before finding their derelict basement. Unable to walk, Violet stayed home with her little dog, she called Albert, in memory of her late husband. Eddie, from a young boy, had always looked after his mother. She couldn't imagine a day without him on her lap. The thin creature never left her side except to root around the cellar. He grabbed the odd mouse or rat, shaking them in his jaws before tossing the dead rodent across the basement floor. He'd allow no one other than Violet to hold him and barred broken yellow teeth to anyone trying to pet him.

One evening, Ruth and Eddie arrived home to find Violet hugging a stiff, dead Albert on the floor. The fire had long gone out, and Violet was icy cold. They hoisted her back into her armchair, still clinging to her dog. Eddie removed the dog and bundled up his mother in all the coats and blankets he could find. Ruth got the fire started again. Together they rubbed her icy hands to get her circulation moving.

At last, the old lady looked up at them. Her wrinkled old face was ravaged by grief. "Got to bury 'em. Tried to, but these legs are no dam good today. My poor little mite's gone." She wailed, "Both me Alberts took from me. Went to sleep in my arms, can't leave 'im the rats will..."Her voice faltered as she dissolved into floods of tears

"I'll do it, Ma. I'll put 'em in the park; he'll like it there," Eddie promised. "You 'ave a brew; sit by the fire and warm up. Don't

76

worry, I'll do it right." He wrapped the tiny dog in his jacket and left.

Violet retreated into herself, not speaking, sleeping on and off all day from that day on. She refused most of her food and became feeble. Around two o'clock one morning, Eddie woke Ruth. "Ma's getting worse; I gotta get the cash to pay for proper nursing." Ruth tried to detain him, insisting a nurse would never come to the cellar. Violet would have to go to the hospital. Ruth implored she would have the care she needed and come back home fit and well. Eddie would have none of it. "Ma's going to no bloody 'ospital. I told you the old girl stays put wiv' us. It's up to me to find what she needs afore it's too late. Never gonna 'av that bag of cash. We need money now, and I'm gonna find some."

"Eddie, please let me come with you," Ruth pleaded. "I can be a lookout."

"No, ya stay with Ma till I come back. If I'm collared, you'll 'ave to take care of her." Aware of her distress, he hugged her. "Don't worry, kid, I won't get nabbed. We'll be okay. Give the others a shake if you need 'elp. They'll get yer grub." He kissed his mother's cheek and whispered, "Rest easy, old girl." Then he took off.

Ruth stayed awake concerned about a hacking cough Violet had developed. On the second night, Ruth made a bowl of vegetable soup and tried to wake the frail old lady. To her alarm, Violet wasn't asleep but unconscious. Too concerned to wait for Eddie's return, Ruth sent someone for a doctor, praying Violet would recover...

The doctor examined the fragile old lady. Turning to Ruth, announced, "This woman needs immediate hospitalization. In her weakened condition, I doubt she'll last the night."

Ruth protested, remembering Eddie's wishes.

The doctor looked around at the squalor with revulsion. "It would be better for her to end her days in comfort than to pass away in this filthy cellar."

Ruth had to agree. Instructed the others to tell Eddie where they were. The ambulance arrived, whisking Violet away to the hospital. Worried, Ruth waited as the staff attended to her. When Violet was ready to move to the ward, a nurse took Ruth into her cubicle. The dear old woman looked so different with the ingrained grime scrubbed from her face. All her matted hair had been cut, washed, and combed. Ruth took the withered hand, leant over, and kissed the old lady. Violet opened her eyes and rewarded Ruth with a beautiful smile before losing consciousness again. Ruth remained in the waiting room, lost in thought, anxious about Eddie's reaction and imminent arrival.

The sound of running footsteps startled her. She went out to the corridor to find out what was going on. An ambulance crew pushing a trolley rushed by, followed by an agitated young constable. Ruth heard him report to a nurse.

"Called to investigate a suspected robbery in progress in Paddington. When I arrived, this big bloke was running from the premises. Well! To tell the truth, being on my own, I was a little unsure; he's a big chap." He confided to the staff nurse, "Couldn't be certain if he would be trouble. I'd just cautioned him when he made a break for it, shouting he would come to the station later. But no, he asked to go home first to see his sick mother and sister. He darted into the road, straight into the path of a lorry." He gulped hard as he recalled the scene. "Turned me up; I can tell you, I've never witnessed a serious road accident before. The poor lorry driver had no chance to stop, hit the bloke head on and flung him over the cab to the other side of the road. He'd just thirty pounds in his pocket from the robbery." The young officer sighed, "Fancy dying for so little."

This description fitted Eddie Ruth, rushed into the examination room. On a trolley lay her beloved Eddie., now peaceful in death. Before daybreak, Violet joined him. Their joint funeral with a full church service was completed a week later. Heartsore and desolate, the sole mourner, Ruth, stood by the graves and knelt down to place two white lilies on the mound of earth. Lost in her misery, she returned to the basement and counted out the few pounds left from the funeral fund. Lingering in the doorway stared back at the dingy hovel. Dark and dismal it may be, but for a few blissful happy months, it was a warm, secure haven.

Closing the door, Ruth said a forlorn goodbye to the only place she'd ever felt cherished and genuinely loved as a family member. Without Eddie as her protector, Ruth was no longer safe.

For days she wandered around the city. "I must move away from London, but where can I go now?" she cried desperate tears as she tramped the streets. aimlessly it began to rain, so Ruth took shelter in the train station., She scanned the destination board and decided to hop on the train to Brighton and start another chapter of her chaotic life.

CHAPTER EIGHT

BRIGHTON ROCKS

Ruth strolled along the bustling promenade. It was a warm, welcoming summer's day in Brighton. There were so many shops, restaurants and hotels along the seafront she was convinced she'd soon find a proper job and be back on her feet. Unfortunately, the move was ill-timed. Others had taken all the available seasonal jobs. Quickly, the little money she had vanished. Without Eddie to guide her and no knowledge of how to exist, Ruth soon became penniless and homeless again. Everything was so different here from London; she knew and understood. In Brighton, a bustling seaside town, the right image meant everything. The residents didn't want her sort on their doorstep. Unlike London, the local markets were full of clothes and tacky holiday gifts. None of the stallholders gave away any food. The arcades and souvenir shops didn't want their customers hounded by filthy beggars. Furious owners shooed her away. Unable to find respite or consolation for her wretchedness, Ruth sank further into deprivation, not paying attention to or caring where she travelled.

The constant effort to keep herself clean became too much of a battle. Her unshakeable depression and despair isolated her. Because of her neglected appearance, no one would offer her a job, so she stopped asking. Well-meaning workers from the many charities offered help, but she brushed them aside. Ruth slept in shop doorways or any dark corner that offered a little shelter from the bitter nights. With the need to survive, no pride remained; she picked up half-eaten food thrown in the gutter outside the many takeaways. Furtively checked the slot machines in the amusement arcades for any coins left behind. From the pavement pub tables, Ruth drained glasses with any drink left.

Desperate for food, Ruth accosted holidaymakers as they left the shops and restaurants, begging for loose change. They either ignored her or shoved her away in disgust. Other street beggars drove her away from the prime sites they used. Others dipped fingers expertly into holidaymakers' bags, stealing purses and disappearing into the crowds. Ruth, desperate for money, always seemed clumsy and bungled it. All she got were accusing glares from her would be victims. She gave up trying, sure to be the one who got caught. One night, a group of drunks had their amusement by urinating on her as Ruth crouched in the recess of a bus shelter. After that, she hid under the promenade, out of sight of the public and police patrols.

As she drifted around the shops in the dawn's half-light looking for food, a scruffy, dishevelled man shuffled towards her.

Caution learnt. Ruth paused to see if he would go away and then realised it was her image in a shop window. No semblance of femininity was left in her shapeless form. In disbelief, she stepped closer and studied the vision before her. Matted, lank hair strung out from under a tattered woollen hat. Draped over her gaunt frame, an oversized, filthy coat. Beneath the months of dirt, her face was a mass of open, weeping sores. How did I let this happen? What a disgusting mess. Her hands covered her eyes to block out the image, appalled at what she had turned into. Huddled beside the sea wall, wrapped in an old piece of carpet for protection against the biting cold, watching as the screeching seagulls fought for discarded scraps of food scattered on the pavement. Ruth stared at the empty expanse of the ocean before her. The incoming tide crept up over the pebbles on the beach. Muttering to a nearby seagull, she voiced her thoughts. "I'd be better finding peace in death." Tears fell down her shrunken cheeks. "I can't do this anymore, no one left I care for, and nobody cares for me. What's the point of this way of life?" The longer Ruth stared at the waters ebb and flow, the more appealing death became.

She went to the end of the pier, bending over the iron rails, and gazed into the dark waters. Hypnotised by the rhythm of the waves as they splashed like her tears against the pier's pillars. Sensing the sea invite her to drop into its icy waters to wash away her wretched existence, Ruth clambered over the rail, ready to drop.

A man caught her around the waist and lifted her back to safety. "Whoa, that's not the way, mate. You can always find a way out of trouble. What's caused a kid like you to be so desperate?" He shrugged. "Whatever happened to you is none of my business; let's get out of this wind." The moment had passed, and with it, her intention. She allowed him to draw her off the pier. At the bus shelter, he squatted beside her. Pulled a flask from his bag and offered her a cup of hot tea. With thanks, Ruth accepted. "Lucky, I arrived early to fish, hoping to catch a few mackerel. Instead, I have caught me a little sprat."

Ruth made no reply.

"Here." He handed over a pound note, "Buy yourself a proper breakfast. You'll feel better with a hot meal inside you, lad. I'm off now; take care." Then he left before she could thank him for the kindness as he strolled away. Hot salty tears of despair mixed with gratitude streamed down Ruth's cheeks.

A few days later, a young woman from the Salvation Army came over to her. She had offered to help many times, but Ruth had turned her away. "Hello, how you are today. My name's Penny. What's yours"?

"Why won't you give up and me alone," Ruth moaned. "Look at me; I'm a bundle of rags, not worth a second glance. A man thought I was a boy!" she wailed. "Just go away. I can get by on my own. Don't need your handouts."

Penny sat beside Ruth, taking hold of her thin hands. The young woman replied with a smile. "Handouts are what the charities give you. A hand-up is what a friend offers. Let me be a friend; what do you have to lose?" Penny suggested they find a house where she would have warmth and security. Ruth shook her head in refusal. Penny pressed on. "We have a few organised squats in Brighton. I can take you to a good one. William, the organiser, 's a friendly fellow. Don't you want to be warm and dry? It's so cold on the pier. If you like it, I can arrange for you to stay. At the least, it can't hurt to have a look."

Penny's persistence, at last, persuaded Ruth to agree. Penny found Ruth a set of underclothes, a thick jumper, a skirt, sturdy shoes, and a winter coat to fit her wasted form in the Salvation Army's clothing centre. At the public baths, Penny cut, treated, and washed Ruth's matted, lice-ridden hair. She applied antiseptic ointment to Ruth's facial sores and helped scrub off the ground-in dirt from her body. Then Penny left, allowing Ruth to relax in a warm bath. An hour later, returned to collect her and escorted her to a large, detached house. Penny introduced Ruth to a welcoming man named William, who managed the squat.

William shook her hand warmly. "Nice to meet you, Ruth. Things are straightforward and relaxed here. There are around a dozen young students and runaways like yourself sheltered here. Everyone either works or has student grants." William took Ruth around the house; every room was clean and smelt fresh.

Penny explained, "All the residents contribute to the supply of foodstuff and running costs like the water and electricity for light and cooking. One group member returned home today, so there is a free space.".

The salvation army paid the initial week's charge for Ruth to take the vacancy. William described the strict division of tasks, such as cooking and cleaning. None of the rooms had beds, but a resident gave her an old, tattered sleeping bag. Ruth enjoyed a hot, filling meal for the first time in many months. The following morning Penny took her to a nearby café after a brief chat; they engaged her as a dishwasher, the wage was more than enough to pay her way. The other residents told her William had his own home but was always on call to handle any problems. He gave the authorities little chance to move his people out of the immediate district. William always had another ready if the Council closed one squat, so none were ever without shelter.

Ruth shared a room with Jane, a serious-looking young girl with a pleasant, open face. Straight bleached-blonde hair hung down to her waist. She was a little older than Ruth and took her under her wing. They were kindred spirits as Jane had also fled from an abusive parent. They soon became firm friends. Five other females lived in the house. Ruth met Beth, a chatty, slim, dark-skinned girl and Barbra, who spent most days buried in a book. The last two were Sally and Margaret, identical twins who were always found huddled together and quarrelled constantly.

The other four residents were men. Peter, a stout, middle-aged, black-bearded Frenchman. Simon a lively, small-boned boy with long, brown hair tied back in a pigtail. Simon's Spanish friend, Anton, a tousled-haired youth of the same build, mocked him over his pigtail. They were all pleasant to Ruth, except for one man called Charles, Jane's particular friend. His nickname for Ruth was hog-face.

Most weekends, Charles's friends invaded the house. All upper-class, mature students. They gathered in the lounge or flopped on the stairs, usually drunk on cheap wine and cider. They discussed world affairs and recited boring poetry. To avoid them, the other residents met in separate rooms. Ruth passed many an enjoyable evening. Anton would cause everyone to roar with laughter at his ridiculous antics. As the night passed, the wine took effect. From below, they'd hear the debates become ever more passionate. The topics discussed were just sought to score points and impress the others. Simon scoffed they had as much knowledge about world affairs as he did. Ruth found them all annoying and full of themselves. Jane's Charles was a short, overweight man; who dyed his sparse hair black and plastered it down with oil. His extended stomach hung over his trousers. A self-centred, pompous fool, his droning voice louder than his companions', Ruth often wondered what Jane attracted to the self-centred bombastic bully who rarely smiled. Much to Ruth's irritation, Jane clung to his side like a leach, declaring how splendid he was. Many times, Charles made unwelcome advances towards Ruth. She'd push him away and remind him Jane was her friend.

Once, while alone in the kitchen, Charles came behind her and stuck his hand up her skirt. Ruth spun around and slapped his face. "How many times do you need telling? Keep your dirty hands to yourself," she snapped. As he lifted his fist to respond, Ruth darted fast behind the table, out of reach, then picked up the nearest chair and flung it across the table.

He yelped in pain as it bounced off him. "Stupid idiot, no need for that," he **snarled**. "Don't delude yourself, Hog-face; it's just for fun. I don't fancy you! Who would?" Then he stalked out.

Tidy and clean once more, Ruth got a better paid part-time cleaning job; once again, life settled for her. Jane asked Ruth to join her at a poetry session at the home of Charles's sister. With no interest in poetry, she refused. Jane pleaded. Charles expected her to bring Ruth. He would be annoyed if they didn't go. Aware Ruth didn't care for Charles, she urged they might find other, exciting people and have a break from routine, so Ruth agreed.

CHAPTER NINE

THE DEVIL' S DEN

On their arrival, Charles's sister, Savannah, embraced them. Obese, in her late forties and dressed in a vivid pink caftan, her thin bright, long orange hair hulled to one side, with lengths of silver cord with tiny gold bells entwined in it. Small blue crescent moons stuck on each of her plump cheeks.

She hugged both girls in a high-pitched, animated voice and gushed, "Oh dear, my Charlie's little kittens. So glad you've come. Two at a time, the little scamp. I never thought he had it in him. Welcome to my humble little nest." Waved them past, showing green-painted fingernails, "Go straight through this hallway; everyone is in the blue room."

Almost bent double with mirth, both girls wandered in the direction shown them. Pulling aside a pair of thick, maroon velvet drapes, they peered into the room. Their eyes took a few moments to adjust to the gloom; Ruth noticed the female occupants wore matching attire to Savannah. The men wore baggy, white, pyjama-like outfits. The smoke-filled room had no furniture but scattered around were enormous cushions. From the ceiling, small glowing lamps gave the place an eerie bluish light. Guests listened with rapt attention to a man squatting in the centre of the room, playing a weird-sounding instrument held on his knees.

Charles spotted them and growled. "There you are, about bloody time get over here""

The girls picked their way over and sat on the cushions. Uncomfortable in the stifling heat, Ruth wiped her stinging eyes and wished she never agreed to come. A powerful smell filling the air made her queasy.

Jane smiled encouragingly. "The perfume is just incense. You'll soon be used to it. Tonight, the readings are from third-world countries. Everything we eat and drink is from those regions to create the right atmosphere. Relax, Ruth, enjoy the night."

A man wheeled in an enormous pan of steaming hot food, followed by another holding a large jug. To her disgust, everyone just plunged their fingers into the pan, scooped up a small portion of the mixture, and then shoved it into their mouths. Ruth refused her share from the pan and waved the man away.

"Take it," Charles ordered. "How can we imagine how the poor blighters live if we don't get right into the atmosphere?"

Ruth replied, "No, thanks, not hungry."

His arrogant, flabby face flushed. "Well, Jane, your friend here is making an absolute show of herself. She damn well better eat it, or I'll walk out right now."

Not wishing to upset or have Jane in tears again, Ruth picked up a handful of the mixture and accepted a pot filled to the brim with the jug's contents. Ruth cringed as she watched the thick brown fluid drip from it. It looked revolting and smelt disgusting, but she sipped the liquid and tried to stop gagging.

Charles yelled, "Not like that, stupid bitch, down it in one." He forced her hand up, spilling the drink over her. "Blood hell ", he howled, filled another pot and snarled. "Drink it. "

Ruth's body shook with indignation. "The pompous pig. Who does he think he is? I don't want the rotten drink," muttering to Jane. "I've half a mind to tip the lot over his head."

Jane shook her arm in dismay. "Please, Ruth, don't make a scene. Charles will be furious. He'll just take it out on me," she pleaded. For her friend's sake, Ruth obliged. The drink tasted vile and burnt her throat.

"Good girl," Charles responded smugly. "Ruth will be one of us yet, Jane. Go on, girl, have another. Live a little, enjoy yourself."

When finished, everyone cleaned their fingers in a water bowl, and another batch of small bowls appeared. Each of these held a transparent liquid. Someone passed around a plate of biscuits coated with a brown paste. These were pleasant and good for soaking up the drink. Ruth accepted each one without further protest.

"Here, try this," Jane persuaded, opening a small packet of white powder. "I'll spread it over this wafer for you. Go on; it will relax you. You'll feel fantastic; try just a little."

Ruth accepted and swallowed, then had another drink to wash the taste away. Gradually, Ruth realised something else was happening In all directions amid a tangle of hands and legs, writhing and squirming naked and partly dressed, bodies giggled and moaned in satisfaction. Amid squeals of delight, they engaged in sexual acts in full sight of each other. She saw some roll off one person straight into the arms of another. Appalled, Ruth had seen enough and turned to tell Jane she was leaving, but Jane, preoccupied with Charles, ignored her. As

Ruth climbed over them, Charles reached up and pulled her onto the floor beside them.

"Not given up already, the funs just started. How about having a trio? I guarantee Jane won't mind! She enjoys a threesome, so will you?" Charles yanked up Ruth's dress and tugged at her panties. Ruth tried to shake him off, but to her dismay, Jane helped him hold her to the floor.

Laughing at this, Jane tried to force more powder into Ruth's protesting mouth and urged, "Isn't he the best? Don't struggle so we can share him like real friends."

In a blind frenzy, Ruth lashed out with hands and feet and screamed, "I'd rather sleep with a dog than your fat ugly old man."

Stung by Ruth's response, Charles rolled off and sneered. "Alright, my fine lady, I can wait. I'll have you later".

Exhausted from the struggle, Ruth lay shocked and drained of energy

. His voice forced her back to reality as he hissed, "I'm in no mood to argue, Ruth, so this round's down to you. I can wait till next time." Then shifted his attention to Jane.

. An odd, sickening sensation came over her. She tried to rise, but her strength was depleted, and she slumped back, sprawled on the floor. She looked in Jane's direction for help, but she was held in Charles's passionate embrace.

Ruth waited for the muddled feelings to clear. Charles's head appeared to split away from his neck and glide away up to the ceiling. As she watched it mesmerised, sudden brilliant, coloured dancing flashes of light hurt her eyes. Beads of perspiration ran like a river down her face. Waves of rising heat alternated with shivering chills that coursed through her body. I must get out, but Ruth stayed glued to the floor. Try as she might, her leaden legs wouldn't move. She screamed for someone to release her. Bodiless hands tugged at her arms and legs like long pieces of elastic. Distant echoes of laughing voices mocked her. Then she was whirling over the heads of everyone, hounded by the dismembered head. The jaws were wide open in a mute scream. Long sharp teeth running with spittle raced towards her; as she ducked to avoid them, they dodged away. Charles's eyes turned into two massive holes with thick, yellow-green mucus streaming from the hollow sockets. She wanted to grab the head and hold it still, but it bobbed and twisted away from her clutching fingers. Her grasping hands, at last, found it. As she hung on, her fingers plunged deep into the pulpy skull, and it disintegrated beneath her clasp. In horror, Ruth threw it from her. A sudden explosion of light and sound shot her up to the ceiling, then burst through the roof into the crisp night air. Ruth woke in the garden, her sweat-drenched body shook, out of control. Drained of all energy, she stretched out in the yard until daybreak. Then forcing herself upright and lurched out of the garden. In fits and starts, Ruth stumbled her way back to the squat.

In her mind, Eddie's voice scolded her. *Didn't I tell yer never go down that road?*

The mixture of alcohol and drugs she'd taken had caused her horrendous ordeal. She hoped William would find her space in another house. When Ruth reached the street, she saw a police car parked outside the squat. Council workers were busy boarding up the doors and windows. Still fearing the police might catch sight of her, she pulled back into the shadows. One police officer was speaking to William, showing him a photograph. Although too far away to pick up the conversation, it convinced Ruth they had come for her, so she ducked behind a hedge until they left. Ruth couldn't stay now; it was time to move and lose herself once more in the familiar streets of London.

CHAPTER TEN

THE JAWS OF HELL

Ruth arrived at Kings Cross station with just a few pounds in her purse. Her confidence had been shaken by what she believed the conversation at the squat was about. During the following weeks, Ruth drifted around safe and invisible amid so many. Content to share her resting place with the most decadent and violent of London's gutter life.

Each evening, Ruth queued at one of the many charity kitchens. Here, she could find a meal and a hot drink. The volunteer workers there urged Ruth to take advantage of the many young people's shelters before she came to harm. Their good intentions received sullen responses. Ruth had no incentive to raise herself from her wretched situation, scorned their well-meant advice, ate her meal, and left.

Dejected and alone, Ruth longed to find the companionship she shared with Violet and Eddie. In the evenings' chill, she joined other homeless people as they crowded at the many bomb sites. They smashed discarded furniture and wood to make a bonfire for temporary warmth. Each night, the vagrants scattered to their preferred resting places. Most of them kept to themselves or stayed in their small groups. One evening, a man hobbled towards her on crutches.

"Ugh! It is a bitter night. Mind if I squeeze in beside you, pet?"

Ruth shrugged her shoulders. "It's a free country."

He squatted down next to her, placing the crutches at his side. "It is now, little darlin," he replied in a soft, Irish brogue, offering her his half-empty bottle. "I pray to Almighty God; it will continue. Take a swig of this to warm your bones."

"No, thank you. I don't like it. I'm warm enough."

"That's good, then. Got a night space sorted?"

Ruth nodded, turning to him. He had a wide open, friendly face and twinkling blue eyes. "Don't want to be out in this chill," banging his arms to warm himself. "My given name is Thomas; what about yourself?"

Ruth told him, then shuffled along and shifted the crutches to one side to make more room.

"Wouldn't believe I was once a fine upstanding fellow, would you, Ruth?" He grinned. "Now, I wander around to pass the time with all these other nameless drifters."

"What happened, an accident?" she asked.

"No, pet, lost this leg in the war, so I did. Wasn't even for my own country," Thomas sighed. "The Red Cross tried to help me, did their best, Lord blesses them. But I was beyond their good intentions, my home flattened by bombs that carried off my darlin' wife and three grandchildren. I had no future or reason to live. Glued to a bottle of whisky to dull my memories. I lived a drunken existence with the dregs of the earth on the streets. Just like these wretched souls," he breathed, pointing to others huddled near the fire.

'Until one bitter, bleak winter's night with no hope. I planned to finish it all. For a Catholic, suicide is a mortal sin. So, I went to a church to make my last confession and pray for absolution. The Holy Father led me out of the confessional box and held me in his arms while I cried out all my pain and loss. He never once chastised me and understood my pain. When all was out, I sat drained and silent. Little by little, the priest convinced me life's too precious to throw away. He spared my soul from eternal damnation. The church found me a berth in an ex-services man's hostel. They handled all the paperwork to set up my military pension, so I'm comfortable enough."

Feeling a surge of sympathy, Ruth stretched out and touched his sleeve.

He patted her hand in a friendly manner. "Ruth, you're a kind, gentle child. I appreciate your company. You learn to live with a weeping heart in time." He bought out his bottle, "I still need this devil's wine to help me make it through the dead of night."

He smiled. "Although most memories are now of sweeter, happier days."

"Why can't you go back to Ireland?" Ruth inquired. "Have your family still there?"

He reached out and touched her cheek. "Ma and Da long since departed this world. My sisters and brothers live there. Not seen them for many a year. Still, we keep in contact occasionally by letter and Christmas cards. I lived in the loveliest village on the emerald isle." His voice trailed off as he cleared his throat to muffle a sob and stayed quiet in reflection.

Ruth touched his arm. "I'm sorry, Thomas. I didn't intend to upset you with all my questions."

Thomas turned to her with sad eyes. "It's been a long time since I told of my life. The good Lord gave me the sweetest flower in all Ireland. Times were hard in Irland, so I brought my beautiful Kathrine here, promising to make our fortune, return and raise a fine healthy family. When our first landlord found out she was expecting our third child, he forced us out. We roamed the street for days, looking for rooms. Notices in windows said no kids, pets, or Irish. Footsore, with the little ones worn out, I took a single room in a shared house."

"It must have been tough."Ruth pressed his arm in sympathy.

"Yes, it was; my Katherine struggled to keep it clean." Thomas shook his head. "It was no use. When it rained, the water poured

99

over the rotting sills, and mould covered the walls. With nowhere else to go, we had to remain. The children were often sick in that damp room and with the London fog. We lost our firstborn to pneumonia."

Moved to tears by the anguish in his tone, Ruth reached out to him.

"Oh, dear Ruth, what a sweet child you are." With a handkerchief, he tenderly wiped away her tears. "They say misery loves company, but I've upset you with my tale; I'll finish now."

"No, please don't, Thomas; I want to listen to the rest of your story." Ruth urged.

"Well, not much more than that, except my Kathrine's spirit died in that foul place. Her gentle voice, once soft as rain on petals, changed to one full of tears. This country crushed her spirit and aged her long before her time. Things were tough; with no work or food on the table, life became an endless battle. When the war broke, I volunteered, so at least she had some money each week." He exhaled slowly. " I lost all of them when the bombs dropped over London. We had so many plans when our world was young; all gone now."

"You still got memories of better times," Ruth consoled.

He smiled across. "What a wise head you have on such young shoulders." Nodding in agreement, he continued. "Yes, I do; in my dreams, I return to my childhood home and stroll again through lush green meadows drenched with sparkling morning dew. Feel my face kissed by the gentle, balmy breeze." He glanced down at Ruth's enraptured face. "Picture this, Ruth, nestled in the hills' bosom sit tiny, blue-washed cottages. Honey-perfumed jasmine tumbles around the doors. The fat cattle, grazing at will on fertile land." Thomas' voice wavered as he thought of his home.

"Ruth, never will you find the grass so green until you look at the meadows of Ireland. Constant soft, summer rain keeps it glistening like in no other land. White smoke from the peat fires drifts away from the moss-covered chimneys on a sharp, frosty winter morning. No choking smog in those gentle hills." He gave Ruth a melancholy smile. "My land is the most tranquil place on earth. If you ever yearning for peace of mind, sweetheart, make Ireland your home. That is the place I long to be. It forever has my heart, but I can never go back. Without my children running in those hills, my soul would die." Thomas let out a long shuddering sigh. "How can I return? I left those shores as a hearty young fellow. My head was full of plans for a rosy future; now, you see half a man. No, I shall end my miserable days in this wretched, soulless city."He chatted on for a while, delighting Ruth with his lilting accent. They were at ease together as the night stretched out before them. A church bell struck nine, and Thomas got to his feet. "I'm off now, pet; I must check in on time. Stay safe, and take care of yourself. God willing, until we meet again, the Angels hold you in their blessed care."

Ruth watched as he disappeared into the gloom. Although destined by fate never to see him again, his words stayed with her.

One bitterly cold night, she came upon a site with a roaring bonfire. Sitting around a large group of squabbling drunken vagrants. Cautiously, Ruth drew back a little. A few feet away, a boy around her age fiddled with a small packet; his hands shook so much he had trouble opening it. Lying next to him, she noticed a ring. Ever the opportunist squatted beside him reached down and stealthfully snatched it up. He turned around quickly, almost catching her action. She touched his hand, pretending to offer help.

He shrugged her away, snarling, "Piss off, slag! Get yer own stuff."

"I'm sorry, only trying to help. You appear to be experiencing trouble with that."

He gazed at her and mimicked, "Oh! Dearie me, I appear to be aving trouble, do I?" He thrust the package out of view up his sleeve. "Fink, I'm fucking ignorant, do yer? Bastard scabby lot yer all the same. Just want free gear; never buys yor own. Fink, if yer gives a bloke the nod, offer a quick leg over, he's gonna give out for free." He growled, "Well, yer picked on the wrongen." Unexpectedly he lashed out and punched her hard in the chest. "Shove off afore I clump ya in the gob."

Ruth muttered, rubbing her chest. "Open the damn packet yourself, go on, hope you spill it. I couldn't care less. Don't want that blasted rubbish."

"Fuck off then!" he snarled. Ruth flinched as he raised a fist toward her.

Ruth turned to move away, uttering heatedly, "Stupid idiot! It'll kill you. Hope you have a nasty death too, pathetic little squirt."

The boy sprang to his feet, knocked Ruth to the ground, and sat astride her. His weight kept her beneath him. He bellowed, "Bastard slag, who the 'ell does ya fink yer talking to?" Waving his arms, he sneered, "Ark at miss La-di-dah, never done anyfink wrong, I suppose?" He sat back on his heels and studied Ruth, frowning in thought. "Anyow, what's a posh bint doing 'ere?" His bony knees dug into her chest. "Come on, answer afore I whack ya." Ruth, too breathless to reply, stared up into his pockmarked face. "I ain't joking; speak up, wotcha after?" He raised his fist to strike again.

Crossing her arms to shield herself, Ruth cried, "Please don't; I'm just looking for a warm place to rest."

His eyes narrowed into blazing black pinholes. His thin lips curled to reveal broken, yellowed teeth he snarled. "I know yor a fucking copper's nark. I'm right, ain't I? A grass for the old bill!"

Ruth tried to insist she was just like him, homeless.

He was having none of it. "Yer right. Like, I'm gonna believe that. Yer mates shoulda told ya to lose your la-de-dah voice down 'er." He yelled at the top of his voice to the others around the bonfire. "Guess what? I got us a copper's nark. Sent 'ere to snoop on what we got. What shall we do with it?"

"Throw the poxy git on the fire and shut that bastard row! I want some kip." came an angry response.

"Nah, that won't work. Shit, don't burn," someone else yelled.

"Cut the whore-faced cow up, and send Old Bill the bits," another suggested

From the darkness, other voices gave advice, and some shuffled over to have a look. Surrounded by a drunken, excited mob, Ruth pleaded her innocence to no avail. Rough hands dragged her to her feet, ripping out fistfuls of hair as they shoved her from one to the other. Ruth shrieked for help, but the sheer terror in her voice spurred on her attackers. The instigator of her plight laughed.

"Listen to the pig squeal. I bet this pile of crap will burn. Let's try it, haven't smelt pork for ages." He looked around for support. "What ya say?" The mob roared their approval.

"Leave it out; she's just a kid," a man thrust through the crowd to help her. "Christ's sake, what's wrong with you" he yelled. Placed himself in front of Ruth, wrapping his arms around her for protection. "Pack it in. You've harmed the kid enough." He sought in vain to draw Ruth to safety. The excited vagrants, in no mind to listen to reason, yanked her out of his arms. Others attacked him, driving him backwards.

"If yer that squeamish, piss off, go on, get the fuck away." her main tormentor ordered.

Defeated, her protector ran off to call the police.

The frenzied mob lifted Ruth off her feet and carried the struggling girl towards the fire's greedy flames. Amid her terror came the welcome sound of police sirens and cars screeching to a halt on the gravelled ground. From the edge of the pack came a warning cry.

"Leggit quick, old Bill's here."

Her persecutors scattered, dropping her inches from the edge of the fire. On hands and knees, she crawled away. The boy reached out, grabbed her legs, and hauled her back

. "No, yer don't. I'll see ya burn yet. Let's see what ya got." He searched her pockets and pulled out a few coins and the ring. "What's this? Then nicked it off me, didn't ya?" he scowled, slapping Ruth across the face. "Not so lily-white then?" He forced the ring onto her finger. "Want it that bad, 'ave it. Can't shift the bloody thing, anyway." He sneered in satisfaction. "There ya go now, makes ya a thief, same as me, don't it?" Keeping an eye on the approaching police cars, he hastily searched through the rest of her pockets and found the little money she had. "Right, this 'I'll do," he muttered. Pushing a small package into her coat pocket, he smirked. "Ere's a little present. Wonder what yer mates will think about that."

Ruth covered her face with her sleeves as he rolled her over into the hot ashes. The boy pulled a thick chunk of smouldering wood from the bonfire and laid it across her back. As the police rushed out of the gloom towards them, he kicked her further into the embers. The smouldering rags began disintegrating, and the hot embers scorched her flesh. Ruth lay still, too numb to realise her clothes were alight. She screamed and writhed in sheer agony, but after the physical assaults on her body didn't have the strength to save herself. A police officer heard the screams; his sharp eyes spotted a moving shape almost indistinguishable amid the burning rubbish.

Moving closer, "Jesus", he gasped, "he's on fire, must have rolled in stupid drunken fool". Ignoring the heat, he yanked the body back to safety. Stripped off his jacket, swiftly wrapped it around her and beat out the embers clinging to what remained of her clothes and smothered the flickering flames

An ambulance crew arrived and rushed Ruth to the hospital for emergency treatment. Her rescuer accompanied her, who needed treatment for his scorched hands. Nurses, with care, removed all the blackened clothing and sped her away to the X-ray department. Once brought back to casualty, a consultant assessed her. In a toneless voice, he dictated his findings to a junior colleague.

"On her body, there are significant and minor burns. They should fade in time. Wearing so many layers of clothes saved her life. Her hair will grow back in due course." He rubbed his square chin. "Despite the beating, no bones are broken. When all the x-rays come back, they'll confirm this." He continued to examine Ruth as he spoke. "There is superficial facial burn damage. The girl has slight swelling and bruising to her spine. That will be painful, but with bed rest, it should heal. It will be a long job to get her fit" Having concluded his findings, he ordered her admission to the wards and prescribed pain relief. As the consultant left the cubicle, he spoke to the attending constable, "Actually, she got off lightly. It could have been much worse. I can't understand them living like that so young. Fallout over drugs, was it?"

"We went through her clothes and just found two tablets. Most likely the illicit kind, but not sufficient to charge her with possession. There was no personal property or anything to identify her. However, she was wearing an expensive ring. We have similar pieces reported stolen of late. We will check to see if we have a record of it." The constable shook his head. "I'm afraid, sir, this is a familiar story. She'll end up in care. These kids are homeless, just faceless drifters with no roots. Most times, no one cares enough to report them as missing." He took out his notebook and sighed. "No wonder they get into trouble. Meanwhile, we'll try to find out who she is, but I doubt we hold a record of her." As he prepared to leave the examination room, he added, "A vagrant flagged us down, or she'd burnt to death.

From my experience, I'd say, whatever happens, she'll go straight back on the streets." He grumbled, "I wonder why we even bother. A waste of time and public money."

When discharged, the police arrested Ruth. The ring had been stolen in a local burglary. She was found guilty of theft and sent to a detention centre for girls in Devon.

CHAPTER ELEVEN

TURNING POINT

The correction centre was an old manor house converted to hold twenty girls serving a short-term custodial sentence. The ground floors are used as staff quarters and offices. Extensive grounds surrounded the house. Behind the property was a small kitchen garden. Most girls worked in the greenhouses or tended to the vegetables for the centre's meals. All duties within the house were performed under close supervision and given to the residents they considered "troublesome."

Ruth arrived at midday in time for lunch. As she entered the dining hall, inquisitive eyes greeted her. A staff member handed her a tray and propelled her towards the serving hatch to collect her lunch. While carrying the loaded tray and looking for a space to sit, a dark-skinned girl rose from her seat and shouted.

"Oi, look. Bloody hell. They let a freak out of the loony bin!" Coming closer, the girl stared hard at Ruth. "Far worse in close-up. You need a paper bag over your head, mate." The dining room erupted into laughter.

"I got one upstairs, Annie," one responded.

Ruth threw the contents of the tray over Annie. Carrots, peas, potatoes, and gravy splattered over her head and dripped down her mocking, twisted face.

"I'll mend; what's your excuse?" Ruth sneered

Annie flew at Ruth; both girls wrestled to the floor with cheers of encouragement from the other inmates. As the staff dragged them apart, Annie screamed, "We're not finished, freak; I'll have you!"

Ruth was locked in the punishment room to cool down. Gazed out the window at the lush green hills beyond and the freedom that should be hers. Ruth dashed her fists against the windowsill and made a silent vow. *If anyone hurts me in future, they'll be sorry. I won't be pushed around again; I've had enough.*

Hostile and aggressive towards inmates and staff alike, Ruth was considered a troublemaker and assigned to the house's domestic duties.

Annie, the home's self-styled leader, egged others on to make Ruth's life difficult.

When the lights went out and the night duty staff retired to an adjoining room. Ruth settled down to sleep. In the early hours, she woke with a start to see a group of girls surrounding her. They sat on the bed, making it impossible for her to move. One held down a towel over her mouth to smother any sound. Anna placed a lit cigarette against Ruth's exposed hand and pressed it into her flesh several times. At last, they released her, satisfied they'd done enough to teach her a lesson.

Incensed, Ruth got up, snatched up a shoe and dived headlong at Annie. Pounded the shoe against the hateful face with all her might. Blood erupted from Annie's nose like a fountain; her friends pounced on Ruth and dragged her off.

The noise alerted the staff. Annie received medical treatment. Annie convinced the disciplinary board she was an innocent victim. The other girls backed up her lies, so she escaped unpunished. Ruth was blamed for an unprovoked attack, lost all privileges, and her injuries were thought to be self-inflicted. The staff put her in a locked room at night as a punishment. At least she felt safe there. During daylight hours, the torment continued. Unused to any defiance, Annie threatened she'd make her toe the line. Ruth hurled back ferocious insults.

With the main doors locked at all times during weekends, the inmates were unsupervised for extended periods. A programme designed to make them behave as an independent group. Ruth spent much of her free time on her bed, staring at her reflection in a small mirror. She grimaced at the face covered with scarlet patches. Her left eye was still bloodshot, and the lid swollen. "God, I'm ugly," she breathed. Her sunken wafer-thin face combined with the stubble regrowth of hair that stood upright. She looked like an old, well-used scrubbing brush.

In the evenings, Ruth spent her free time in the small library to relax and be sure of being left in peace. She found perfect harmony lost in the magical world of books.

Unpleasant and unapproachable, she quickly became the ideal target for ridicule and scorn, known as the red freak. Ruth loathed them all and vowed to escape as soon as possible and burn the hated place behind her.

One evening, Ruth, enjoying the solitude of the home's library, heard the door creak open.

"Yes, the bookworms here. Come on, quick," a girl called out. Around a dozen others entered the room. One pushed a chair against the handle to jam it. They came towards her, led by Annie.

Ruth jumped to her feet. "What now?" She pointed a finger at Annie., "I told you before, leave me alone, or you'll be sorry. Go on, clear off, and leave me in peace."

The group showed no signs of going. Troubled by their slow approach, Ruth barked, "Are you deaf? Shove off, find somebody else to annoy, leave me alone."

"Don't panic, freak. It is not your company we want. We wondered if such an ugly sort like you ever had a good fuck!"

Annie smirked. "So, we thought we'd find out. Catch hold of her girls; get her kit off quick."

Ruth was swiftly stripped and held down on the carpet.

"Look at the freak!" cried one of her attackers. "She's covered in red splotches and got bright pink nipples."

Another sniggered. "That means ain't had no little bastards yet, doesn't it?"

"Spread her legs; let's find out if she's still a virgin," Annie instructed. Then forced her fingers inside Ruth.

"Come on, Annie," one girl urged, "is she or not? The suspense is killing us."

"Wait a minute," Annie complained, "Christ's sake! Keep her still, can't you? There's enough of you; stop her wriggling about." Withdrew her hand and exclaimed, "Poor cow, just like we thought. Never had a fella, not likely to either, with a face like that." She roared with laughter. "Oh, dear me, you've no idea what you're missing. Well, freak, I'll give you a treat. Who's got that bottle?"

Someone passed an empty sauce bottle to her. As Ruth squirmed to break free, Annie sat between Ruth's splayed legs. Forced the bottle between her legs into her body. Driven insane with pain, Ruth bit hard into the nearest arm. The girl shrieked and released her hold; Ruth pushed Annie off and rolled free. She raced around the library, hurling books, files, and chairs at her assailants. She picked up the discarded bottle and smashed it against a table. Then lunged at Annie, dug, and twisted the jagged glass deep into her throat. As Annie collapsed to the floor, her life's blood made a crimson pool beneath her. She gasped and spluttered her last breath.

The horrified onlookers made no attempt to help their stricken leader. Instead fought with one another to escape. Ruth, naked, demented with pain, armed with the broken bottle, chased her tormentors through the corridors. They sought the safety of the common room and hastily barricaded the door. Huddled together in absolute terror as Ruth's fists pounded on the door.

At last, her wrath spent, she pushed against a massive cabinet beside the wall. Rocked it back and forth with all her strength until it fell and blocked the doorway. "They won't get past that!" she growled.

Then she raced back to the library and dressed without a second glance at the inert body sharing the room. Looking at the shambles of the library, she had to **escape** before the staff returned. Ruth remembered Annie smoked and searched the blood-soaked body but discovered nothing. Without emotion, she turned the corpse over to release the jacket trapped beneath and found a box of matches in a pocket. Ruth ripped out the pages of a book, made a small pile beneath the heavy curtains, struck a match, and waited. Soon the flames licked the hems of the curtains and shot across the ceiling. In no time, the room was ablaze. Hiding in a stairwell as the fire alarms rang, she waited unnoticed as staff unlocked all the doors to empty the building. Ruth took her chance and ran down the back stairs and out of the building.

During the evacuation chaos, she slipped unnoticed through the gates left wide open for the fire engines. Ruth lingered and watched her tormentor's silhouettes in the barricaded blazing room with grim satisfaction. They clawed at the secured window, trying vainly to escape the encroaching flames.

CHAPTER TWELVE

A RESTING PLACE

To avoid the major roads, Ruth kept to the fields and lanes. She wandered through the countryside but discovered hours later she had travelled in a circle. In the late winter, the barren earth offered little food, finding only berries and raw vegetables. Her stomach rumbled with hunger. She slipped unnoticed into chicken sheds on the isolated farms, rammed chicken feed into her mouth and packed her pockets with eggs. Then, safely out of sight, devoured the raw eggs in the hollows of hedgerows.

In a small village, Ruth hovered outside a greengrocer shop, waiting for a chance to steal something from the outside display. The suspicious shopkeeper asked what she wanted. "Looking, that's all." She grinned and waited until he was distracted by a customer. Then she grabbed two large apples and shoved them into her pocket. The enraged man rushed out. Ruth pushed the bench, scattering his produce all over the pavement, and darted off with the man's curses ringing in her ears.

She flopped down on a grass verge outside a bramble-covered cottage and tucked in with relish to the apples. Ready to move on when she glanced over the fence. An old man wheeled a barrow full of vegetables into a shed at the bottom of his garden. Huddled low and unseen, she watched him work. As dusk fell, his wife called him to finish for the day. He leaned his tools against the shed and locked it. To Ruth's delight, he used a simple padlock to secure his shed. Ruth waited until the cottage was in darkness.

The full moon bright in the cloudless sky gave the garden some light. Taking care to stay in the shadows, Ruth sneaked through the gate and snicked down to the shed. With the prongs of the garden fork, it was easy to break the lock. It clattered on the slabs, and Ruth looked towards the cottage, but it remained in darkness. What a feast she had!

A vast array of preserved fruits, pickled eggs, and spicy chutneys sat on the packed shelves. Hanging from the roof, sweet brussel sprouts. Stacked boxes of apples wrapped in blue tissue paper and sacks of other winter vegetables were on the floor. Stacked on the floor were bottles of home-made wine. After weeks of near starvation, Ruth ate and ate. She opened and gobbled up the preserves and discarded open jars, unfinished in her greed to open another. She pulled the corks out and tasted the wine until finding some she liked. Ruth drained one bottle after the other. Unused to wine, she stumbled around the shed. Knocking many containers from the shelves and sending them crashing to the floor. The result of a full stomach and the wine took hold. Ruth fell into a satisfied drunken stupor until the indignant old gardener roused her.

"What are you doing in here? This is private property!" With his hands on his hips, he looked at the devastation and groaned, "What a waste! All this food ruined; you'll pay for this, my girl." He rummaged in a drawer and pulled out another padlock, growling, "I'm calling the police." Ruth got to her feet; the man waved a warning finger at her. "Oh no, you don't; stay right where you are." He dashed out the door, slammed it shut, and replaced the padlock.

"No, please wait!" Ruth jumped to her feet, banging on the door pleaded, "Please don't. Not the police; I was so hungry. I'm sorry for the mess. Give me a chance to make it up to you." To her relief, he reopened the door.

Looking at her dishevelled state, the gardener frowned. "How will you do that, then? Got money to pay for this damage?"

Ruth shook her head in misery.

"Thought not. What's it to be then, my girl?"

Terrified that he'd call the police, desperate to convince him not to, her words came rushing out. "I'll work for nothing to repay you. I'm a hard worker and much stronger than I look. You won't be sorry, I promise," Ruth assured him.

He considered her suggestion, tucking his braces between his fingers. "I am getting on now and find it harder each year to do the garden and prepare everything for sale at markets."

He leaned against the wall, "What's happened? Been in an accident?"

"Yes, but I don't want to talk about it," she muttered, desperate to gain his sympathy and give herself time to run away. Ruth bowed her head, buried her face in both hands and sobbed, forcing out tears that rolled down her cheeks.

His voice softened. "All right now, lass, don't get in a state. I can use a little help if you're up to it." He rubbed his gnarled, arthritic hands together, considering the advantage of some manual help. "Two weeks' work should be enough." Still irritated by the damage she had caused, he grumbled, "First, to clear up this mess you've made. You can do the heavy digging in the garden to make up for what's already wasted."

Ruth eagerly nodded her head in agreement.

"You can sleep in the old washhouse. There is a water pump with a privy nearby. I'll bring out a camp bed. Plenty of wood to light the old boiler in there to keep warm. Still sharp cold in the night." Ruth breathed a sigh of relief as he continued, "My wife will fetch a meal out each day. Don't come into the house, are you willing? It is hard, backbreaking work. Either accept this offer, or I will call the police."

Thankful for this reprieve, Ruth replied, "Yes, please, thank you"" Her voice came out in a frantic rush. "I'll do anything you want. I'll work from dawn to dusk if you like, it doesn't matter how hard. I'm stronger than I look, you'll see."

He smiled and chuckled at her outburst. "Hold on, their lass, I'm no slave driver. I can't deny the work won't be easy" he turned away, satisfied with the arrangement.

"Right, then. Come to the back door; I'll leave a bucket and broom. Clean up this mess first, and I'll ask Mary to fix you breakfast and a mug of tea later."

Ruth waited, smiling outside the kitchen as he returned to the cottage to tell his wife, Mary. Through the open window, Ruth heard her rage screeching at the top of her voice, "You're a stupid soft fool, Ted Taylor! What are you thinking? We know nothing about her. We'll be murdered in our beds."

"Don't exaggerate; we've nothing to worry about." Ted laughed. "My guess is when she cleans herself up and heals, she's attractive." Mary spotted a wry smile on his lips. "She has the loveliest, sea-green eyes." He shook his head "Shortest hair I've ever seen on a girl, though. Anyhow, do us good having a young person around."

Mary's voice grew shrill. "Still the same old fool! After any bit of skirt, have you forgotten your past affairs? Want a young one now, is it? I took you back time after time. I won't go through that humiliation again. Good God, man, you're old enough to be her grandfather. Get rid of her; she might do anything. I shan't rest a moment till she's gone from here. If you don't call the police, I will."

"No, you won't, ya silly woman; our doors are locked every night. She's just a young kid who's had a rough time, she's staying, and there's an end to it."

With his wife fuming, Ted returned and handed Ruth a bucket and brush. "Take no mind of Mary. She's a silly old woman; she'll come around given time."

Ruth doubted Mary ever would. While Ted quarrelled with his wife, Ruth resolved to stay put as long as possible. She had to tread carefully; this secluded cottage was a perfect hiding place. One month turned into four; Mary brought her meals out each day without further protest but never uttered a word. Ted picked her flowers from the garden and often brought small presents back from the market. Ruth often felt Mary's eyes on them as they laughed and chatted as they worked. She delighted in his company and smiled inwardly at his comic attempts to flirt with her.

Ted confided in Ruth, seated together in the wash house after another row with Mary. "Despite her sharp tongue, Mary's a good wife and has forgiven me many times for past affairs. There is no excitement now in our marriage. We settled down now to a comfortable slipper and pipe life," He looked at Ruth.

"It shames me that I fell out of love with Mary long ago." Taking hold of Ruth's hand, he spoke with trembling emotion. "A man has needs, even at my age," then sat back in his chair and mumbled softly. "Such a comfort having a young thing around the place."

Ruth knew he wanted more; she noticed how his old eyes devoured her. However, she felt content living there, convinced Ted wouldn't make any unwelcome advances.

One morning, from the cottage, Ruth heard shrill voices rage. "Over my dead body!" screamed Mary. "I won't have that thief in my house. If she does, I'll leave."

"Suit yourself, Mary. I'm bringing her inside the cottage when I return from the market. The girl can sleep in the spare room. You do as you think best."

Ruth helped Ted load his van for the market, insisting she was happy to leave things as they were. She didn't want to cause distress to Mary by moving inside.

"Washhouse is for dogs; I'll not have you treated like one any longer," snapped Ted as he drove away.

Mary stormed out to the washhouse screeching at the top of her voice, "Go on, clear off right now!"

Alarmed, Ruth stammered, "What have I done? Tell me, Mary, please don't send me away. Wait until Ted returns, and I'm sure we can sort things. I enjoy living here."

"You're a thief. I need not give the likes of you an explanation," Mary yelled, her ample bosom heaved as she gasped. "You won't come inside my house while I still got breath. I saw you making eyes at my Ted." Ruth protested. Mary would have none of it, bellowed, "Don't bother denying it, Seen it with my own eyes. Giggling and whispering together. Dirty trollop. He's old enough to be your grandfather. You should be ashamed leading on the old fool." She raised an angry hand, silencing Ruth as she opened her mouth to reply, "Don't say you haven't." Her voice rose to a wild shriek, "Only one fool in this house, and it's not me""

Ruth picked up the hoe and walked down the garden, meaning to stall Mary's tirade at least until Ted returned. Mary wobbled after her, "are you deaf." She roared, "Go on, get out this minute, or I'll call the police"" As she followed Ruth around the garden and back inside the wash house, she kept berating Ruth. "I bet you're on the run. Why else should a slip of a girl stay on here? You never once went through that gate, hiding away in my home. I'm sure there is a reason, not a good one either. I'll be bound."

It was plain no reasoning or pleading would change Mary's mind. With Ted away, without a doubt, she'd call the police. Ruth couldn't risk that, so with no choice, she nodded in agreement, "All right, Mary, have it your way." Throwing down the hoe in surrender. Ruth moved around to pick up the gifts Ted had given her and announced, "I'll leave right now. "

Mary dashed them from her hands, grabbed Ruth's arm and pushed her out of the washhouse. "Never mind taking anything. Nothing here is yours; you came here with nothing. Now clear off the same way."

Ruth tried to shake free; the older woman stumbled and fell backwards, hitting her head on the concrete boiler. Ruth looked down at the blood trickling from Mary's ear in anguish. She shuddered as Mary's sightless, wide-open eyes fixed on her, full of loathing.

"Oh! My God, she wailed. "No one will believe this is an accident!" Ruth scribbled a note to Ted before running off across the fields.

After the undertakers took Mary's body away. Ted found the note from Ruth

I never hurt your wife, Ted; please believe me. I will never forget your kindness, but I can't stay.

Despondent, he bowed his head and wept. His tears were in part for Mary but also for the loss of the young girl he'd fallen in love with

CHAPTER THIRTEEN

HALCYON DAYS

While she rested in a lane near a small wooded copse, a young boy and a man carrying bundles of willow and hazel twigs approached. The man spoke to Ruth. "Hello, youngin, where are you off to on this lonesome track?"

"Nowhere much, Just travelling."

"Look like you could use a good feed. When did you last have any grub?"

She shrugged her shoulders.

"I go by the name of Nelson; this scrawny little mush is one of my chavvies, Levi. We're on the road travelling, same as you. Tell you what," He invited, "stay and help the boy cut more hazel twigs from this hedgerow. We'll carry this load back to the trailer; my woman's doing a bacon pudding with boiled spuds for supper. You're welcome to share. How's that sound?"

Ruth's mouth watered at the thought, so she agreed and helped them collect more willow. With their arms loaded, they returned to the campsite. On arrival, the treo were greeted by seven inquisitive children and a round-faced, heavily pregnant woman.

"Found this young stray on the road, Rosie," Nelson hollered. "Fetch another bowl. This girl's so skinny she'll blow away in a good wind."

Rosie told Ruth to sit around the fire. Hung from a hook over the glowing logs, an enormous pot bubbled full to the brim, its aroma overpowering and inviting. One of the children passed Ruth a steaming bowl of delicious food.

As they all sat eating, Nelson pointed out the children. "That freckled-faced girl is Polly, our eldest at eleven years. Levi, you've met; he's ten. Next, with hair as black as night, comes Rachel; she's nine. The others go, Lottie, Phoebe, Jasper, and Bessie, downwards to our Ambrose." Laughing, he pointed to the last child. "That little barrel at the end is baby Joseph." He glanced over at his wife. "I reckon by the looks of their mother, she'll have another afore morn. On our way to Epsom for Derby Day, give you a lift as far as Sutton. That suit?" Nelson asked. He looked over at his wife as she arched her aching back and sat back with an effort. "Has your time come, old girl?"

Rosie nodded yes. Ruth looked on, fascinated, as Nelson set up an odd-shaped shelter. Polly placed two sparkling metal bowls inside, filling one with warm water. Then he spread out a ground sheet, some clean cloths and a bundle of rough rags.

"I'll keep the pot going on for the washing," Nelson called as he completed his preparations. "There, all done." He lifted Rosie. "In ye go, old girl, come on, Polly, help that mother. You too, Ruth."

"Me?!" Ruth shot her head up. "I don't know what to do."

"You're a woman, ain't ye? It'll come naturally. You'll see." He called Rachel, "Put the little ones to bed and mind them." Nelson lit his pipe and settled down by the fire.

That evening, Rosie went into labour. The girls rubbed her aching back as she groaned and shifted about, trying to get comfortable. They wiped her sweating body with the rags dipped in cool water. A few hours later, Polly sent Ruth out to collect the hot water with orders to keep the other bowl warm. Mesmerised, Ruth watched, mimicking every heave. Rosie hardly made a sound as her child pushed his way into the world. Polly deftly cut the cord as she'd done many times before and passed the chubby baby to Ruth.

"Wipe him over with that water," Polly ordered, pointing to the second bowl, "Wrap him up with this." She passed over a soft square of muslin. With her heart pounding in her chest, Ruth held the slippery child. They rinsed the blood from him with care, wrapped him as directed, and passed him back to the exhausted mother. Polly called out to her father. He came into the tent with a steaming hot cup of strong tea for Rosie. Admired his new son while Polly and Ruth helped Rosie back into the trailer.

"Another beautiful boy to carry our name. We'll call him Alfred," Nelson proclaimed, handing him to Rosie, who put the child to her breast. Once satisfied, she passed the contented baby to Rachel. She laid Alfred in a prepared box and covered him with a sheep's fleece, cosy and safe, while Rosie, exhausted, slept.

Polly called Ruth back to the tent, and they cleaned all the gore away, folding up the soiled linen for washing. Then they wrapped up the afterbirth in a separate cloth. Polly handed the bundle to her father, who buried it deep in the ground, safe from foxes. He said a brief prayer, thanking God for the safe birth.

"Why's your father doing that, Polly?" Ruth **asked**.

"That's what our new baby lived on inside. Once the baby is born, it dies. So, it gave life to his life; all life must be buried," Polly explained wisely.

They all settled in their beds for a well-earned sleep. At first light, after attending to the baby, Rosie cooked breakfast on the fire. Ruth was astounded.

"We don't lay a bed just because we bring another soul into the world," Rosie smiled as Ruth tried to make her rest a while. "Work to be done, no time for slouching.

The children practised dancing and the songs to sing to entertain the racegoers who'd threw them a penny or two in appreciation. Ruth watched in awe as Nelson and Levi used small knives to whittle wooden pegs from the willow sticks. With great dexterity, they fashioned delicate rose-shaped flowers in the same manner in preparation for sale at the Derby fair. Rosie taught Ruth how to make small bunches of heather and fern. Together, they created meadow primrose posies and filled up two large wicker baskets, ready to sell door to door.

The sleeping space in the trailer was tight. Nelson, Rosie, and the baby shared a raised bed. On the floor underneath, the young ones slept snug and warm. Ruth slept in the old comer van they used to tow the trailer with the other older children. She learnt how to skin a rabbit caught by Nelson with his ferrets. How to pluck a stray chicken he'd found for Rosie to prepare a tasty stew. The food they consumed all came from the land. The children would run at the field's edges to scoop up whatever vegetables they could pull or cut. It all went into the cooking pot. Ruth had never eaten so well. The family took to her as one of their own. She learnt how to work the doors and what to say to the housewives to encourage them to buy. Ruth added pink or blue ribbons to the primrose baskets. "They can hang them over the baby cots for luck," Polly grinned.

"I think you must have some gipsies blood. Let's call these Ruth's baby baskets." Rosie laughed.

As they offered the pegs, flower posies, and sprigs of white heather and fern, Rosie offered to tell the women their fortunes if they gave her a shilling or two. Ruth listened to Rosie read their palms and stifled a giggle as the woman gasped with amazement at Rosie's words and nodded in agreement. Ruth thought fortune telling to be a load of rubbish. But the women seemed convinced, so there was no harm done. The family took Ruth to heart and invited her to stay with them as long as she wanted.

Rosie carried her full basket on one arm; Alfred was tied snug and safe in a blanket wrapped around her body. The older girls took turns selling and keeping an eye on the children. Ruth swore they had the devil in them. Many householders feared the gipsies would curse them if they refused to buy. They dipped into their purse, grabbed the heather bunches, and slammed the door. Others swore or spat at them, often calling them filthy thieves.

Sitting around the fire one evening, Ruth asked Rosie to read her hand for a laugh. Rosie refused. "the spirits don't give the gift to be used for fun. I know you don't believe, Ruth." Poking the fire, making red sparks fly into the darkness, Rosie chuckled. "Tell you what; come with us to the fair. We'll ask the Grandmother, and then you'll see. She's terrific, got the gift and taught me the ways."

131

"Maybe we'll have you married off to a fine Roma lad," Nelson chuckled.

Ruth watched the races, full of admiration for the magnificent horses as they paraded past. She trembled with excitement as, with pounding hooves, they galloped to the finish. Her sides ached from laughter and amusement at the little ones' cheek when they jumped on the fairground rides, then leapt off before the owners came for payment.

A memorable evening passed, relaxing in a field set apart for the gipsy vardos and caravans. Old friends and relations greeted each other with warm enthusiasm. Then moved around to the individual fires to chat and sing vivid stories of times long past. Disagreements often provoked light-hearted arguments. Entranced by the melodic sounds of rich, coarse voices singing, Ruth found her feet tapping to cheery notes from the many accordions and fiddles. Joyous laughter filled the warm summer air.

On the last evening, Rosie took Ruth to her Grandmother's trailer as promised. "Here she is; grandmother wants her fortune told." Rosie motioned Ruth to sit beside the fire and returned to her children.

The old woman took hold of Ruth's hands to study her upraised palms. Suddenly horrified, she released her grip and scowled, "Girl, I see evil, dark secrets in your past and future." She brushed down her skirts, rose and demanded with a shudder, "Get gone from here, bring no trouble to my family."

Confused and a little shaken, Ruth returned to Rosie.

"That was quick; what did Grandmother say?"

"Nothing important," Ruth lied. "I think she was too tired and needed her bed." "Fortune telling's all nonsense, anyway." she picked up a pot to fetch water and shrugged her shoulders.

The men went to Epsom village late in the afternoon, meeting in local pubs for a farewell drink.

"There'll be fights with the locals afore this night is out," sighed Rosie. "Always the same when they gather to drink. Someone says something, arguments lead to fights, and they all have a go. Then there'd be hell to pay; they never learn. Be home later, battered and bruised, but they'll do the same next year. None as daft as a man in drink. My blokes as bad as the rest. He'll come roaring home eventually, the worst for wear, silly sod." She heaved herself up and sighed, "Best get these chavvies fit for bed; we are back on the road early morn."

But by the following day, none of the men had returned to the camp. Rosie sat by the fire, wringing her hands. "Something must have happened. Why doesn't someone come and tell us? I'm that worried; it's not like him."

One of the other wives came yelling through the field, "The gavvers got them locked in the cells. Eva's boy, Jack, just returned; his mother sent him to the village to see where they were. Our men were fighting last night; bust up the boozers. Went from one pub to the next. Thrown out each time for starting trouble, they went mad, so the gavvers were called and chucked them all in jail. The landlords say they must pay for the damage. They got to divvy up one hundred and fifty pounds each. We gotta to pay it today. Those that can't must stay in the nick. God's sake, they must have caused a riot." Rosie went into the trailer, collected the baby, and gathered all the money earned at the fair. With the children trailing behind, all the women marched to the police station to pay for their men. As Rosie, Ruth, and the children crowded into the small police station, waiting for their turn, Rosie nudged Ruth, pointing towards a poster on the wall. It showed that Devonshire police wanted Ruth for arson and murder. Her heart stopped dead.

Rosie whispered, "Go back afore they spot you. Move on, quick!" She hastily pushed Ruth out the doorway.

The sharp-eyed desk sergeant spotted her. He leaned over the counter for an unobstructed view, but the girl had gone. As Rosie approached the desk, he asked, "Who was that young girl you just pushed out?"

"No idea, sir," Rosie replied. "So many fresh faces this year."

"Hmm, looks familiar." He frowned, going forward to peer at the notice board. "You'll be in big trouble if you're lying, understand?"

Rosie slung the money at him. "Just let my man out. We'll be away. Don't want to hang around. Need to move to our next resting place." As Nelson joined them, Rosie, frantic with concern for her family, told him about the station wall poster. They hurried back to the trailer.

"What have you done, girl?" Nelson asked. "Tell us true, so we know what's what."

In a subdued tone, she told them of her life in the detention centre. Ruth confessed to starting the fire before escaping, but not the killing of Annie.

Horrified, Rosie crossed herself, "Oh, mother of God! The Grandmother saw it didn't she? Sweet Jesus, what's to be done?" she appealed to Nelson.

"Gather your stuff together," He shook his head. "Bloody hell Ruth, you got to leave here right quick. No one will hide you now. You've got to be gone afore the gavvers come here."

Ruth, with sorrow in her heart, kissed the children goodbye.

Rosie gave her a parcel of food and a small amount of money to keep her going, then hugged her tight and wished her well. She held both Ruth's hands in her rough ones. With tears flowing down her rugged face, she whispered, "We'll never forget you, girl. You're in our prayers forever."

Ruth jumped into the van. As they raced off, two police cars were heading towards the field.

Nelson dropped her off at Sutton railway station and advised, "Jump on the first train, don't matter where it's going. I pray the Lord forgives you, Ruth; you did a terrible thing. I got to hurry back so the gavvers don't tumble. God be with you."

The next train due was going to Kings Cross; she had just about enough for the fare. Ruth sped off into the unknown, her dreams dashed once more.

CHAPTER- FOURTEEN

A TIMELY BLESSING

Back in London, Ruth could hide straight away and blend in as another homeless sixteen-year-old beggar. Living the life she seemed fated for. While sheltered in a church from a torrential rainstorm during a christening ceremony. She noticed a smart handbag and a thick winter coat on a pew a few feet away. Tucked in behind a pillar, Ruth waited for her chance. Stealthily, she moved forward, keeping an eye on the family. Picked up both items and retreated unseen. Resisted the urge to run—tiptoed out, closing the church doors without a sound. Once outside, threw off her dirty jacket, put the warm coat over her threadbare dress, and scudded. Ruth waited until she was far from the church before opening the bag. Inside, found a purse holding sixty pounds in notes and loose change. Stuffed it in her pocket and rummaged through the remaining contents. Letters, cards, and bits of rubbish she threw aside. At the bottom of the bag, she found a small box. Ruth opened it, on a silk cushion lay a tiny silver bracelet. Too sweet to throw away, she put it in the purse's side pocket, dumped the bag in a nearby bin, and then gorged herself on an enormous meal. Hunger satisfied, she leaned back in the chair. Ruth linked her hands behind her head and breathed, "Phew, I'm stuffed." Ruth glanced at the food scraps on the plate before her and muttered., "waste not want not," and scooped another mouthful. Thought for a moment about her victim and shrugged her shoulders. "Anyway, I bet she's got a stack of money and a warm bed each night. Ruth's lips twitched, "Stealing from a church. I'll never go to heaven now".

After finishing her second cup of tea, Ruth wondered where to go. *"If I waste this windfall, I'll be a fool. This is my chance to change this life. Perhaps I'll try Glasgow this time. I should find work in a smart hotel with my experience; no reason I can't begin again.*

Ruth hurried to the station and bought a one-way ticket. With a few hours to wait before the train's departure, she purchased a bar of soap, a small hand towel, shampoo, and a comb. Passed a shop selling cheap clothes, looking down at her attire, muttered, "I must get rid of these rags" Ruth entered the store and purchased a complete outfit and new underwear. She quickly washed in a lady's toilet and lathered up the soap to clean her hair. Looking in a mirror for the first time in months. Her face, although deathly pale, was now bright and clear. Her hair had grown enough to smooth into order. Pulling on the coat, satisfied; at least she now looked healthy. She counted out her money, surprised to find she had only a few pounds left. Things were a lot more expensive than Ruth remembered. Wandering around to pass the time, Ruth heard the familiar sounds of a violin following the music to its source. Sweet hidden memories flooded back as she listened to the man play. Tears filled her eyes as she saw once more an image of Eddie standing in this busker's place. Without thinking, Ruth opened her purse and emptied all the money into his small box.

"God bless you, girl; thanks to you, my kids will eat well this night. May good luck follow you today." The busker smiled in gratitude.

Ruth nodded and turned away, a deep longing tugging at her heart. She took out the bracelet and tucked it safely inside her bra, threw the empty purse into a waste bin and returned to the train station. Onboard, Ruth settled down in a window seat. To start yet another journey, convinced this time to find a new life in Glasgow. The carriage filled. With satisfaction, she saw that now, looking presentable, no one glanced at her. She draped the coat over her legs and wriggled until comfortable, settling down with the busker's words still in her head. *I could use a few blessings.* Ruth mused before she slipped into a sound sleep.

A sudden jolt roused her, throwing her to the floor. A second violent jolt followed; the train had hit something on the track. With bone-shaking vibration, the carriage rocked back and forth. Ruth never forgot the scream of steel on steel like a banshee wailing her final lament. The engine bumped over the rails, its wheels juddering as they dragged along the ground. The carriages tipped over and hung precariously over a steep embankment. Showers of gravel smashed the windows, showering the passengers with razor sharp pellets and glass. The train twisted on its side and came to a shuddering, grinding halt. Unimaginable chaos ensued as passengers were thrown from their seats and into each other. Luggage plummeted from the racks like shooting weapons, inflicting further injuries. Finally, the train came to an abrupt stop; the air filled with the sounds of muffled moans and shrieks of panic. Tilting carriages rocked to and fro. A long moaning sound of ripping metal was followed by complete silence, and then with a final roll, the carriages left the track and hurtled down the steep bank. It was all over in seconds but seemed to happen in slow motion. So, horrifying and disorienting. The stench of smoke and burning oil was nauseating.

Held fast beneath a man's dead body, Ruth called for help. After what seemed like an age with no one coming, eventually heaving and pushing with all her might moved the body aside and struggled free. She tried to rise, but trembling legs buckled beneath her. Ruth cried something she had not done through all her recent miseries. A woman came to her side, cradled Ruth in her arms, and stroked her trembling body.

"It's all right, my dear; you're suffering from shock. Try to get out into the fresh air. You'll be fine in a little while. Here, let me help."

Ruth stood upright with the woman's support and gasped in horror, seeing blood all over her coat and legs. "Oh my God, I'm hurt. Where's all this blood coming from?" she wailed.

The woman looked her over. "Now, now settle down. You're fine, only a few cuts on your legs," removing the coat, holding it up, and shaking Ruth's arm in reassurance, "See here, the blood only on this, my dear."

Unconvinced, Ruth gave herself a frantic examination, twisting around to view as much of her body as possible. With relief, she realised the blood wasn't hers. She'd escaped with just a few cuts and bruises. Ruth turned to thank the kind woman, but she'd moved on. Dizzy and sick, needing fresh air, Ruth picked a pathway over groaning injured, already dead, or dying casualties and scrambled over a jumble of broken seats and glass. The unnerving shrieks reverberated throughout the crashed train. Plumes of smoke seeping through the carriage walls fuelled her panic; Ruth looked for a way out through the haze of choking dust. Rushing towards the nearest shattered window, Ruth barged past others heading in the same direction

A man shouted for calm and tried to block the surge. "Take your time," he advised, "Rushing like this will just cause more harm." The desperate passenger's overriding desire to survive pressed on, ignoring his pleas. Ruth yanked back a woman reaching up to the window and took her place. Stuck half in and out, wedged between two others, finding it difficult to breathe, she squirmed and wriggled in vain. Ruth felt hands on her backside shove her, sending her tumbling headlong onto the embankment to safety.

Ruth soon revived in the fresh evening breeze and then tried to comfort those about her severe injuries until the emergency services arrived. Suffering from shock paid no attention to the scattered wallets and purses of her fellow travellers. An oversight she later regretted. Those who found their way out from the wrecked train sat with wide vacant eyes or staggered about, overwhelmed with shock. The carriages at the back of the train hung to the edge of the track. Able passengers scrambled out and rushed to assist those still trapped and injured. The survivors emerged with head injuries; some were carried out unconscious and laid next to the tracks. For many others, it was too late. Before long, Ruth heard the sirens of emergency service vehicles close by. After receiving first aid and being given a warm blanket, Sat, at the side of the track, to her dismay, learnt the train had travelled just as far as Yorkshire. Twisted wreckage littered the verges. The thick, rancid smell of burning filled Ruth's lungs. Many passengers were trapped under others, past help. The ambulance and fire service members arrived to attend to the injured. Glad to be alive, Ruth recalled with gratitude the busker's blessing. Ruth watched in horror and sorrow as they extinguished the fires and lifted many blackened bodies out to cover by blankets on the side of the embankment. Unable to watch the grisly sights or the plaintive pitiful cries of pain all around her, she slipped away unnoticed, passed all the bright flashing blue lights of the emergency vehicles. Setting off, she hoped in the right direction for Scotland.

On such a chilly night, having lost the coat, she was glad of the blanket. Hoping to find a lift to her journey's end. But getting a ride was more challenging than Ruth thought. Many drivers stopped but sailed on as they realised it was a young girl. One driver leaned out of his cab, looked at her dishevelled state, shook his head and remarked,

"You shouldn't be looking for a lift, girl. All sorts travel these roads, my love, be careful. My firm doesn't allow it but look here." He put his hand in his jacket and passed her a note. "I got a daughter around your age; I'd be worried sick if you were mine. Take this tenner, go to the next village, find a B-n-B clean up and catch a train in the morning much safer." Ruth thanked him and walked on.

At last, one lorry stopped; bearing in mind what the other kindly man had advised, she hesitated, but she was exhausted and needed to rest. Ruth climbed in and lay back as the miles sped away. The driver studied her, "You're a right mess. What you been up to, a runaway Ah!?" he grinned. "Hit the road myself around your age."

"No, just travelling."

"Got folks in Glasgow then?"

"Yes, that's right."

Ruth had a sense of foreboding about this person; the way he looked at her sent shivers down her spine. Shut her eyes to avoid further questions and dozed off.

She woke to a hand tugging at her clothes. "Stop that!" Ruth pushed his groping hands away. "What do you think you're doing?" They had parked in a lay-by.

The driver had expected no trouble. "Come off it, girl. I didn't pick you up for nothing. You pay for a ride on the road." Ruth reached for the door handle. He roughly crossed an outstretched arm over her chest and anchored her to the seat. "No, you don't, my girl, pay up or put out. Your choice, what's it to be?" he snarled.

Ruth pulled out the five-pound note and threw it at him. "There, pig, which should cover your petrol," she snapped.

"Oh, for God's sake, thick bitch, I don't want your money. Don't be so melodramatic. Come on; just a quickie; I'm well ready," he coaxed.

Ruth bit down hard on his arm, he recalled in pain; she reached for the door handle. "Keep your ride; I'll walk." She opened the door and jumped to the ground. Forgetting the lorry cab was so high, she fell over, lost her footing, tumbled down the steep bank and lay winded on the grass verge.

"Come back, ya silly prat," he roared, "You'll catch your death. We're in the middle of nowhere out here!" As he started the

144

engine, he bellowed out of the cab window, "You'll freeze to death on these moors. Come on, last chance, jump in."

Ruth ignored him. He yelled, "Bollocks! Suit yourself; I don't have time to worry about a mardy cow," throwing out the blanket. He thundered, "Keep to the roadside, or you'll get lost." He slammed the lorry door shut and drove away. Alone and afraid on the dark moorland, Ruth collected the damp blanket and wrapped it around herself. A car slowed beside her as she struggled, and a young woman rushed to her side.

"Are you alright? Good job, we pulled in for a rest. Has he hurt you?" she inquired.

"No, I'm all right," assured Ruth. "I had a lucky escape."

"Bastard! Didn't even give you your luggage, the pig," the girl retorted. "Where are you heading to?"

"Glasgow, I've got family there," lied Ruth.

"We're going that way. Can give you a lift as far as Gretna."

Ruth, glad for the offer, accepted. Soon they were speeding along the road. The girl's name was Sally, she chattered away while her boyfriend, Steve, drove. "We're eloping to Gretna Green to get married. Both our parents arranged a big wedding with all the trimmings. We told them we wanted a private ceremony. Just married without all the drama. The old folk wouldn't hear of it, so we planned this a few weeks ago. Steve made all the arrangements needed; I'm so excited!" she giggled as Ruth congratulated them. "I tell you what," Sally replied, "We need to find two witnesses. You can be mine. What do you think, will you?" She placed a gentle hand on Ruth's arm. "Please say yes."

"Look at the state of me," Ruth complained. "I'm a mess."

"Soon fixed; we're about the same size. I have a full case of outfits with me. We'll find a bed-and-breakfast place, have a clean up, and grab a meal. My treat while Steve finds the second witness." Swept away by Sally's enthusiasm, Ruth agreed.

After the ceremonies, Sally kissed Ruth, saying, "Thank you so much! We're off home to face the music. Can't imagine what the parents will say." She shrugged her shoulders and giggled. "But maybe they'll give us a party. You can keep the clothes." Sally opened the car boot. "Here's a spare jacket; I'm afraid it's rather thin, but it will keep the worst chill away. Glasgow's about sixty miles; you should find another lift soon. Don't accept one from a lone driver, this time, mind." Ruth waved them off and resumed her journey.

CHAPTER FIFTEEN

THE HAND OF FATE

Reluctant now to accept a lift, it took Ruth three long weeks to reach Glasgow, each day desperate to find shelter, hungry and frozen to the bone. She tried to find work and food on the way, but she refused because of her dirty clothes and lethargic appearance. Stealing food whenever the opportunity arose. Ruth continued her journey. She arrived in Glasgow, weak and ill from the icy winter winds and persistent rain. Ruth cursed softly. "What a fool I am! Should have picked up a few purses lying around when the train crashed." While beating her arms around her body to warm herself. Ruth felt the child's bracelet tucked inside her brassiere. She pulled it out and sighed in relief, "Thank God!" then she remembered seeing a pawn shop a few streets away. "I should get a few pounds for this, enough for a decent meal." Ruth hurried to retrace her footsteps, praying the shop would still be open. She smoothed down her dress and tied back her tousled hair to make herself as presentable as possible. She need not have bothered. The man at the counter didn't give her a single glance. Ruth handed over the bracelet and waited. The pawnbroker counted out twenty crisp pound notes into her shaking hand. A scruffy pair behind her watched the transaction and followed her from the shop. Ruth's only thoughts were of the long-awaited hot meal. Clasping the money tight, oblivious of the impending danger, when she spotted a fish shop sign, her pace quickened, almost tasting her meal as the aroma drifted towards her. The stalking pair closed in, pushed her aside, and tore the precious money from her grasp. They left her sprawled on the pavement. Defeated, she crawled into a doorway, hoping to die and leave all this misery. All day Sunday, the icy rain lashed down. Ignored by passers-by as just another city drunk, Ruth lay too weak and ill to rise.

On Monday morning in the grey dawn, two street cleaners walked through the alley, pushing their wagons before them. One spotted the girl and stopped to inspect. "Come on now, hen, get up; you'll freeze here. Where's your coat?" Ruth tried to reply, but no sound came. The man called to his companion, "Tom, Tom, come over, have a look at this wee lassie."

"Leave her be, Colin," advised Tom. "She'll be another wee waster, drunk herself silly on cider, I bet."

"No," insisted his friend, "She's in a bad way. Come and look." He removed his duffle coat and wrapped it around her frail body.

Tom touched her ice-cold hands and face and had to agree. "I'd say she's near death; we should phone for an ambulance." While they waited, Ruth slipped into unconsciousness as Tom held her close in his warmth.

The next time, Ruth opened her eyes to find herself in a warm bed between crisp white sheets. Comforted and secure, she relaxed and slipped into a peaceful sleep. Ruth woke to find her hand held by a freckle-faced girl around her age.

"Hello, how are you today? We have been taking turns to sit with you, so you wouldn't wake up alone. I'm that glad it's my turn. My name's Sadie; what's yours?"

In a weak voice, Ruth told her.

Sadie chattered at a breath-taking pace, fluttering her tiny, dainty hands as she talked, describing her large family. "I'm the eldest. Then comes Maggie, who's fourteen, followed by our eleven-year-old twins, Alison and Fay." She smiled. "Next in line is Sally, three years old, a right little monkey, full of mischief, and then the apple of our Dad's eye, baby Robert." Sadie folded her gesticulating bird-like hands for a second, then babbled on, "With that lot, our two-bed flat feels like it's bursting at the seams." Sadie finished her tirade by telling Ruth how her father and his friend had found her. "They rang for an ambulance. You were suffering from exposure and malnutrition."

Sadie got up. "There, my gabbing fare wore you out. Try to sleep now; I'll be back tomorrow. I'll leave you in peace. You'll have lots of visitors now. I can't wait to tell them you're finally on the mend."The little figure trotted off out of the ward, turning to give a cheery wave. The soft, melodic tone in her voice was soothing.

Ruth looked forward to the regular visits from her rescuers and their families. The hospital almoner enquired if she had somewhere to live and offered her a place in a local hostel, but Ruth declined: she had her fill of hostels. Margaret, Sadie's mother, asked Ruth if she would like to contact any family members.

Ruth lied, "No, family, there's just me now." Fending off further questions, Ruth assured them the almoner had arranged hostel accommodation. She would move there when discharged and be fine.

"Hostel indeed. All by yourself, I dinna think so. Look at you, just skin and bone, need feeding up," Margaret huffed. Looking into Ruth's face, she asked, "How old are you?"

"Sixteen, soon be seventeen."

Margaret clucked and shook her head. "Sixteen", she repeated, "the same age as my Sadie. I'm that worried about you, Ruth; far too young to be on your own." Margaret took hold of Ruth's hand. "Why not stay with us until you find your feet?" Nagged each day by the enthusiastic family, Ruth finally agreed.

Tom, Margaret, Sally, and Robert slept in one bedroom, the three girls in the other. Sadie and Ruth shared a bed tucked into a recess in the living room, snuggled up close to each other on the cold winter nights. Each Friday night, in front of the fire, the little ones splashed in a large tin bath, screeching as they played, sending water all over the floor until reprimanded by their mother. The older members retreated to the public baths to wash and escape the noise. Somehow, Margaret kept her house spotless.

She took great pride in the children's appearance, making sure they were tidy each day. Although they were short, Sadie shared all her clothes with Ruth until she found employment and contributed to the family's small income. The girls enjoyed going to the dance hall together. Tom insisted they came home before midnight. Ruth accepted his gentle dominance with mild amusement and smiled with Margaret as he proclaimed himself master of the house.

On her seventeenth birthday, the family gave Ruth her first ever party. Margaret made a cake in secret. When friends and relatives had gathered to wish her well, Tom turned out the light, and the children marched in holding the surprise, lit with bright candles. Loud voices sang Happy Birthday as she received it with delight. Such kindness was too much for Ruth; she burst into tears of happiness and gratitude and stuttered her thanks.

They all hugged her and laughed. Sadie grabbed hold of Ruth and kissed her straight on the lips. Like a bolt of lightning, an electric shock raced through her body. The stunned expression on Sadie's face it was clear she felt it too. The children laughing and giggling pulled them apart, the moment lost and forgotten. Tom handed her a silver heart-shaped locket identical to the one Sadie had. A friend had brought a camera to take photos and mark the occasion. Together they picked out the best picture of them side by side. Tom had copies made and fixed them into the girl's silver lockets. They promised each other they'd wear them forever. Time spent with his loving family was the happiest and most carefree of her young life. At last, she believed her days of wandering were over.

Tom and his friend Colin took their families on a working holiday picking hops in Kent each summer. That year, they invited Ruth to join them. The work was hard and backbreaking, but she soon got used to it. They squashed together in a tiny, sparse tin hut both families shared to reduce costs. Each evening, the parents sat chatting, swapping stories and silly jokes. Ruth discovered contentment and belonging that she never dreamt of experiencing again. All the young ones ran wild, enjoying the free space to play away from the smoky city.

The next hut was occupied by a smaller family with young boys. They shared the sleeping area with two adult workers, both men. One was a loud-mouthed, arrogant man, around thirty years old, called Jerry Finch. The second man, Sam, was the complete opposite, small and friendly. He cut down a tree branch and made a rounder's bat for the children. Sadie set her cap at a handsome young boy, and he returned her interest. The competition was fierce as hut challenged hut. Spectators grew hoarse as screams of encouragement roared out during the games. The summer sped by. They often disappeared for hours, walking through the countryside.

Ruth took an instant dislike to Jerry, who was lazy and rude; he never did a full day's work, often found back at the hut sunning himself while others worked on until dusk. He always grumbled that the work was hard and the pay too low. The charge hand reported him to the farmer, who gave him a final warning to pull his weight. Ruth noticed how Jerry followed young Fay about. He pretended to join in the chase games but always singled out Fay to catch. Ruth cringed at the way he leered at the outline of Fay's youthful body through her thin dress as she stretched up to gather the hops. Sam, also suspicious of his interest in Fay, tried to stay close to him. Ruth took it upon herself to be Fay's guardian, never leaving her out of sight while Jerry lurked nearby.

One afternoon, Ruth and Fay took the young ones back for tea. They collected the children and set off back to the hut. With the children washed, fed, and settled, Ruth sent Fay out to enjoy the sunshine. Sitting on a chair outside, drinking and smoking, Jerry called Fay over to him. When Ruth looked out of the window, he pulled Fay against him. Forced her hand onto his groin and, with one swift movement, removed her panties. Ruth rushed out as Fay tried to fight him off and barged into his massive frame. Jerry didn't see her coming and was knocked off balance, stumbled and lost his hold on Fay. The distressed child dived behind Ruth for protection.

"Leave her alone, you disgusting creep!" she hollered. They sped back to their hut. "Go inside, lock the door, Fay," Ruth ordered. "Your dad will fix him." Terrified, Fay scurried inside and closed the door. Now incensed with rage, Jerry made to follow. Ruth picked up the rounder's bat, stood to face him, and brandished it, barring his way. "Get past me first, slimy toad!" Ruth cried.

"Right, my girl, you asked for it," he growled, catching the bat as it swung towards him, and snapped it in half like a twig. Slapped Ruth hard in the mouth and lifted her off the ground. Despite her screams and struggles, he carried her to his hut. His colossal body blocked the only exit. Ruth staggered to her feet, breathless, demanded he let her pass or she'd tell the other men about him.

Jerry shoved her to the floor, "Tell who you like; I'll be long gone from here. Not before I give you what that juicy kid would have got. I'm in the mood now; you spoilt my fun." He unbuttoned his trousers and gazed down at Ruth, smacking his lips in anticipation. "Take that look from your face, girl. You might even enjoy having a real man inside you," he smirked.

"You dare touch me!" Ruth warned, her heart beating fast. "I'll report you to the farmer; he'll call the police."

"Report me, will you?" He sneered. "Not before I knock you from here till next week. Threaten me, stupid bitch! Who do you think you are? I'll teach you what happens when you mix with the big boys."

The door swung open, and Sam stood there. "I knew you were up to no good, dirty great pervert. Leave her be!" He rushed at Jerry, his fists flying; Jerry knocked him aside. He scrambled to his feet and charged again.

Jerry mocked him. "Stupid little prick, don't start what you can't finish." He bent down and picked Sam up with ease. Placed massive muscular arms around the small man, locking them together and squeezing hard, Ruth heard Sam's ribs crack. Jerry kicked him into a corner like an old rag. Ruth tried to run for help, but he stopped her mid-flight and punched her head and body, knocking her down to the floor. In a fever pitch of excitement, he tore off her clothes. Ruth squirmed and fought in vain to push him away. "Good girl, go on fight me," Jerry breathed, "I love a struggle. It makes it much better."

Screamed for help at the top of her voice. Jerry put his rough hand over her mouth to silence her. Ruth sank her teeth into his fingers, drawing blood.

"Bloody little bitch!" he yelled in pain. "Do that again, and I'll go after the other one."

Ruth fell silent and lay still; in her head came Violet's crackling advice again.

If a bloke ever tries to take ya, Ruth, don't fight. He'll 'urt ya worse, even kill ya. No sense in getting 'urt for what you'll give away one day. Take your revenge later; it'll be all the sweeter.

Breathless with excitement, Jerry continued stripping her until she was stark naked. He straddled her and leaned back to unzip his trousers, wetting his lips as he gazed down at her. "I would have had you before if I knew what a cracker you are." Despite her protests fondled her breasts, squeezing hard. Ruth arched her back, straining to remove his weight. Jerry misunderstood this movement. "Great, ready now, are you? I should have known that with a body like yours, you'd be hungry for it." He pushed her legs apart and uncovered himself, moved into position. "Give me all you got." He pressed down on her, smothering her face with wet slobbering kisses, and then his mouth was on her breasts, sucking and biting her nipples. Moving his hands to her hips, he pulled her forward. Breathless with excitement, Jerry entered her. Ruth suppressed a scream as he tore her insides, praying the horror would soon end. After an eternity, he shuddered in satisfaction and rolled away.

Raw and bleeding, Ruth staggered to her feet. Jerry sat back on his knees and moaned. "Good Christ! Never took you for a virgin. I'm right sore. You're right." He leered at her. "Enjoyed it, didn't you? A man can tell; sorry for hitting you. Lost my head; it will never happen again. I promise we're right together. I know how to do it in lots of different ways. Don't worry, I'll look after you; I got a good job back home. What do you say? How about coming with me?" He looked ridiculous, standing with his trousers hanging open and a pathetic look of adoration in his eyes.

"Rather do it with a dog," Ruth screeched. "If that's the best you got, I suggest you go back to the drawing board. As for going away with you, I don't intend to spend my life with a sexually incompetent. I need a real man, not a useless cabbage." Old Violet was right; as she blasted him, his expression was sweet revenge. Enraged, Jerry lunged at her. Ruth brought her knee into his groin with as much force as possible. While he was doubled over, Ruth shoved him backwards. Unbalanced, he crashed to the floor and cursed her, holding his injured manhood.

"Jesus Christ," he moaned, "Fucking bitch, I'll get you for this. " Bent double with pain, he lurched across the room towards her, stumbled against a table and dropped to his knees.

Ruth picked up a solid glass ashtray and whacked him with it. As he fell face down, she jumped on his back. Blind with rage, she repeatedly smashed the ashtray against his skull. When too exhausted to lift her hand, she threw it aside. Ruth rose as his blood and brains oozed onto the floor.

Sam called feebly, "God's sake Ruth, what have you done?"

"Serve him right, the pig. Animals like him deserve killing," Ruth snarled,

Sam groaned as he attempted to stand. Ruth, still naked, rushed to his side, eased him to his bunk, and then wet a tea towel to wipe his bruised, battered face.

"I'll be all right, love," he responded to her concerned questions, shrugging aside her thanks for trying to help. "Get away now, girl, fast and far. I'll tell them all what happened, but you better get going straight away" Sam gave her a weak smile and winked. "Be a good idea to dress first."

Ruth grabbed a blanket to cover herself and returned to her hut. She brushed aside Fay's anguished questions, dressed, collected her handbag, packed her suitcase, and then gently spoke to Fay. "I have to go away now, sweetheart. Give everyone my love; everything will be all right; Jerry can't ever harm or frighten you again."

Ruth got a bus to Newham, the closest large town, and booked into a boarding house for the night. Relaxed in a long hot bath to wash Jerry off forever. She fingered the facial bruises, relieved they were superficial and easy to cover with makeup. In the morning, she took a train back to London. With three weeks' pay in her purse, she determined never to be destitute again. This time, she would create a good decent life for herself, no matter what.

CHAPTER SIXTEEN

A LOVELY LIFE

Ruth made her way to the west end to find work in one of the many hotels, cafes, clubs, or bars. Ruth accepted a position as a counter server in a coffee bar. She could start at once. It wasn't live in, but it was a start, so she took the job. During the day, a customer told Ruth of a decent, nearby well-run hostel for young women. She followed the directions at the end of her shift and found herself outside a large grey building. A pleasant smell of disinfectant hung in the air. At the reception desk, a smiling middle-aged woman greeted her.

"Hello, my dear. Can I help you?"

"I'd like to rent a room, long term, please."

"We have two places available," the woman told her. "This may be your lucky day, my dear. We are a female-only establishment with no male visitors in the rooms. The deposit is ten pounds held against any damage to furnishings. The rent with meals is eight shillings a week in advance." She concluded, "Are you able to prove regular employment?"

Ruth confirmed she had a job by showing the letter her new employer had prepared for her. The receptionist handed her a registration form. "Good; fill in this form. I'll take it to the office."

To her relief, the woman returned with positive news. Her application was approved; she informed Ruth that the weekly charge included two healthy meals daily in the dining hall on the ground floor. Then leading Ruth to a side room handed her a fresh, laundered bedding bale. Leading the way to the second floor showed her the spotless communal bathroom for that level's residents. Then to a spacious, bright room with three single beds, three wardrobes, and small bedside cabinets. A colourful curtain gave privacy to the tiny sink in one corner. Soon Ruth received the warmest welcome from the two girls she'd shared the room with. Sandra and Alice were both in their late twenties. Sandra, tall and slim, was a very glamorous young woman. Alice, in comparison, was short and dumpy but had the sweetest disposition and was always full of merriment.

They dressed in the most up-to-date fashion; all the outfits were revealing and skimpy. To satisfy the work regulation of the hostel, they worked part-time in a nearby factory. They said they did occasional evening work in the service industries. Neither offered further information, but Ruth was no fool and quickly realised they were prostitutes. Often both girls would be flat broke and need to borrow a few pounds from Ruth. On other days, they arrived back armed with bottles of cheap wine and presents. Ruth pointed out that maybe they should save money for rainy days.

"Daft little dope, stop being such a worrier! Spend it while you can. You're a long time dead!" they cried, laughing at her.

One evening, Ruth returned to the hostel and found all their belongings packed and the girls ready to leave. Alice told her they had found a flat. Ruth's heart sank in a weak, despondent voice near to tears; she congratulated them, "I am happy you found somewhere nice, but I shall miss you both."

Sandra put her arms around Ruth. "Dozy little sod. You're coming with us. We've packed all your stuff too and given in your notice. Here's your damage deposit; we drew it out; we didn't think you'd want to stay here without us. We need you to help us pay the rent and drop us a few bob when we're skint. You do want to come, don't you?"

Ruth, delighted, agreed

The flat had three good bedrooms: a spacious main room, a small kitchen with a full-sized cooker, and a spotless bathroom. When Ruth finished opening every door and cupboard,

Alice asked, "Do you like it?"

"It's gorgeous, but it must cost the earth. Are you sure we can afford it? We don't earn all that much" It had been a while since the girls told Ruth they worked as prostitutes. They were her friends. However, she wondered if she'd have the same relaxed attitude when they brought clients home. Ruth decided what happened behind closed doors was none of her business.

"Stop worrying all the time about money," Alice replied, "Sandra and I have it all worked out. With our own place, we'll go upmarket and make a mint."

Over the following weeks, they settled into a routine. Ruth worked long hours in the coffee bar and hardly ever saw the other two. They would be still in bed when she left each morning and often out when she returned. They agreed that if one girl wanted to bring a friend home and use their own room to entertain, the others wouldn't be in the way. Just as Ruth expected, men called for brief visits throughout the night. On a rare free afternoon, Ruth decided it was time to give the flat a good clean. She passed the old couple who lived in the flat opposite theirs, struggling up the stairs, their arms full of shopping.

"Here, let me help," she volunteered.

"Oh! Yes, thank you very much. These stairs get steeper each day." Passing over the heavy shopping bags, the old lady exclaimed, "I'm right puffed out."

As her husband unlocked the flat door, he inquired, "Early finish day is it, my lovely?"

Ruth smiled, "Yes, thought I take this chance and catch up on my cleaning while the place is empty."

"Fancy a cuppa before you leave?" the woman asked. "We're having one; need a rest after carting this lot about."

Ruth accepted, warming to this old couple called Lizzy and Robert Miller over tea. She discovered they'd walked down the aisle over fifty years earlier. Robert had worked for the gas board all his life and bragged they held many shares in the company. With those and their life insurance s would mature soon, they'd have plenty to see them through their old age in comfort.

"We're on the list for a council bungalow; can't come soon enough," Robert sighed as he rose from the chair. " I'll grab forty winks while you girls have a natter."

Lizzy showed Ruth their many photo albums, her eyes full of pride, pointing out their three boys killed during the war. Before Ruth realised, the afternoon whizzed by, and it was too late to start her intended cleaning. From then on, Ruth made a point of stopping by to make sure they were okay. They left a contented Robert to his book in a comfortable chair while she went shopping with Lizzey. Ruth spent many pleasant hours in their company, listening with rapt attention as they reminisced about times long gone. Lizzy taught Ruth how to use a treadle sewing machine to make simple dress repairs and alterations. She'd often remark how lucky people were with clothes coupons no longer needed rationing finished and material so easy to come by. Ruth spent Christmas Day with them. After an enjoyable dinner, she listened politely to the queen's speech on the radio with her two old friends. Ruth made sure she was with them as the bells rang to welcome the new year of nineteen fifty-two with them.

Finally, they received an offer of a bungalow in Wandsworth. Ruth helped Lizzy wrap all her treasures, ready for the move. Together, they measured and made up new curtains. Ruth arranged for the gas and electric services at their new address. As the men loaded the removal van, her heart was sad. They had become such a large part of her life she would miss their times together. Robert made her promise to come and see them often, which she did, but the travelling distance made it difficult.

Ruth longed to return to Glasgow and meet up again with Sadie, whose friendship she missed so much. Ruth convinced Sam would have told what happened at the hop farm and would welcome her short visit. On a free weekend, she took a train to Scotland full of excitement and rushed to the old tenement block imagining how happy and surprised her old friends would be to see her. As she turned the corner, all her hopes came crashing down. The entire area was in the final stages of being demolished. Distraught, Ruth asked around the remaining occupied buildings if anyone could tell her where the family had gone. She discovered that most tenants had moved to a new estate in East Kilbride, but no one knew Sadie's family's new address. Crestfallen Ruth returned to London.

CHAPTER SEVENTEEN

TEARS FOR ALICE

After a pleasant evening spent with Lizzy and Robert, as Ruth opened the front door, she overheard the wireless playing, knowing someone was home. As she prepared for bed, the phone rang. It was Alice's voice, gasping for breath.

"Where's Sandra, Ruth? Fetch her, for God's sake! hurry."

Ruth dropped the receiver and banged on Sandra's door. "What's the matter?" Sandra demanded, opening the door a little. "no blooming time to chat. Got one on the boil in here; make it quick."

"It's Alice on the phone. She's in trouble; it sounds awful. Come on, before her money runs out." Ruth, agitated, yanked her arm.

"All right! All right! I'm coming," Sandra grumbled, shook Ruth off, grabbed a housecoat, popped it over her shoulders, half closed the door, and murmured, "Won't be a jiffy, darling, help yourself a drink." Irritated by the interruption, shoved past Ruth and headed for the phone.

Sandra snapped, "What's up, Alice? I've got a generous punter impatient for action. " Sandra's voice altered, hushed with foreboding. "Alice, love, take it easy. Tell me where you are, and I'll come for you." She hesitated, "Hold on, mate, don't move. I'm on my way." Flew back to her room and brushed away the questioning Ruth. "Sling your hook, mate," Sandra ordered her guest. "Got no time for you now." Not bothering to dress, dug in her pocket as she pulled on her coat. "Where's my bloody purse? I need a taxi." The disgruntled man left, slamming the door in a temper.

At last, Sandra addressed Ruth. "Send for a doctor, Alice's in trouble. Sounds like she's hurt really bad. I'm fetching her home."

Twenty minutes later, she returned with Alice dripping blood all over the floor, supported by herself and the taxi driver. Sandra tried to give him a tip, but he protested. "I can't take it, miss. Wish I knew the lunatic that did this. He needs locking up for sure. Seen her around, a pretty little thing. Not any more, poor mare; he did a thorough job on her. The bastard, been better if he'd finished her?"

It was a good hour before the doctor showed up. "Good God! You should have called for an ambulance, not me," he proclaimed as he examined Alice. "Fetch me a bowl of warm water and a clean towel."

As he worked to stem blood flow, they looked at the full extent of her injuries in disbelief. A ragged slit ran down both cheeks to her throat. Her lips parted with swelling, revealing missing teeth.

Sandra ran for the bathroom to be sick. Ruth stared transfixed with horror as blood oozed from Alice's mangled face.

Unable to do more, the doctor insisted, "This woman must go to the hospital at once before she dies from blood loss." He muttered, "Too much valuable time lost." Turning to Ruth, he asked, "Where's your phone? Heaven knows what they can do for her."

Later that day, the girls returned to the flat. Alice needed over a hundred stitches and an emergency operation. Once out of surgery, they hooked her up to machines in intensive care. A police officer remained at her bedside, hoping for a statement from her.

When they returned home, Sandra sank into an armchair. "Christ, Ruth, what a mess. If the poor little cow comes through, how can she work with her face like a jigsaw? Be better off dead." Sandra whispered, "What bloke will give her a second look now? I told her to be wary of the weird ones. All Alice saws were thick wallets; now, look what bloody greed's brought her."

Throughout that night, incapable of sleep, the girls chatted about their lives, sharing long-hidden secrets. Ruth learnt that Sandra, from eleven years of age, molested her mother's string of boyfriends.

"Social Services put me in a kid's home. I soon ran off. Was homeless until an old bitch called Lou promised to look after me. Old bag, she did that all right; locked me in a room, belted me black and blue till I agreed to bed down with old men who preferred them young." With a sardonic grin, Sandra explained, "I tricked a punter into believing I'd go with him if he got me out of there." She chortled at the thought. "Should have seen the old bitch's face. When he threatened to inform the authorities she was using a child for prostitution, she almost shit herself," Sandra laughed. "Old hag couldn't wait to get rid of me. What a prick that daft sod believed my promise. Fat chance," she snarled. "Slimy pig left him high and dry. Found me a place, just a dump. At least I had a roof over my head. I worked the streets, keeping every penny I earned for myself, and have done ever since."

Ruth felt strangely comforted by Sandra's story and confessed all that had passed before they met.

Sandra flabbergasted. Gasped, "My God, you're a dark horse! I never guessed you'd be capable of murder. Talk about still waters. Still, sounds like they had it coming."

Alice refused to help the police, so her assailant stayed free. One evening, she slipped out of the hospital. No one ever saw her again. Sandra believed Alice dived into the Thames to end her life and stated,

"I would have done the same rather than look like my face went through a meat grinder." Sandra became tormented by Alice's fate. Over the next few months, she drank a great deal and refused to trudge the streets alone, insisting that Ruth came with her. At Sandra's insistence, Ruth stayed in the next room with the door open while she entertained.

Ruth became too drained to do her work and lost her job. Taking care of Sandra was soon her full-time occupation. Drunk, violent, dishevelled, and unwashed, the offers for her time dwindled away. Ruth worked as a barmaid in a club where street girls gathered. Falling behind with the rent, they were evicted from the flat. Ruth approached the hostels, but with Sandra blind drunk clinging onto Ruth's arm, they were turned away. In desperation, she took a cramped bedsit in a boarding house. Sandra refused to be left alone and slumped over the bar, demanding another drink. If denied, she became aggressive and screamed verbal abuse. The management threatened to sack Ruth if she didn't control her friend.

Ruth once to refused to give her more money. Sandra explode.

"You owe me! Who took you out of the crummy hostel? Poor Alice and me, that's who. Didn't mind taking from us in the good times. Didn't care how we got it, either, did you?"

Startled by such venom, Ruth reached out to pacify her.

Sandra shoved her away. "Don't touch me, ungrateful cow. Pretending to be so innocent, you're no better than a pimp. You can't wait to be rid of me too. Go on, admit it. Shall I go like Alice? If you want me gone, say so. I bet you do. No more stupid Sandra around. Well, you can bugger off; I don't need you. Go on, sling your hook." Rising peered at her reflection in the mirror and ran short nail bitten fingers through her messy hair. Shuffled in her dressing table drawer, found, and applied a wobbly slash of lipstick. She yelled, "I can go by myself and bring in money. I'm not past it yet, whatever you think, little miss perfect."

Ruth threw up her hands in resignation. "Oh! Right. Opened her purse; stop that damn yelling."

Sandra turned, her eyes blazed like twin slits of fire. "Bollocks! I don't need your precious money or anyone else's." she bawled, propelling Ruth towards the door.

In exasperation, Ruth growled. "Fine, suits me; you take care of yourself, I'm off. All you do is whine and drink yourself stupid every night. Well, you can wallow in self-pity on your own."

Ruth shook herself loose from Sandra's grip and pushed her aside. Sandra lost her balance and stumbled over a chair.

As she scrambled to her feet spat out, "Murdering bitch! You ain't so lily-white, are you? Remember what I know, cross me, and I'll tell the cops no problem. Don't think I won't either!"

Ruth paused, alarm shooting through her at this announcement. She'd forgotten Sandra had the ammunition to destroy her.

Fleeting relishing the shock on Ruth's face, then repentant, Sandra whined. "I'm sorry, Ruth, I would never split on you; my gob runs away with me; I'm scared. Can't you understand I'll never cope on my own? We're mates, please don't leave me. I'll quit the drink, stay home, chat, and have a giggle like the old days."

Her reformation was brief; soon, she was worse than ever. Her rages at home and in public towards Ruth continued. Never sober, consistently aggressive. Soon lost and annihilated all her former friends. Ruth struggled to take her home as she shrieked and cursed at imaginary insults from the other girls. Ruth had no alternative but to remain.

The consequences of Sandra's malicious revenge were too dire to contemplate. She resented having to care for her day after day with no respite. However, afraid that Sandra would betray her, there was no escape. Sandra's jibes and accusations no longer hurt. The constant tantrums became second nature, a heavy burden carried through each weary week. Ruth felt trapped, having to work as a slave for a wage spent on alcohol for Sandra. They were in danger of losing the room, as they owed so much rent. Sandra often searched Ruth's purse, taking any cash to buy another drink.

The other prostitutes watched Sandra's decline with mixed feelings. In her prime, she had left them far behind in looks, so richer pickings had all been hers. Now she never got a second glance. Ruth had many admirers; her hair had grown back as luxuriant as ever. She scraped it back in a bun to avoid male attention and wore no makeup. Despite that, Ruth had a natural beauty that shone through no matter how she sought to appear unattractive. The street girls felt sorry for her and criticised Sandra for exploiting her misplaced loyalty. They tried to coax Ruth to join their ranks, pointing out how much better off she'd be. One day, having endured yet another drunken scene and at the end of her tether, Ruth broke down and sobbed with frustration at the emptiness of her life.

One girl called Babs tried to console her. "Listen, Ruthy, we can't work out why you let Sandra walk all over you. It doesn't have to be like this. I have a friend who runs a discreet, private nursing clinic. If I ask, might take Sandra on to dry her out."

Desperate and worn out, Ruth, willing to clutch at any straw, listened as Babs continued.

"You're a fool, slaving all the hours god sends to make ends meet." Babs pulled a card from her bag. "Look, I can ring now. The clinic is expensive, but lying on your back a few hours a day, you'll soon have the cash to pay for the treatment. Stop whenever you like and let Sandra go her own sweet way."

Others listening joined in, assuring Ruth the first time was always the hardest, but after that, it became easy.

"Do it while you can before Sandra drives you to a premature grave.". Babs pressed the card into Ruth's hand.

The prospect of being free appealed. Babs' advice made sense; becoming a working girl seemed the only way to raise sufficient money for Sandra's treatment. Ruth received instructions on how to remain safe and avoid getting pregnant. Because she needed to learn the ropes, another girl offered to chaperone her. Aged nineteen, Ruth embarked on the next stage of her life.

CHAPTER EIGHTEEN

FIRST AROUSAL

Initially, they insisted Ruth change her image. At the end of their efforts, they examined their creation with pleasure. Now dressed to seduce, they all agreed she looked perfect. Ruth instantly saw herself reminded of the little girl wearing a bright yellow dress in the mirror. Then thought she looked so grown up and elegant. How did Mrs Wallace decide to offer her a job?

She agreed it showed off her figure well, but it was not what Ruth would have adopted. The makeup they applied was too heavy, and her outfit was far too revealing. The skirt, already tight, had a split up on each side. A low-cut top revealed the top of her breasts; the look was finished with donated beads and bangles that rattled with each movement.

"What's this?" uttered an elegant woman who drifted into the club. "Another girl?" She studied Ruth. "My name is Viviane; I expect you've heard of me." Large velvet eyes peered. "Wait a minute, I know you're the skivvy tied to that waste of space over there. Deluded fool!" She waved a bejewelled hand towards Sandra, who responded with a limp wave. "how long have you joined the ranks of the damned now? What's your name?"

Her face scarlet, Ruth lowered her eyes and replied, " Ruth and today will be my first time."

"Hum! I see." Viewing Ruth's attire, sniffed in distaste and drawled, "Get me a drink, darling, and come over, sit by me a while." With all eyes on her glided to a table, Ruth scuttled behind her, fascinated. A high-class call girl, Viviane's visits to the club were rare. But as she owned a local brothel using some of the club's members for the rougher side of the sex market, she knew all the gossip. Dressed in a stylish, soft green pure silk suit with tastefully matched expensive accessories, far outshone anyone else in style and poise. With feline grace, she lowered herself into the chair. Well aware she was the centre of attention, she informed her enraptured audience, "One of my top girls has let me down at the last minute." She shrugged her shoulders. "Can't be helped, but I need another girl tonight." Viviane concentrated on Ruth. "You're not from around here, are you,"

Ruth shook her head.

"Thought not," Viviane sniffed, "It makes a change to meet someone in this part of town who doesn't drop their H's. Despite your lack of experience, will you come with me, Ruth?" She drummed long nails on the tabletop, waiting for an answer.

Perplexed why she picked her, Ruth asked, "What do I have to do?"

"Stand up," Viviane ordered. "Turn around; let's have a proper look." Viviane screwed up her nose in disapproval. "Hum might do something. Nothing too complicated for your first time. Although, not dressed like that, come home with me. I'm certain I have something suitable." She picked up her handbag and prepared to leave. "Come on, my taxi is outside waiting." Ruth paused and glanced over at the dishevelled, drunken Sandra. Streams of saliva dribbled from her mouth. Viviane pressed her elbow.

"Well, Ruth?" she pointed in Sandra's direction. "What's it to be? A lifetime with that albatross around your neck or a glimpse of the life you could lead. It is up to you. I won't wait. It's now or never." Ruth decided and followed her. Closed her ears to the incessant screeching from Sandra.

That evening, they prepared to go to a casino in the west end. Ruth looked sensational in a gorgeous blue cocktail gown. She let her long auburn hair cascade loose over her ivory shoulders. Ruth paraded for Viviane, who nodded in approval. "I can see I'd better not call on you too often. The way you look now might take away my clients." She suggested they bought a drink at the bar to relax, "We're engaged in entertaining important clients.

Stick close by me and follow my lead. My regular girls will be here soon; I won't leave you alone."

Watching other couples vanishing for a brief time upstairs, Ruth's courage failed as the hours ticked by; she clung to the hope the clients might not appear. Viviane had been plying her with strong drinks all night, and as they took effect, Ruth relaxed and was a little intoxicated when the clients arrived. There were four of them. Three Turkish men dressed in expensive intelligent suits, the fourth, a tall, slim youth about eighteen years old, his silk suit seeming to dwarf his slender frame as he remained on one side with his head bowed. Two other young, attractive girls joined them later. While Viviane spoke to the men, the girls told Ruth that Çocuk often accompanied them. Viviane and the girls followed them upstairs to a vast, luxurious suite. Once inside, Viviane told Ruth to remain in the main room with Çocuk. All the others retreated into the bedroom.

Ruth waited on tenterhooks, not sure what to expect. Çocuk raised his head. Her heart skipped a beat. He was so handsome, took her breath away. A light olive complexion, hair as dark as night curled over his collar, full sensuous lips smiled at her. Ruth thought she would melt into his wide brown eyes. She'd expected him to be a mild character, but he confidently invited her to relax beside him on the couch. He told Ruth he came from Italy and worked first as a car valet to support his mother and younger brother. Then the three older men befriended him.

They were generous, so he accepted their demands. Full of compassion, Ruth reached out to touch his arm. He brushed her hand away, his face hardened with indignation.

"Don't you dare pity me! This is my choice; no one forces me to do anything." He dragged her to the windows and mumbled in her ear. "I will be the lowest of the low, creep, crawl, perform despicable acts for their warped pleasure, anything to get what I want."

His fingers nail dug into her neck as he drew aside the velvet drapes and forced her to look out. "See that city down there? Everyone, there will know my name one day and tremble at the sound." He nodded towards the bedroom. "My given name is Rego Calvo, but those men call me Çocuk, which is Turkish for a dog," His lip curled as he growled, "I allow them to defile me for payment."

Ruth glanced sideways at him; his jaw tightened in determination. About to ask his name, but seeing his thunderous, unapproachable expression, Ruth decided not to pry.

He announced, "One day, I'll be the one who's rich and powerful, and they will lead the life of a dog." He spun her to face him; his sensual eyes became dark slits full of menace that blazed into her. "In a few years, everybody will respect and fear me. I'll do whatever it takes; anyone who stands in my way will pay."

With a deep, shuddering breath, he released her. Pushed aside a strand of inky black hair that tumbled across his face. Gently he cupped her face in his manicured soft hands, "Remember, Ruth, in your life, this moment is a stepping stone."

Two hours passed before the occupants returned to the living area. The older men settled into the many comfortable chairs. The three girls sat on the floor at their feet. Ruth couldn't help wondering what part she played in the evening's performance.

One man yelled, "Come on, Çocuk, get started. Make a decent show; there's a handsome payment for you."

He drew her from the chair and whispered, "Don't be nervous, Ruth, this is your time. Relax and let me do the work". Cocuk lowered the zip on her dress and unclipped her bra; in one swift movement, her panties were around her ankles. His eyes never left her flushed face. Humiliated by gasps of admiration from the watching men, Ruth felt a desperate urge to run out of the room but couldn't move. In a flash, Rego stripped off, turned her from him and brushed his lips over her neck. As his hands circled her slender body, he hardened against her. Ruth pressed her flesh into him. His fingers drummed around her breasts, Ruth visibly quivered with each touch. She had never experienced such emotion and shivered with delight. Rego continued stroking her with a deliberate, meticulous rhythm, rocking her body in time with each movement. He moved tantalising, fleeting fingers around her groin. Turned her back to face him and dropped to his knees. Travelling upward, used his mouth, tongue, and hands to explore every inch of her yielding body.

In Ruth's mind, chaotic perceptions of arousal heralded uncontrollable fires of emotion swiftly followed by an ice cold sensation. She touched his head, gliding trembling fingers through dark, thick, wavy hair and implored, "Oh! My God, don't stop, don't stop. "

Rego continued fondling her with infinite tenderness, blowing soft air streams on her skin as he progressed. He lowered her to the floor in one rapid motion and moved over her body with inquisitive hands.

Ruth responded to him, oblivious to the spectators. Her senses awakened. Pulled him to her, dizzy with desire; beads of perspiration glistened on her impatient body. Ruth arched her back, ready to accept him. Every nerve stretched to breaking point, but Rego made her wait for what seemed like an eternity.

At last, he entered her; Ruth wrapped her legs around his back and groaned in delight. A raw sensual poignant need overwhelmed all inhibitions forgotten as her body rose with him. Ruth experienced her first exquisite organism; all too soon, it was over.

Rego kissed her softly and murmured, "Just a stepping stone. Ruth"

Brought back to reality by vociferous applause from the onlookers with cheers of "Bravo! Well done, Çocuk." Ruth got to her feet, flushed red with embarrassment, gathered her clothes, and dashed into the bathroom to dress.

Viviane accepted their payment and escorted them out. Ruth glanced back and saw the boy, still naked, follow the three men to the bedroom at the door. Rego caught her eye and gave her a knowing nod. Ruth read the defiant glint in his eyes and hoped she would meet the fascinating man again. After handing each girl their payment, Viviane arranged taxis to take them home. As she sped through the empty streets, Ruth couldn't believe the number of notes in her hand and promised herself she wouldn't work for long as a back-street prostitute. Viviane's lifestyle she aimed to follow. However, Viviane never asked for her again; her club companions joked Ruth was too much competition.

Desperate to earn enough to send Sandra to the nursing home, she started to work the streets with other prostitutes. When the first client had his rancid, fat, sweaty body astride her, his foul breath caused Nausea to wheal up inside her. As he huffed and puffed throughout the performance, a thought kept buzzing in her head *What on earth am I doing? There must be a better alternative to defining myself in the back seat of a car with this lump of lard.*

Ruth occupied her head with thoughts of her delicious moments in the casino. As her client rolled off, he lay still, panting and wheezing washed out. Ruth was relieved by how soon it was over. She looked at him somewhat comical with his trousers around his knees, his plump face rosy red as he gasped for breath.

Concerned, Ruth shook him and yelled: "Bloody hell, don't have a heart attack. " But couldn't help a slight smile thinking, *what a reputation I'd have killed off my first punter.* With forced consternation, asked, "You, all right?"

He stuttered, "Be okay in a minute. You're a real goer; I'll use you again."

 Then she was hustled out of the car onto the pavement, and a ten-pound note thrust in her hand.

Ready for the next client and the next.

CHAPTER NINETEEN

THE ABORTION

O h! Christ," Ruth wailed in dismay; it suddenly dawned on Ruth that she hadn't had a period for a while. The last thing she needed was a child. She had nothing to offer, no home or security.

Worried sick, she confided in Betty, the barmaid. "Insist on condoms," she advised, "You must remember, no sheath, no business. Your too late now, ya daft prat. Take my advice; get rid of it quick," Betty whispered, "You'll be worthless with a kid hanging around your neck."

Ruth glared at Betty, aghast. "I can't! It would be murder, a sin!" appalled she'd mirrored her father's words.

"Rubbish," scoffed Betty. "How far gone are you?"

"Haven't had a period for six weeks, can't remember."

"There you go, bloody hell!" Betty sniggered, "You're such an innocent; don't you know anything? How's it murder? It's nothing, just like a seed. As for it being a sin, daft cow being on the game rules you out for the nunnery."

Ruth gave a wry smile at this analogy. "I'm sure I'd muddle through somehow."

"Don't be so bloody daft," Betty scowled, "You can't work with a kid in tow. If your dates are right, that should do the trick. Shift it take lots of boiling hot baths, and drink loads of gin. Don't hang about either. The longer it stays, the harder to shift."

After three days and many scalding baths later, nothing happened, plus she'd drunk enough gin to float a ship. Ruth returned to the club and took Betty aside.

The barmaid frowned. "Humm, are you sure you did what I suggested because something should have worked?"

Ruth nodded and replied, "Yes, all of it."

In muffled tones, Betty leant close. "Tell you what, Ruth, I've got a friend who knows a woman who might help. She has a sure-fire way to shift it; it won't be cheap. About a ton and a half in advance; can you handle that?"

Ruth frowned and echoed, "A ton and a half, what's that?"

"Oh, Christ," Betty grinned, "Forgot you're a country girl and not one of us. Remember, too, what she does is always risky. And illegal, so keep your gob shut. Give me something as a deposit; a score will do. That's twenty quid to you, posh tart. The old girls' charge is a hundred and fifty quid, right " Betty smiled, "I'll take Sandra to my place for a day or two until you recover

With no alternative, Ruth handed Betty the deposit. A week later, knocked on a door in a small street of terraced houses. An elderly woman greeted her. "Ruth, is it Betty's friend?"

Ruth nodded.

"Right, best you come in, dear; I'm Edna; how far you gone?"

"I can't remember for sure when I last had a period; it might be eight to ten weeks or even more."

"Hum!" Edna put her hands on her hips. "Gets complicated that late on could be a problem; let's see what we can do."

Ruth had second thoughts. " I'll leave it, Edna; sorry to have wasted your time." She turned towards the front door.

Edna darted in front of her, "Oh no, pet, don't dash off; of course, you're nervous. You've come this far, don't back out now to regret it later." and ushered Ruth back to the room. "Nothing to it, promise. A mix-up with dates often happens. I fix up lots of girls with no problems. My guess is you're only a few weeks gone."

Ruth was sure all the old woman wanted was the money. Then remembering Betty's dour prediction of what was to come; she hesitated

Sensing Ruth's compliance, Edna coaxed, "Best not to lose any more time, pet; let's get on," she patted Ruth's hand, "Nothing to fret about, my dear. I'll soon have you fixed, all right?" She held out a grubby hand for her payment, stuffed the money into her apron and warned, "What I do is illegal. Keep your trap shut, or we'll both be in trouble with the law." Edna ushered Ruth into a cramped, untidy room. "My dear, take off your knickers. Lie down on those towels. I shan't be a minute."

She left the room, coming back almost bent double under the weight of an entire basin of steaming water. A drawer produced a cheese grater and bar of Lux soap and pulled out a long rubber tube apparatus. To Ruth's bewilderment, the woman using the grater scraped the soap, letting the flakes fall into the hot water. When done, immersed the tube to force the water through it, creating bubbles. When satisfied, she carried over the bowl and squatted beside Ruth. Edna told her to raise and separate her knees; she stuck one end of the tube between Ruth's legs, forcing it deep into her; the other end remained in the bowl. She held the tube down in the suds and squeezed it until the soapy water flowed through the tube into Ruth. The warm water flushing around her abdomen was an odd sensation and made her feel queasy. Five minutes later, it was over; the tube was withdrawn.

Ruth was advised to remain still and left alone. Afraid to breathe, she waited. Nothing had happened. When the old woman came back, Ruth protested. Edna snorted. "Have patience, love. It can take a few hours. Sometimes this way doesn't work. Depends on how much out your dates are." As Ruth dressed, Edna ordered, "Off you go, home straight now. Stay in for a while. If no luck, this time, pet, there's the crochet hook or the elm stick. I use that as a last resort. Costs more mind, but I offer a cut price for past clients. I know how to use them and guarantee results. There is a greater chance of problems afterwards, though." She hustled Ruth to the door and murmured, "Don't forget dear, get in touch if any of your friends need my help," tapping her arm urged, "Hurry yourself back now; catch your death in this rain."

Ruth stayed until almost dawn, waiting and waiting. Convinced the experience had been a complete waste of time and money, she retired to bed. Within an hour, she ran to the bathroom with agonising cramping pains. The insides of her legs were sticky with slime. Dizzy and sick, positive she was going die. Ruth held her fists hard against her mouth to suppress the rising screams. Burning pressure gripped her as she sat on the toilet, a rush of liquid, syrupy blood-filled globules agonisingly propelled out of her body. Straining with effort, Ruth forced herself upright and

189

turned to flush the mess away. Placing her hand on the chain, she paused, unable to resist the impulse to look. To her horror, the longer she stared, the more convinced Ruth became that a solid form was floating in the water. Dropped to her knees on the floor and pulled a towel from the rail. Placed both hands into the gore at the bottom of the pan. Distraught put what she held in her shaking fingers out on the towel. There was a diminutive form with recognisable limbs. The foetus was at least three to four months.

"Oh, my Lord," Ruth whimpered. "I must have fallen pregnant on that night with Viviane. My God, what have I done? It wasn't just a seed; Betty told me filthy lies." The cramping pains in her stomach were ignored. As a profound sense of loss hurt like nothing she had ever experienced. Transfixed on the mass before her eyes. Ruth moaned. "Poor little mite, I'm so sorry. May God forgive me; I never shall!" she wailed in misery; salty tears of regret ran down her cheeks. Ruth whispered to the blood-streaked form on the towel, "I'll call you Lark, poor baby. At least I can bury you." She wrapped up the towel, too weak to stand, and crawled out to the garden. With the rain still pouring, the ground was soft, so she scraped a deep hole with her hands. Heartsick, she buried her lost child and prayed for the little spirit of her baby. Her voice cracked in grief, sobbed, "God, if you are there, this child is innocent. Take this little life I destroyed and make Lark's pure heart sing again." Ruth fashioned a rough cross from stones and crossed herself. Too weak to rise, too unhappy to care, Ruth crawled in ferocious pain back to the bedsit and tore off the soiled, blood soaked nightwear, then yanked a cover off the bed. She lay on the floor for two days; the pain in her body was nothing compared to the anguish in her heart. Sleep brought only constant visions of a screaming child ripped from her body. Ruth vowed she'd never go through an abortion again.

Soon she had her regulars; most men relieved themselves, paid and left. Others would make no conversation other than asking the rate, consent, perform, and drive away. Sometimes, a client would want a "relationship." Ruth learnt how to decline without offending. Many assumed they were special, so the sex would be free and abusive when asked to pay. Ruth soon discovered to take the cash first. Some wanted more than explicit sex. Stag nights' group sex or watch her perform a sex act with another woman. A few subjected her to vile threats and insults, reminding her she was a dirty whore, and they wanted their money's worth.

The last night she worked the streets came when her mind, distracted with thoughts of Sandra's latest rant, got into a van with what she thought was a lone punter. He pulled into a deserted factory car park, got out, and ushered her to the back of the van. As the doors opened, Ruth saw two more men inside, sitting waiting. She backed away, insisting group sex was not what she did. The driver lifted her up and threw her into the arms of his companions. One barged against the doors while he struggled to hold Ruth fighting to escape. The van doors flew open, and they both toppled to the ground. Ruth got to her feet and ran, her heart pounding in terror, sure they would kill her. She stumbled, lost a shoe, regained her balance, and hobbled on. Gasping for breath, her lungs were about to explode. Her legs, like wooden weights, would not move faster. The men caught up and pushed her back to the van roaring with laughter; all three viciously raped her. Satisfied, they chucked her out and drove off with the van's tyres screaming.

Ruth staggered to her feet to the nearest road before collapsing. A passer-by found her lying in the gutter and called an ambulance. Her face was severely bruised and swollen. With three broken ribs, a fractured arm, and shaken to the core, Ruth couldn't work. When she recovered, she was too frightened to be on the streets. Forced to endure Sandra's rants and rages, as she accused Ruth of being stupid for not taking better care. However, it was plain Sandra was annoyed that Ruth's drop-in earnings restricted her alcohol intake. Ruth worked from the comparative safety of the club's private rooms. Conscious if she wished to follow Vivian's lifestyle. The tarty image had to go and choose her clients with care. Ruth reverted to wearing tasteful outfits and discarded the heavy makeup.

One girl chuckled, "Blimey Ruth, we've got our very own Viviane."

Sandra continued to drink herself into oblivion each night while Ruth earned for both of them. As the girls had predicted, she was a success, quickly managing the fees to send Sandra off to the nursing home, assessed as having manic depression with suicidal tendencies. Ruth arranged a private room in a secure psychiatric hospital.

Ruth's previous struggles with poverty had made her thrifty. She always saved as much as possible in a post office account. She cajoled one city stockbroker into opening a bank account in her name by posing as her father and handing over the necessary references. Her bank balance grew, as did her list of regular clients.

Soon Ruth could afford to lease a flat and no longer needed to use the club's rooms. She bought a headstone for Eddie and Violet and made her last goodbye. While tidying up the gravesite and arranging a small posy of violets, she spoke to them. "I'll not come again. You would be so ashamed of what I did to survive. With all my heart, I wish things had been different. I would sacrifice everything to change my way of life to make you proud. We never know where our life will lead. I'll never forget you. You both will always live in my memories and heart." She turned and walked away.

On an escorted visit to the hospital for treatment for alcoholism, while they waited in a sideward, Sandra attacked the attendant and swiped her handbag before running off. She bought a large bottle of vodka. In a drunken state, she toppled down the steps at Euston Station. The fall broke her neck. Ruth paid for it but didn't go to her burial. At last, she was free from all responsibilities.

CHAPTER TWENTY

WINDS OF CHANGE

L onging to find solitude and serenity away from smoke-filled pubs and nightclubs, endless parties, and feckless men who ran home to their wives. Ruth decided it was time to move on. With valuable financial guidance and support from one of her stockbroker clients, Ruth invested a substantial part of her earnings in stocks and shares. They performed well, making her a prosperous woman.

Ruth never forgot the picturesque way Thomas described his home in Ireland as they'd sat together so long ago. She often thought how wonderful it would be to find such tranquillity. Unknown to her acquaintances, Ruth made several weekend trips to Ireland using a false passport to start the search for her ideal cottage.

In due course, an estate agent showed her a blue-washed, tumbledown cottage surrounded by a small stone wall. A mile away from the nearest village, approached only by a narrow winding lane. Sweet-smelling honeysuckle smothered the building. The agent apologised for the condition of the property. As he pushed a path through the tangle of twigs and leaves and heaved aside the rickety wooden gate. A rotting timber plank fell down and clattered to the ground. Ruth picked it up and rubbed away years of moss and grime. It read 'Jasmine Cottage.'

"Perfect," Ruth sighed. Around the door, lintel, up to the roof, night-scented jasmine clung to every crevice and cranny, and thick twisted vine covered the tiny lead-glazed windows.

" I'm sorry the roof is in such a dreadful state, and the garden's a jungle of wildflowers." The estate agent rambled on about a local man she could call on to clear away the rubbish and landscape the garden,

Ruth decided to leave it wild and natural. Apart from a little general tidying, to allow the wildflowers to continue growing. The front door opened to a generous living room with an inglenook fireplace. Three narrow windows allowed the room plenty of natural light. Ruth loved it.

The estate agent led Ruth through the cottage and showed her a roomy kitchen dominated by a massive black cooking range. The remaining unstable cupboards clung on by loose brackets to the walls. Thistles and weeds squeezed up through slits in the damaged stone floor. Ruth picked her way through the rubble and saw a narrow archway set to the side of the kitchen. Two crumbling concrete steps led to a scullery at the rear end of the dwelling. It contained a blackened, cracked double sink with a long-handled iron pump to draw up water. On the rickety back door hung a rusty tin bath.

Eager to explore upstairs, she opened a door in the living room, which led to a winding stairway. With care, she tiptoed up the small, creaking stairs. The cottage had one decent sized and two tiny bedrooms. A box window in the largest room looked out on an overgrown back garden. A dilapidated sentry box toilet covered in wild roses stood in a corner. The whole place needed a considerable amount of work.

The hovering agent advised Ruth, "It will take a substantial outlay of capital to restore the property, Miss Morris." Leafing through his file, murmured, "It may be difficult to get a mortgage.

"That's not an issue. I'll pay cash. "Ruth announced

Cash buyers were few, thinking of a hefty commission; he tried to entice her to view some modernised cottages a short drive away.

Ruth loved the quaintness and charm of the bedraggled cottage; the agents quickly accepted her offer. She sold her excess belongings and moved into a hotel an hour's drive from her new home. A builder recommended by the agent soon made it habitable. Ruth used this time to pass a driving test and purchased a vivid yellow sports convertible. In a pet shop, she noticed the cutest puppy. Unable to resist, a pair of enormous brown eyes and a wagging tail bought him for companionship and named him Thomas.

It was all Ruth dreamt of absolute peace and isolation. She spent many pleasant hours pottering around the garden or taking long solitary walks with Thomas. They explored lush, green-dressed meadows that rolled away for miles without a single building. Ruth gazed with pleasure at how they melted into the folds of stark, mist-topped mountains. Ribbons of blue, white-flecked water slithered through the hills and tumbled like teardrops through the moss-covered banks into the stream. At peace with herself, exhaled in pleasure, *Thomas was right. This place is paradise on earth. Hidden in Ireland, I can lead a normal life without fear of arrest.*

Ruth caused a stir as she whizzed through its narrow lanes in her bright yellow car. Most of the strait-laced older villagers viewed her with obvious disapproval. She smiled in mild amusement as young men whistled and called out as she sped through. Ruth decided to have an indoor plumbing system installed. Rushing to the outside toilet in the freezing rain and the massive pump in the scullery shooting out ice cold water defeated her resolve to preserve the place as original as possible. It should be no problem to convert a bathroom and toilet from one bedroom and have efficient heating for her comfort. Ruth wanted everything finished before winter, so she agreed to engage him and asked the shopkeeper to make the arrangements. The shopkeeper said he knew a local jobbing builder with a large family to support who'd be grateful for the work. He added she wouldn't have to wait weeks for him to start.

Ruth answered her door Monday morning to a tall man in his mid-thirties. Dressed only in a light housecoat of translucent white silk, her cheeks flushed like a schoolgirl. As his liquid brown eyes almost popped out of his head. Ruth became self-conscious and tucked herself behind the door.

"Good morning, Missus, I'm Andrew, your builder," he said in a soft Irish brogue. "Come to see to your plumbing and look at the building work that needs doing."

Confused by this stranger's effect on her, Ruth led him into the scullery. Her pounding heart threatened to leap from her chest. She fled upstairs to compose her emotions, every pulse throbbing in her trembling body. Taking a long time to choose out her most becoming dress, brushed her thick, luxuriant hair with care and draped it over her shoulder. Satisfied, she looked stunning made her way back downstairs.

"Everything all right?" Ruth murmured.

Andrew turned to face her and gaped open-mouthed at her image. "Eh Ye-yes," he stammered and twisted away, crouched down to inspect the sink's antiquated plumbing.

Hovering in the doorway, Ruth smiled smugly, well aware of the vision she presented.

Ruth couldn't take her eyes off Andrew as he began to dig down to inspect the ancient outside water pipes. The mid-day sun beat down on him as he toiled, drenched with sweat; he removed his shirt.

Ruth gasped; he was beautiful, lean, and athletic.

Andrew returned to the kitchen and struggled to fix his lust-filled eyes on Ruth's face but kept dropping his gaze to the contour of her body, barely concealed beneath the flimsy dress. Ruth noted with pleasure that her appearance aroused him, although he attempted to hide behind his tool bag.

"How long will the work take?" She asked serenely, even though her heart raced.

"Seven or eight weeks. It's an enormous job. I'm afraid it won't be cheap. I bought it down as low as I can," Andrew handed Ruth a scrap of paper with the quote on it and sputtered in response. "I can start in the morn if that suits you."

Ruth agreed; she didn't care how much the estimate was or the time it would take. As she closed the door behind him, the cosy cottage seemed empty. Ruth spent a curious, languid day unable to concentrate, tossed and turned most of the night. She rose early to prepare herself for his arrival. Long hours crawled by until Ruth heard his van rumbling along the lane. Her head spun, shaky with excitement, and trembled at the prospect of being near him again. Forced herself not to rush to the door. She waited for his knock, her heart beating like a drum.

The weeks flew by all too fast. Ruth was entranced by the musical rise and fall of his soft voice, his amiable smile. She tingled with pleasure when she caught him watching her with brown eyes full of admiration. Ruth learnt about his wife, Dawn and his seven children. He told her of his wasted youth.

"I was a devil for the girls," he'd laugh, "I messed up getting Dawn pregnant. I never loved her, but she's been a good wife. Still, I can't help wondering what might have been if I'd remained free. I'll stick around until my youngest is grown, and then I'll l travel the world. See all the things and places I missed."

Ruth listened and watched as he worked. How she ached to hold him, have his firm young body tight to hers. It became harder to control her overwhelming desires. Unable to tear her eyes away as in the hot summer days, he stripped to the waist. She lusted after his taut, tanned body. Longed to caress each inch of muscle moist with perspiration. She took herself off to walk Thomas in the meadows to subdue her rising passions. In the confined space of the cottage, they often brushed against each other.

While collecting logs from the woodshed, she stumbled over a tree root; he caught her and held her in his arms for support. Ruth pressed her body against him, unable to stop herself, leaned into him and savoured the moment. He kissed her full on the mouth. Ruth felt a shivering thrill and returned his kiss. She collected herself together and pushed him away.

"No, Andrew, you're married; this can't, mustn't happen." She hurried back to the cottage.

Breathless, she hurled herself onto her bed, fighting a powerful impulse to return to his arms. All too soon, the last nail hammered home. Andrew made no mention of the kiss or attempt to touch her again. The need to reach out and possess him all these past weeks had been torture. However, married and with children, he could never belong to her.

His face was bright red looked down at his shoes and spluttered, "Right, missus, no more to be done. I'll take my leave if you're happy with the work."

In abject misery, Ruth nodded. She'd plunged head over heels in love with a man she could not have.

"I'll send my bill in a day or two." He packed his tools and walked out of her life without a backwards glance.

CHAPTER TWENTY-ONE

STOLEN HEART

Ruth froze motionless behind the magazine stand in the newsagents unseen by two chattering women who entered deep in loud conversation.

"That car belongs to the tart from Jasmin cottage; my man has been on hot bricks since he finished work up there, always looking for any excuse to return. From the first day, never stops talking about her."

"I bet you can guess how her sort got her money, can't you?" her companion sniffed.

The newsagent waved in Ruth's direction to alert them. But they, intent on their gossip, ignored his frantic signs.

"On her back, where else?" the other sneered. "Yes, you're right to worry. I said so from the start. Mine keeps on about how hard life is for a lone woman with no man. They chase her like dogs after a bitch in heat. Marriage-breaker, she is. Parades around in that flashy car. Turns all their fool heads with her sly eyes and brazen manner. Damn fools besotted; they are as if she can't manage a shopping bag! Makes me sick. It won't be long before she gets her claws in one of our men. I'd go up there like a shot, warn the slut off, make sure she learns what's what."

The man behind the counter tried to show Ruth's presence again, but they chattered on

"Huh! Yes, you're right," the other agreed. "He sits in his chair with a stupid dreamy look and a silly smile. I talk to him but get no answer till I yell. Didn't I catch him scowl at me as I got undressed for bed?" The voice rose with indignation. "Compares me to that skinny bitch, I know it. Says he's too tired and turns away when I snuggle up to him in bed." She blew into a handkerchief. "He's always been that way inclined."

Her confidante consoled, "There now, pet, don't upset yourself. After seven children, no doubt in that direction."

The woman gave the agitated shopkeeper a withering glance. "He wants that flighty piece in his bed. Now the work is finished, he's sullen and snappy. Almost lives at the pub, anything, rather than at home with me. He'll not do anything again for her; I won't stand for it."

The shop door clattered as Ruth made a hasty retreat. At the noise, both women turned and saw Ruth cross the narrow street back to her car.

One opened the door wide and shouted: "I'm sure I don't care if that brazen madam heard us; we only spoke the truth."

Ruth muttered, "One of those spiteful cows must be Andrew's wife, but I gave her no cause to talk like that. A sob escaped as she gulped back her tears. "Why is life so unfair? "her hands shook so much she dropped the keys. Ruth felt their hostel eyes on her as she started her car and sped away.

Dawn came to the cottage on the pretext of presenting the bill. As she made out the cheque, Ruth remarked what an excellent job Andrew had done, and she'd be glad to use his services again. Ruth noted with satisfaction how plain Dawn looked.

Dawn drew her woollen shawl tight and snapped, "Andrew won't be available for a long time. He's got a backlog of work for his regular customers. He'll have no time for casual jobs." As Ruth showed her out, Dawn suggested she find another worker from the nearby town.

The conversation she overheard in the shop and Dawn's curt tone convinced her Andrew was hers for the taking. Ruth's first impulse was to rush out and find him, lock him in her arms and never let go, Aware of what people would say if he deserted his family. She sat in the garden with Thomas and spoke her thoughts to him. "What the matter with me, boy? I chose this place to lead a normal life; besides, he's got a family to support. I can't expect him to leave his children". Ruth rubbed Tom's ears as he gazed up at her with big brown adoring eyes.

"You liked him, didn't you, pet?" she visualised the probable outcome and realised how futile it would be. "Don't want to be called a marriage wrecker and ruin any chance of being accepted by this tight-laced community. We found this place to settle; we don't want to ruin what we have. We must forget Andrew, continue our lives, and allow him to do the same. The entire village will despise me and need to move on again," she got up and slipped, the dog lead on. "Come on, boy, we'll have a walk and stop daydreaming."

So, Ruth continued her lonely existence. With a packed lunch, she walked miles over the meadows with her beloved dog, her only companion. One day when passing an isolated cottage, Thomas barked. "Be quiet, boy; what's the matter with you?" She bent down to fondle his ears when a faint cry came from the cottage. Ruth hooked the dog's lead over the gate and walked up the narrow path. A dog appeared at the front door; he crouched low and growled. Ruth couldn't leave if someone was in trouble, but the dog looked fierce. She pulled out their lunch from her bag and threw over a ham sandwich. The dog dived on it and had it down in less than a minute. She tore off a piece of mutton pie and threw it over. he snatched it up, so Ruth threw another and another, inching forward all the time. The dog wagged his tail, his moist eyes locked on her hand until all the pie had gone. Thomas had never played with another dog full of excitement; he bounced up and down and slipped his collar. Ruth called him back in a panic, but Thomas paid her no heed and ran up to the bigger dog. They sniffed each other both tails began to wag. The older dog seemed to like Thomas. Ruth threw down the last piece of cake. Both tails went into overdrive as they woofed it down. Ruth breathed an enormous sigh of relief and stretched out her hand to pet the large dog; he pressed his head into her.

"Well, only hungry, were you, pet?" both dogs settled down on the step together. "All bark and bluster, typical man."

She opened the paint, peeled the door and stepped inside. The only light in the cottage streamed past the small, latticed windows. The stone windowsills had jars of faded spring flowers. In the grate, a charred wood log remains long since out. The sparse furniture was old but well looked after; a thin layer of dust covered their surface. She made out someone huddled in a tattered armchair covered with coats. Ruth crossed over and pulled back the top coat; an aged face of an old lady stared at her, and a pair of pale blue eyes blinked.

"Oh, praise be to God," the old woman shuffled in the chair. "been here for days hoping someone would come. I heard the dog bark, knew it wasn't mine, too squeaky for Rex."

"What's wrong? Can I help? "Ruth bent over the old lady

"I fell over on a cracked slab in the kitchen, hurt my foot three nights ago, knocked me sick, I can tell you. Hobbled to this chair, been here ever since, but it swelled overnight; now I can't walk."

"Here, let me look" Ruth examined the injury, "Yes, it is swollen; it might only be a sprain. I'll make a cold compress that should reduce it," she rummaged in her bag. "Take a couple of these aspirins to help ease the pain. Would you like a cup of tea?"

Ruth found a tea towel in the small, spotless kitchen, ran it under the cold tap and wrapped it around. The old lady's ankle. "How's that?".

"Oh, much better, thank you. I'll be as right as rain now; the district nurse calls every Monday. She'll look if my foot is not right by then." The old lady smiled. "What's your name? Mine's Bridget."

"I'm called Ruth; now, how about that tea?" Ruth called out as she busied in the kitchen, "When did you last eat, Bridget? Can I fix up something?"

"Could eat a horse, so could poor old Rex. If it isn't too much trouble, you'll find some cold pork, tatties, and parsnips in the larder."

"No trouble at all," Ruth smiled, "happy to help. Rex is fine; he finished our packed lunch."

While Ruth tended to the fire, Bridget said, "You're the one that brought Jasmine Cottage."

"Yes, so lovely now I had it fixed up."

"Thought so," nodded Bridget, "the English woman they all hate. Out to pinch all their husbands."

"No," Ruth grinned, amused at Bridget's outspokenness, "I'm fine as I am. I don't know why they all dislike me so much."

"Can't you guess," chortled Bridget. "You're attractive, well-dressed, single. Seem to have plenty of money. What's not to hate?"

"That's so unfair. All I want to do is fit in."

"Ach! Pay them no mind, narrow-minded lot. I never bother with that sort. To tell you the truth, I wouldn't spit on half of them if they were on fire. Some decent women live in the village; they'll come round. You'll see; just be patient."

"I hope so; I'm often lonely with no one to talk to except my dog. I wish I could find something useful to do. Each day only blends into another," Ruth got up. "I'll tidy up," and dusted and polished the furniture while Mary gabbled on.

"Tell me about it, pet; dogs are such pleasant companions. Don't know what I would do without my Rex. I spend days here and never see a single soul either." She stopped to sip her tea and gulped it down in satisfaction. "You make a good brew, Ruth.

209

Now, where was I?" Bridget cradled her cup while she recollected her train of thought. "Oh yes, I remember you asked how I spend my time. On fine days, I bike to the village, visit my Patrick's grave, and chat with him. " She pointed to a vase on the nearest windowsill, "which reminds me those flowers need fresh water."

Ruth jumped up to replenish the water. When she returned, Bridget continued.

"The district nurse comes once a week'; she's kind and always stops for a cuppa. She's better than a newspaper telling me all the juicy gossip." Bridget clapped her hands together. " You must meet her sometimes. I am sure you'll get on."

Ruth set out Bridget's dinner and took her leave. "I'll pop by again tomorrow when I pass to make sure you're all right."

She held Ruth's hand, "Yes, please do. I should like that and thank you for your help. You're a good girl. I'll be sure the village hears about it too, so I will."

Over the next three days, Ruth called in to check that Bridget had warmth and a hot meal. She promised to pop again when Bridget was up and about.

True to her word, Ruth stopped by Bridget's cottage often. Rex bounded out to greet her and play with Thomas Ruth always rewarded him with a treat and a quick pat. One day Bridget was with the district nurse.

"Hello, my darling," Bridget beamed, opening her arms to embrace her in welcome, "This is the girl I told you about, Catherine, who saved my bacon. She did, for sure."

Catherine offered her plump hand, "So pleased to meet you, Ruth. Thanks for what you did for Bridget."

"It was nothing. I'm glad I was around," Ruth instantly liked Catharine.

"Bridget tells me you're at a loose end most days. Is that so?"

"Yes, that's true. Do you have something in mind?"

Catharine crossed her ample bosom. "Be most grateful for someone to call in on my elderly patients. Say midweek, for an hour. With such a large area to cover, I can only manage once a week," sighed Catharine, "I worry about some of the frailest. Do you think you could do that? "

"Oh yes, love to,"

"Right, I'll come soon with a list. You've got your own transport, right? If you have any problems, contact me through the surgery by phone. I can't thank you enough." She got up and hugged Bridget. "I think you found me a treasure; I'll be off now." Taking Ruth's hand, said, "You have no idea how good it is to meet you; I'll be visiting you soon."

"Thank you," responded Ruth, "This is just what I need. I look forward to it."

Catherine chuckled, "Be careful what you wish for, Ruth; once word gets around, there's a new volunteer in the parish. You'll be swamped with requests."

Catherine was right over the next two months; Ruth had many appeals from the village's voluntary organisations and beyond and visited Catherin's patients once a week. She did hospital transport, helped at the retirement home, village bazaars, and jumble sales. Stepped in as an emergency receptionist at the doctor's surgery. Ruth worked long hours volunteering at fundraising events; her tireless efforts earned her grudging respect and a few casual female friends. Her days were full and satisfying.

The only fly in the ointment was Andrew. He seemed everywhere, badgering her for further work at the cottage. Offering to chop wood, clear the garden, anything. His blatant attention renewed gossip. She'd tried hard to be accepted all these past months, and his blatant attention could sabotage her efforts. Although every bone in her body cried out for his touch, Ruth steeled her heart and refused.

After a village jumble sale, he caught her alone, busy clearing up.

"Jesus, Ruth," he moaned, gazed at her flushed face, and pushed back a stray damp lock of hair on her troubled brow. "You're so beautiful, like a delicate butterfly." He took hold of her before she could fly away, his voice hoarse with emotion. "Ruth, don't make me suffer any longer, sweetheart." He held her upturned face and kissed her. "You're on my mind every hour. I know you're the same, don't deny me any longer. I can't bear it."

Ruth pushed him away and whimpered, "No, Andrew, I can't; we mustn't. Leave me alone." Then she fled from the hall in tears.

Ruth ached to share a few stolen moments in his arms. Her days passed in fantasising how perfect they could be together. Each night in her dreams, they walked in the meadows planning a life together, arm in arm.

While walking in the lane with Thomas, she saw Andrew striding towards her. Andrew dropped to the ground, wrapped his arms around her knees. Pressed his face into her dress and whispered, "Ruth, I shudder when Dawn touches me; the hurt in her eyes shames me. What can I do? I long for your soft breath on my chest every morning. You want me too; I can tell by the look in your eyes I'm begging, please stop this torture."

Ruth bent forward, "For pity's sake, Andrew, get up before someone drives past; you know how tongues will wag if we're seen. Go back to your wife and children. We will never be together."

He blinked away tears. "Ruth, I have my pride. I'll not ask again. Will you come, yes, or no?"

"I can't", Ruth mumbled.

With an aching heart watched the only man she ever loved disappear down the lane. What she felt for Andrew was no longer just the need for their bodies to entwine; this love was so deep it hurt and consumed her every hour of the day. Ruth wasn't sure if Andrew loved or just desired her. She couldn't bear to find out. Her heart would shatter if it were lust, not love. A passion that lasted only until the chase was over and fulfilment satisfied. Then, like all the men in her life, run back to the arms of his wife.

Summer slipped away, and Ruth wrestled with her thoughts as winter approached. When Andrew met her in the village, true to his word, he turned and walked away in the other direction. That hurt Ruth more than she could bear.

In the small hours, she sat at the bedroom window. Finally, Ruth decided to take happiness while she could, thinking *Dawn had had the past fourteen years to make Andrew happy and failed. He was shackled to a wife he didn't love and seven children who depended on him. As convention demanded, he'd sacrificed his wild adolescent dreams of travel to do the right thing by Dawn. Why shouldn't it be his time now?*

Ruth reached this stage in her thoughts by overriding desperation to snatch a moment in time and, after that, what would be. She put Thomas on her lap and murmured, "My life is pure misery without him. I must know if he loves me, the person; if not, I'll risk him breaking my heart. No need for him to desert his family. We could meet secretly in the hills and find

214

an isolated place, so no one need be hurt". Ruth found a notepaper and an envelope and wrote:

My life is empty without you. I need you in my life. Fleeting short times together is all I ask. I'm here, will you come?

Marking the envelope "personal," abandoning all pride, she set out to find him; Ruth spotted his van parked outside a house. Unseen, she slipped the letter under the windscreen wiper blade.

A few days later, after her morning bath, dressed in only a housecoat, Ruth heard his van rumble up the lane, to her delight. Andrew leapt out. She rushed through the door and down the path straight into his embrace. He smothered her face and throat with long, lingering kisses, eased back and held her at arm's length.

"Ruth, you're a devil temptress in my dreams, my thoughts, and every waking hour. I have never had such an ache in my heart. Dawn is an excellent wife, always cooks a good meal, our home is spotless, and I love my children. But you must know I can never leave them."

Ruth, breathless, uttered, "Oh darling, I don't want you to desert your children. I'll take whatever time you can give."

Andrew lifted her in his arms and carried her back to the cottage. As the door closed behind them, they gave way to ecstatic passion and made love on the passage floor. Ruth moved her hands over his thick shoulders, along his muscular arms and around to his broad back, holding his muscular body against hers. At breakneck speed, they undressed one another Andrew kissed the length of her jawline, moved on to her throat, and eased her gently to the floor. Ruth wrapped herself around him as he entered her, conscious only of the soft cries of delight that escaped her gratified being.

Each meeting was an exquisite secret, confident they avoided prying eyes. They met near an old, deserted shepherd's hut in the hills. Both lived only for their time together. In the soft twilight, they strolled through the meadows, made love, and stayed locked in each other's arms under the stars. These precious hours slipped away too fast. When the time came to part, they'd cling to each other, reluctant to leave. They both wanted more but worried about Andrews's children; they left things as they were, stealing every moment they could.

One morning, to Ruth's astonishment, Andrew burst through the cottage door, his face ashen as he held her in a tight embrace.

"Dawn's found out about us. She confronted me today."

Ruth's heart skipped a beat, breathless murmured,

"Oh, Andrew, no. What happened? We've been so careful. We have to finish," Ruth gazed into his troubled face.

"Not careful enough, it seems. Dawn's been mithering me for a while. She questioned why with all the work, no extra money was coming in. First, I tried to convince her it was only a run of bad and late payers. Dawn was not stupid, and she knew full well something was wrong. I've not shared her bed for a long time, so with her suspicions and the village gossips spouting their poison, it came to a head during a row this day. I should have known some busybody would delight in telling her,"

Tears rolled down her cheeks, "Oh, sweetheart, I'm so sorry, Andrew. What did you do?"

"I told her the truth," he watched her expression change

"Oh, my God, you didn't. Why?" She gasped.

"To be with you forever with no more lies."

"But we can't," Ruth protested, "everything has been wonderful while it lasted. I worked hard to fit in. This will ruin all I strived for."

"Ruth," he cried in anguish ", don't you love me anymore?"

Her voice broke between heart-rending sobs, replied, "Losing you has been my biggest dread, but we knew it could never last. I love you more than my life, but now it must end."

"Well, it's done; too late to go back. I won't lose you; I can't," Andrew declared,

"No, it's not too late; she loves you," Ruth insisted, "Go back, make it up with her. You can say it was a moment of madness. Whatever it takes, we can't keep seeing each other."

Roth jumped in alarm when he slammed his fist on the worktop. "A moment of madness," he spat out, "is that all it meant to you?" His handsome face darkened in anger; he grabbed her arms and shook her. "Woman, I would give up my life and family. All you care about is your reputation. How can you be so shallow?"

"Let go; you're hurting me." Ruth cried out

He roughly shoved her away, sending Ruth reeling across the room. She had never seen this side of Andrew, and it terrified her. To calm the situation, she explained: "Andrew, you don't understand my life. Until I came here, it had been so chaotic. Here, I'm accepted and feel I belong. Can't risk losing all I worked for."

He knelt before her and sobbed, "What about life with me? I can't bear the thought of living without you. We can face any hurdles if we stick together."

Ruth stood by her decision, "This isn't what I want, Andrew. Go back, beg your wife's forgiveness; there is nothing for you here."

Stunned, he stood frozen in astonishment, unbearable despair etched across his face. His voice was flat, and his words cut through Ruth like a knife.

"Frolic in the meadows was all I meant to you. It breaks my heart to realise my true worth." He turned away, shoulders hunched, "I'll not beg anymore. I can tell what's important to you, and it's not me."

Ruth slapped her hand to her mouth as he slumped down the path and out of her life.

As Ruth predicted, Dawn forgave Andrew and tried to forget what had happened. Their troubled life carried on but was never the same. As long as Ruth remained, the temptation was still there. Dawn wished and prayed her rival would soon return to England. Ruth's resolve and heartbreak had been in vain. Everyone knew of the affair and blamed her for leading Andrew on. Over the next few weeks, the requests for help fell away. When Ruth drove into the village, those she talked to were barely civil. Others turned their backs and snubbed her. The damage was done. Ruth, on a lonely stroll, found herself outside Bridget's cottage.

Bridget's always pleased to see me. I haven't visited her for ages. God only knows I need a friendly face. As she walked up the path, the door flew open. Bridget glared at her; the old woman threw her arms to wave Ruth away.

"Get gone!" she snarled, "After what you did to that young family, you're not welcome here."

"But why? I thought we were friends."

"Friends, is it? Huh! Not no more, we're not," Bridget retorted, holding tight to Rex as he tried to greet Ruth.

Taken aback by the disgust in her voice, Ruth reached out to her, "Bridget, please don't be like this. I need someone to talk to."

Bridget moved out of reach, "Don't you lay your sinful hands on me, girl."

Ruth pulled back and dropped her arms to her sides.

Bridget took out a handkerchief, blew her nose, and continued, "Tell you want, is it? Pity you didn't just talk instead of bedding someone else's man. I'll have no truck with the likes of you." She shook her grey head, "I thought you were a good girl. Your soft voice and gentle ways had me well fooled, no mistake. This has opened my eyes." Bridget pursed her mouth in contempt, "Your sort makes me sick." She hobbled to the door and flung it wide open. "Get out I'll not breathe the same air as you. Don't come here again. I want nothing to do with a marriage wrecker on your way," Ruth walked down the path as Bridget slammed the door behind her.

Ruth despondently walked away, left to her solitary existence once more. The unbearable void in her heart without Andrew grew in severity every day. As she dressed to go to the large shops in Kilkenny a few miles away, Ruth looked at her reflection in the mirror; and murmured, "I should never have sent him away. What difference did my sacrifice make? If I followed my heart, I'd still be shunned, but at least not as miserable. We could have faced the world together and been strong." She finished dressing and sighed, "It's too late now. I hurt him so much. Why didn't I grab happiness and hang the consequences when I had the chance?"

In torrential rain, Ruth felt the car shudder; she pulled to the side. The tyre had burst. "Bloody hell", she swore, "I'll get drenched." While struggling to change the wheel, a van drew up, her heart almost jumped from her chest. It was Andrew.

"Get in the van out of this rain; I'll do that," he ordered.

When done, he got into the seat beside her. Andrew looked at Ruth, shivering and dripping wet. He took out his flask. "Here," and passed her a cup of steaming tea. "Get that down; you'll catch your death."

She gulped it down, trembling still not so much from her sodden clothes but the closeness in the confined cab of Andrew, sitting stony face beside her.

Ruth passed the cup with her thanks back to him. As their fingers touched, a spark like an electric shock passed between them.

Andrew grabbed her hand, drew it to his lips and groaned,

"Oh, Ruth, how I missed you. Say you feel the same, or I'll go mad," He tilted her face and kissed her.

Despite herself, Ruth responded. They sat for a long time in a silent embrace.

"Take me back, Ruth," he pleaded, "I should never have walked away, but your cruel words shattered my world, and a man's foolish pride drove me out."

Ruth resisted even though her heart screamed at her to say yes. She caught her breath and whispered.

"What about your family and friends? They won't let you."

Andrew replied, "The only friend and family I need is you, Sweetheart. I am so lost without you. I drink myself into oblivion each night to forget and ease the pain of losing you." He pushed back into his seat. "To my shame, wrapped with my needs, I neglect Dawn and the children. It isn't the life I wanted for them, but to endure my pain, I can't help myself." He held her on his lap; she nestled into him. Andrew persevered, "Say yes, and I'll be there this night. No power in this world will keep me away." he implored, "Say the word, Ruth, and I'm yours forever." He watched her expression.

Unable to contain herself, Ruth snuggled into his chest. "Oh! Sweetheart," she breathed, "I've been so lonely and miserable without you, missed you every day." Her heart beat like a thousand painful drums in her chest, restricting her breathing. Her voice choked with emotion; she clung to him and stuttered, "I should never have sent you away. I'm so sorry I hurt you. I'll never do that again." All her energy spent, she lay against him and sobbed, "I can't imagine living my life without you. I need you beside me so much." Ruth drew in a deep, shuddering breath. "Darling, the biggest mistake of my life was losing you. The pain in my heart has been unbearable. Come back home and back to my arms."

In reply, her love smothered her in rapturous kisses.

Late evening, Andrew drove up the lane and back into her life.

CHAPTER TWENTY- TWO

IN THE NAME OF LOVE

Settled in front of the fire, Andrew told Ruth what happened when he told Dawn he was going to leave her.

"She attacked me like a mad woman, grabbed a pan and tried to smash it across my face. I had to push her away; Dawn slipped up and fell over, so I took my chance and walked out. As I left, she ran out of the house, screeching with all the neighbours listening," Andrew drew a deep breath. "Now everyone knows, no point in hiding. We have one last hurdle to cross, Ruth; no more secrets. Let the world see we're together. I'm going back to fetch my stuff in the morning."

"I'm coming with you," announced Ruth.

"Might be trouble, Ruth, be better if I go alone," he warned.

"I am coming, and that's that. We'll face whatever comes together,"

As they parked outside his house, Dawn rushed out, furious, and pointed at Ruth.

"What are you thinking? How dare you bring that tramp to my door?"

"Don't make a show of yourself, Dawn," Andrew ordered, "I'll get my things, and we'll be gone." He went into the house to collect his belongings. Dawn raced behind him; each time he came out to load the van, she clutched hold of his arms to stop him. In frustration, he pushed her aside. Dawn lay on the pavement, sobbing. Andrew bent over and lifted her back to her feet. "I'm sorry, Dawn, are you hurt?"

She clung in desperation to his jacket. "Hurt! You talk of hurt?" she wailed. "What about your children? Has that bitch turned you against them as well? "Andrew scowled. Dawn resorted to tearful pleading. "Don't do this, Andrew, I beg you. She's a cheap slut from England playing with you. When she tires of you and goes after someone else's husband, where will you be then? Disgraced in the eyes of your family and the church."

Andrew pulled her back to the doorway. "For Christ's Sake!" he implored, "Woman, stop this. I'm going, and an end to it." Andrew kept on loading, ignoring the distraught woman's pleas and tears. Dawn threw her arms around his legs and held on tight. Exasperated, he untangled himself, tilting up her anguished face. Weary of her, he muttered low.

"Dawn, you know full well there was never love between us. I only married you because you were carrying our Kevin. I never denied you're a good wife and mother. I was always faithful. Even though I had enough offers." He raised his voice and pointed towards a group of young women. "Even with your so-called friends." Some of them lowered their heads; their cheeks flushed red with guilt. "I stayed true to our marriage vows."

"Didn't stop you from bedding me, did it? After seven children, how can you say we had a loveless marriage," she protested in anguish. Please don't leave me! Think of the children." Her pitiful voice was full of suffering; Dawn tried once more to appeal to his moral sense. "Andrew, I'll take you back again like before. As if this madness never happened. I swear we won't speak of it again." Turning to the crowd of onlookers for support, cried out as tears streamed down her face, "Everyone here knows your mind's twisted by that trollop. They won't hold it against you."

The onlookers nodded and murmured their agreement.

"There, look, see, no one blames you. "Dawn glared in Ruth's direction. In desperation, Dawn played her last card, "The Holy Father will give you absolution for this terrible sin. Come back to your family where you belong."

"All this talk is pointless," Andrew threw up his arms in frustration. "Woman, I'm only a man with a man's needs. Our children won't go short; I'll provide for them, but I am leaving this house today." He walked back inside.

Dawn rushed to the van, yanked open the door, grabbed Ruth's hair, and dragged her onto the stony road. "He's my man, mine! Do you hear me? You'll not have him!" The incensed woman banged Ruth's head against the ground. The gathering crowd egged her on. Andrew heard the commotion, ran out, pulled Dawn off, and dumped her on the doorstep. She curled up in a corner and howled like a wondered animal in despair and desolation.

Ruth lay semi conscious in the middle of the road. Andrew kissed her pale, bruised face. "Oh, my love, I tried to avoid this." He cradled Ruth in his arms, smoothed back her tousled hair and whispered, "Be away soon sweetheart; there's one more thing to do." Andrew turned to face the onlookers. "See this woman; she is my life. I'll be at her side till the day I die. I am leaving this place what you lot think means nothing." He looked over at Dawn; as shocked neighbours surrounded her, Andrew directed his last remarks to his distraught wife. "I am sorry, Dawn; I never set out to hurt you." He lifted Ruth up in his arms, carried her back to the van, and drove away.

One afternoon, while Andrew was out with Thomas collecting wood for the stove, the parish priest called Ruth invited him inside, but he declined.

"Miss Morris, I'm Father Michael, the parish priest. What I have to say is best said here on the doorstep. This is not a social call; I am here to beg you to end this abominable wickedness. What can a person like you want with a simple village man? He'll bring only trouble and shame." He reached out and held her arm. "I can't believe you don't know or care about the pain and misery you caused. Have you no conscience or thought for his wife and those innocent children?" His voice softened as he cajoled. "Miss Morris, it's in your power to finish this sinful affair. Just send him back to them. Dawn is a staunch Catholic, so she will never agree to a divorce, you know that. Are you content to live in sin? Settled into a life you've no right to? God will never forgive you."

Ruth interrupted his preaching and pulled her arm away from his clasp. "We love each other, and I wish he were free. Divorce or not, I won't give him up. I'd sooner tear out my heart than lose him." The look of disapproval on the priest's face made her blood boil. She fumed, "Doesn't your precious church preach that love conquers all? Isn't that what the Bible says?" Ruth leant towards him, "We are together now; I will never send him away. I have nothing more to say to you. "Then she slammed the door shut

the priest walked back out of the garden, turned at the gate and bellowed ", More shame on you. I'm warning you no good can come of such wickedness. One day you both will pay."

Late evening, just as they were about to retire, loud, angry voices shouted for Andrew to come outside. He pulled back the curtains; Dawn's four brothers were in the garden. They roared for Andrew to come out. Ruth tried to restrain him, but he would have none of it.

"Best face them, Ruth," he said. "I've expected trouble from them," and went outside to face them. Together, the four men attacked him. He tried to fight back, but the odds were impossible. Ruth picked up the fire shovel, rushed out and pounded at the nearest man until he knocked her aside. When the brothers had exhausted their revenge, one pulled Ruth up and threw her down where Andrew lay slumped on the grass.

"Tell your man there not to come to the village unless he wants more of the same. There'll be no work for the gobshite hereabouts. We'll take care of our sister and the children. You're welcome to him; may you both rot in hell!"

After the brothers left, Ruth helped Andrew to the car and made her way at breakneck speed to the nearest hospital. Two days later, she brought him home. Andrew had cracked ribs, facial bruising, and a few stitches in his head to show for his ordeal. Ruth cherished the time together as she fussed over him. He laughed when Ruth refused to let him put a log on the fire.

"All this spoiling. Be careful, girl; I don't get used to it," he chuckled. "It suits; you'd make a great little skivvy."

When Andrew recovered, he searched for work again. Ruth made sure they sat down together to a full breakfast each morning. She noticed her skirts were becoming snug. Ruth made a beeline for the bathroom most mornings. Having had seven children, Andrew knew a thing or two. He waited to hope against hope Ruth would announce she was pregnant and complete their happiness. One evening, to his delight, she wrapped herself around him in bed and whispered,

"How do you feel about baby number eight."

He sat bolt upright as if the news had come as a surprise. He lifted Ruth out of bed and danced with her around the room. "How far gone are you?"

Ruth smiled at his enthusiasm. "I think about three months. I was waiting to make sure before I said anything to you."

Something changed as a different expectant air settled in Jasmine Cottage. Delirious with joy, they waited for the joyful event. Even with her swollen body, Andrew adored her. During the waiting months, they grew closer. The high passion of their first night didn't expire. Each time their bodies met was as wonderful as the first.

But now, there was a golden treasure to come in the shape of their firstborn.

CHAPTER TWENTY-THREE

TIME TO PAY

While at the sink preparing dinner, she heard the gate slam. Peered out of the kitchen window. A group of children huddled in the garden, deep in conversation. Bewildered, Ruth dried her hands and opened the door to face six pairs of brown eyes.

The tallest child thrust a jar full of coins at her. "I'm Kevin, the eldest of Andrew Kenny's children. Our Mammy and the Holy Father say you stole our Da. All the relations tell us you're a wicked person. Ma says if Granda, God rest his soul, was still here," he solemnly crossed his chest. "He would come up and take a horsewhip to you." Biting his trembling lips, he continued. "Everyone says you take things you got no right to. You have a black heart and do anything for money. So, we collected these pennies from all our savings to buy our Da back."

Ruth looked into Kevin's proud, stern face, moved by his distress as he struggled to speak. Ruth pushed his jar away in refusal.

"Keep your money, pet; I never stole your father; you can come here anytime. He lives with me but loves you the same. Come back later; he'll tell you so himself."

One of the smaller girls tugged at her skirt."Mammy said you're an ugly whore, but you're pretty. Please let Da come home; he's ours, not yours."

Ruth reached out at a loss for words and took her tiny hand."I'm sorry, sweetheart, I can't do that. Do you want to wait for him?" the little girl moved forward.

Kevin pulled her back. "No, Connie, we don't go into a whores house," he glared at Ruth. "We want our Da at home. Mammy cries all the time. So does the babbie at home. Will you send him back, yes, or no?"

"I can't; I'm sorry," replied Ruth.

"You are ugly, so," the boy shouted. "Ugly and dirty black with a wicked evil soul. Mammy's right, come on," Kevin commanded, "we be wasting our time here. Hope your bastard child dies, and you too." With that, he stormed away up the lane with the others trailing behind him.

Unable to settle on a wild, stormy night, Ruth listened to the wind roaring through the trees. Wondered how much longer Andrew would be. Fierce hammering at the door startled her. When she opened it, Dawn was halfway back down the path.

"Andrew's had a terrible crash with a lorry," she screeched. "They say he's dying. I went to him, but he wants you, made me promise to fetch you. Be quick; there's not much time."

In silence, the two women sat together in the taxi. Ruth felt Dawn's eyes bore into her, glanced across; pure hatred contoured her flushed, tear, stained face,

Dawn snarled. "All your fault, this is. If he stayed with me, it never would have happened. I'd like to tear you apart; looks are all you got, no heart."

Ruth dashed inside the hospital, praying Andrew would recover and come home. A doctor blocked the doorway to stop her from entering the room.

"Don't go in there, my dear, in your condition; it wouldn't be wise."

Ruth pushed the doctor aside, approached the bed and froze in absolute shock. Andrew lay pale and silent, his handsome face unrecognisable. She clutched at the child inside, moaning in despair. Brought his hand up to her lips and kissed each finger.

With heart-rending sobs, Ruth begged, "Sweetheart, don't leave me; I need you so much."

Andrew opened his eyes; his voice was so weak and faint Ruth had to lean forward to hear.

"Ruth, no tears; you have my heart in life or death. Take care of our baby; promise you'll never forget me."

"Never, never. Don't leave me; Stay with me, sweetheart. I can't live without you," Showered his face with tear-drenched kisses. As her lips touched his, he took his last breath.

."Oh! No!" Ruth screamed, "No, God, not this." Shook his inert body, trying to force life back into it, ready to give her own so he might breathe again.

The room swam before her eyes. Hearing her cries, Dawn crashed into the room, followed by her brothers. She shoved Ruth aside and fell across her husband's body. Her screams resounded throughout the hospital; her brothers pulled their sister away.

Turning to Ruth, her face contorted, Dawn shrieked, "I hope you're satisfied. Dirty slut! He'd still be alive if he weren't rushing back to your bed. Now, neither of us will have him. "her lips curled as she snarled "Just remember, I'll be the one to lie beside him when I go, not you. His body and mine will mingle until eternity as if your time with him never was. I swear you'll never have a moment's peace." Her voice faulted as she struggled to speak, taking hold of her rosary torn from her throat. As the beads bounced on the floor, she snarled, "I'll curse you till the day I drop dead. Don't think you'll come to Andrew's funeral either. I'll swing for you first." The deranged woman lunged towards Ruth as her brothers restrained her. Dawn screeched, "Get her out of my sight; leave me to grieve my husband."

One brother dragged Ruth from the room. He bellowed, "Woman, you destroyed my sister; take your bastard back to England. May God strike me dead, and I'll see you burn in hell for what you've done to this family." Then threw her to the floor.

Blinded by tears, Ruth stumbled along endless deserted corridors looking for an exit sign. All she wanted was to go home and be alone with her grief. A wave of nausea rose in her throat and threatened to spew out. Ruth barely made it to a toilet in time. Squatting on the floor, her head hung over the rim of the pan, she vomited until nothing was left. The pains became stronger. Ruth clutched her stomach as her waters broke, flooding out over the tiled floor. " Oh God, not yet; it's too early. Don't let me lose our baby. I must find help." Pressing her arms against the wall for support struggled to her feet. Staggered along until her legs gave way, then crawled on her hands and knees. One corridor led to another stretching out before her with no one in sight. The pains increased and came swifter with growing intensity. Frantic and fearful, Ruth screamed for Andrew. With one last burning pain, she felt a solid form between her legs; her baby had entered the world, exhausted; Ruth lay immobile.

 In an instant, hordes of people surrounded her. Someone picked up the baby and dashed off. Until a nurse knelt beside her and, in a steady, soothing voice, said: "Come on now, pet, done the hard work all by yourself."

"Where are you taking my baby?" Ruth cried with waves of panic rising, sure something was wrong. Ruth appealed to the attending nurse, "Is it all right? Please take me to my baby; I want to hold it."

Ruth was taken to a side room and examined by a midwife to ensure the afterbirth was all out and no stitches were needed. The nurse gently patted her arm, "There now, don't fret. I'm sure your child's fine, a little premature, that's all."

"Please tell me, is my baby all right? What is it, boy or girl?"

The midwife muttered a brief, brisk response, stating she would find out as soon as possible. She left a junior nurse to clean Ruth up. The nurse made her comfortable but avoided direct eye contact with her charge. Ruth had a deep sense of foreboding, sure they were hiding something terrible from her. Left alone to deal with her vivid imagination and fears. Each time Ruth closed her eyes, the last torturous moments with Andrew returned. The scene played over and over like a stuck record. The conviction that her child had died hunted her.

Ruth turned her face into her pillow and groaned, "Andrew, why did you leave me? Now I lost our baby; I know it. I don't know if we've got a boy or girl." In anguish, Ruth moaned, "I'm so sorry, my darling. So sorry."

A woman entered the room with a clattering tea trolley. It seemed a long time since she'd seen anyone. This added fuel to her fears. Determined to find out, manoeuvred herself through the edge of the bed.

"Hello, there. Where you off to?" I'm Mags, brought you a nice hot drink. Nothing like a cuppa after having a baby. She smiled. "Plenty of time to walk about." She eased Ruth back between the sheets. "Heard yours was in a rush?" Passed Ruth a cup, "Here you go, my love, a nice cup of tea."

As she sipped the welcome drink, Ruth asked, "Where's the premature baby ward?"

"Just at the end of this corridor. Is that where you were off to?" Taking in Ruth's worried face, took her hand, "Not to worry, they're marvellous here; your baby will be fine." Mags soothed, "Now drink up your tea like a good girl. Try to rest; you got many sleepless nights ahead with a new baby. I should know; I've had six." She smiled and left the room.

Ruth rolled over the bed's edge as soon as the door closed, determined to find the unit, but her legs buckled. As she collapsed, the teacup fell from her hand and smashed.

Halfway down the passage, Mags, alarmed at the sound, rushed back in. "Oh my God, child, you're not strong enough to walk about." She helped Ruth back into bed and tucked in the covers.

Ruth sobbed, "Please give me a hand; I never saw my baby. I'm sure that's because it's dead," she wailed. Ruth tried to rise again and failed. Held on to Mags, pleading in frustration, "I must see for myself. Will you help me? I'm begging you, please?"

Mags bent over and cradled Ruth's trembling body in her arms. She rocked Ruth like a child until the cries ceased.

"There, there," she crooned. "Settle down; you'll make yourself ill. I'll see if I can find a wheelchair. If I don't, you'll just do yourself a mischief." She smiled. "Could cost me my job, though. Promise it's just for a quick peek, then back, and we might get away with it." Ruth gripped her hands and kissed them in tearful gratitude.

When they entered the premature baby unit, Mags called the nurses, "Just brought over a mum for a few minutes, Ok?" The busy nurses waved them in.

Searching the incubator's name tags, Ruth held her breath when she read a pink card with the words, Baby Morris. Looking down at a tiny doll-like baby wrapped in a white blanket, Ruth burst into tears of profound relief. Turning to Mags, bursting with pride and relief, gushed, "I got a beautiful girl, and she's just perfect."

"Yes, she certainly is," Mags agreed, turning the wheelchair towards the door. "Come on, before we get found out. Back we go. Feel better now, pet?"

Grateful beyond words, reluctant to leave, but now she had the precious image in her mind, Ruth slept. Eventually, she was allowed to briefly visit the unit and hold her baby's tiny hand. Then, as the little girl grew stronger, they allowed Ruth to hold her in her arms. Ruth choked with regret when the tiny fingers grasped hers for Lark, the child she'd aborted so many years ago.

Ruth walked to the ward window and looked up to the starlight sky. Then gazed at the bundle nestled in her arms; she had Andrew's chestnut-brown hair and honey-coloured eyes. Ruth whispered, "Can you see her, sweetheart? Our baby is so beautiful and perfect. I'll tell her all about you." Ruth sighed as tears fell on the baby's downy cheeks. "Daddy's with the Angels, but he'll always be in our hearts and watch over us from heaven. " Despite Dawn's rants and threats, Ruth would never lose him; his image would live on in this beautiful child. She named her Lucy as they had planned.

On her return to the cottage, she found her little garden had been wrecked. She'd forgotten to lock the door in her haste to see Andrew. Open to the elements, the floor was drenched by rain and full of wind-blown leaves. Cautious, Ruth stepped inside to discover the house trashed. All her furniture was upended, the cushion covers slashed to ribbons. The kitchen cupboards were emptied, and food lay scattered and rotting on the floor. On the wall, in black paint, a sign read, "Feck Off Prossie." She placed Lucy safely in the crib Andrew made. Then, she remembered Thomas; the poor little mite hadn't eaten for over a week. He wasn't in the house; Ruth searched for him in the garden and fields. At last, she found him underneath a large bush, covered in maggots, his head drenched in congealed blood and, nearby, a hammer. Someone from the village had killed the harmless creature for spite, Ruth quickly buried him.

She took Lucy to visit her father's grave; the heart-shaped wreath she ordered lay torn to shreds by the rubbish bin. Dawn's doing, Ruth was sure. Night after night, youths hurled mud, eggs, and abuse at the cottage. Ruth crouched in the kitchen corner, terrified, no longer with Andrew to protect her, and held Lucy tight in her arms.

 With no food in the house, she had to go to the village shop. The owner slammed the door in her face and changed the door sign to "Closed." She received the same response at the chemist and petrol station.

As she passed, some villagers spat, "Go back to England and take that bastard with you!"

Ruth made no answer as she fought to create a path past them. Fearing for Lucy's safety, sped away as stones bounced off her car. They were no longer safe and would have to leave as soon as possible; Ruth's dream lay in tatters. The priest had been right. Losing Andrew, the love of her life, was too high a price to pay.

Later that night, she woke to the smell of burning, thick smoke seeped under the door. Ruth snatched Lucy from her cot, wrapped a cover over her and opened the bedroom door. The entire lower floor was ablaze; greedy flames snaked up the stairs. Sick with terror, Ruth slammed the door shut and rushed around the room in a blind panic.

She rolled a blanket at the bottom of the door to block the smoke, dashed to the window, lifted the latch, and looked out. The drop to the ground was too much. Her frantic cries went unheard above the sounds of broken glass. As timbers surrendered to the flames under her feet, she felt the heat of the inferno beneath them. Thin trails of choking smoke seeped up through the floorboards. Ruth screamed and prayed for someone to come to save them.

Using water from a flower vase, soaked a jumper and placed it around Lucy to dampen the blanket. Then she saw the lights of cars and vans racing up the lane. Men from the village had spotted the glow on the skyline and smelt the smoke. They dashed up to investigate Ruth screamed to get their attention, but her voice was lost in the fire's roar.

The cottage roof caught fire as the flying sparks danced up to the sky. The rescuers found no safe way through the intense flames, so some raced around the back, shielding their faces from the extreme heat. With streaming red raw eyes, they peered through the black dense blinding smoke. One man spotted Ruth hanging out of a window. Unable to get close, they tried to persuade her to throw Lucy out to them. However, with fingers of flame darting out from the walls, she was too afraid. A van crashed straight through the garden; the driver positioned it as close as possible to the blazing cottage. Two men climbed up on the van's roof. One held the other round his waist. He stretched out as far as he could and shouted to Ruth to drop Lucy the few remaining feet. Ruth hesitated; the man yelled sharply.

"Kill yourself if you want but save the child." The hairs on his arms were being scorched, and flying embers landed on his head and shoulders, burnt through his cap and jacket. "Come on. I can't stay here much longer." Ruth remained frozen in terror at the window, looking down at him. He hollered, "In the name of God, woman pass that child down now. "

The man holding him shuffled his feet as the paint on the van's roof blistered. Afraid the heat would ignite his van's petrol tank, the driver blasted his horn, shaking Ruth into action. She threw a thick rug over the smouldering window ledge, leaned out and released her precious baby into outstretched arms. Then she jumped onto the van's roof and tumbled safely to the ground. With no water supply, she looked on in despair as her dream home burnt to the ground.

An ambulance arrived, sped them away to the hospital, and treated them for smoke inhalation, but they were fit to be discharged the next day. The priest offered her temporary shelter but made it clear it was only for the sake of her child. To her horror, the fire inspector discovered that petrol had been poured through the letterbox and started the blaze. They'd found an empty can dumped in the lane. The inspector told her he had to send a copy of the report to the police headquarters. However, he added there would be fingerprints on the petrol can, so they would find the arsonists. Ruth couldn't afford to have the police involved. Afraid they had her photo and fingerprints on record, then realised who she was. To claim any insurance for a police investigation involved bringing to light her false details was more than she dared to risk.

Ruth knew she couldn't stay in Ireland; her dream was lost. It was a bank holiday weekend, and any cash had been lost in the fire, leaving her with no available money. Luckily, she parked her car further up the lane to leave room for Andrew's van. As always, she forgot to remove the keys and chequebook from the glove compartment. The priest, eager for her to be gone, gave her funds from the parish poor box to fill up with petrol and go to Belfast. Ruth sold the car to pay hotel fees, buy new clothes for herself and Lucy, and catch the ferry back to England.

CHAPTER TWENTY-FOUR

CHANCE MEETING

Ruth searched for an affordable (room to rent card) in the newsagent's window. Although not what she would have chosen, but there was nowhere else. It was far too small, and they had to share a bathroom and a windowless kitchen, both often left filthy. The rents in London for suitable places were much higher than Ruth remembered. Three months in advance, a large deposit and references required these she couldn't supply. She used her own name with no plans to travel again. Ruth registered the baby as Lucy Page. Six other tenants, including drug users and drunkards, filled the cramped rooms. Arguments and violent fights were a regular occurrence. Their room had mould stains on the skirting boards and every wall. When it rained, the water dripped in through the warped windows. Ruth often took Lucy to the park in her free time as a break from the bleak room. In a café she visited, Ruth got to know a young married couple. During their conversations, she learnt they also lived in a dingy bedsit and hated it. They told her they had no problem getting false references but couldn't raise the money needed for a deposit. Ruth suggested a way to secure permanent accommodation for them and solve her situation at the same time. The couple asked a friend who ran his own business to supply false references for Ruth. In exchange, she agreed to give the couple the amount they needed. With references secured, Ruth found an unfurnished basement flat in a pleasant area of Bayswater. It had direct access to a small garden. She bought some decent second-hand furniture and cheap household items. Ruth missed Andrew, but in time, the pain eased; she gave Lucy all her heart and love. Ruth received a bank statement on the day her child took her first faltering steps. Because of all her additional expenses, her savings had dwindled. Her remaining shares were not performing well and not worth keeping, so she had to find work fast.

She lost her national insurance card and birth certificate in the fire. Ruth began work in a small dressmaking firm that employed casual workers and offered cash in hand. She found a young girl to look after Lucy. At the end of her first week, to her dismay, there were just a few pounds left after paying Lucy's child-minder and the rent. Although Ruth hated the job and the time it took away from Lucy. With no other skill, she had no choice but to stick with it. At the factory, she learnt dressmaking skills, bought an old treadle sewing machine in the market, and placed a card in the local shop, advertising dress alterations, often working far into the night. This added income brought small treats for Lucy. Selling her depleted shares meant she could open an accessible saving account for Lucy's future. Ruth plodded by each week, eventually getting used to managing on reduced funds.

One Easter holiday, Ruth took Lucy, now a bright, delightful two-year-old, to a funfair. Enjoying the wonder and delight on the little girl's face. Apple-round cheeks flushed pink as Lucy beamed at the bright lights and jiggled in time to the music. She squealed with delight on the merry-go-round, her tiny hands waving with joy each time she passed Ruth. Limpid brown eyes shone with excitement as she pulled Ruth from ride to ride. Before leaving for home, Lucy begged to go on the toddlers' roundabout again.

While Ruth waited for the ride to end, she felt a tug on her arm; a hesitant voice asked, "Your Ruth? Ruth Page, isn't it? I would recognise you anywhere. How are you?"

Ruth turned, and a brassy-haired woman stood behind her. Bemused, she looked at the woman who appeared to know her well, but Ruth couldn't place who she was. Thick makeup, a revealing dress, she must be someone from the club. But who? Not wishing to offend, Ruth smiled and waited, hoping to as they conversed would remember.

"Fancy seeing you after all this time. I love funfairs, don't you? I thought I would treat myself to a candy floss in passing. You remember me, don't you? Wendy, from the club?"

"Yes, Wendy," Ruth lied, "How are you? Still working at the old place?"

"Never mind about me," Wendy questioned. "What you been up to? You still look fabulous; time's been kind to you. You look better than ever, lucky bitch," she remarked with good humour. "It will surprise the girls when I tell them I saw you. Let's go for a drink, and you can tell me what you've been doing."

The ride ended, and Ruth lifted Lucy out. Wendy knelt in front of her, running long, painted fingers over the child's tight brown curls. As Wendy brushed her flushed cheek, Lucy gave her a sweet, tired smile.

Wendy gushed. "What a poppet, so cute. I would die for such long eyelashes. Worn out, lovely little thing. Yours, I can tell." She looked up at Ruth. "Got married, did you? I always said you would make good. Where's your bloke then?"

"No, no, bloke, only Lucy and me." Lucy tugged at her dress, pleading for one more ride. Ruth smiled. "Last time then, sweetheart, it's getting late." She placed her back on the children's ride. "Tell you, what if you're not in a hurry? I live nearby in Bayswater." Ruth suggested, "Why not come back with us? We'll buy a bottle of wine on the way. I'll put this little mite to bed; we can have a proper chat away from this noise." Once home, they settled in the living room; Ruth poured a glass of wine each. "Come on then, tell me all the gossip," Ruth prompted.

"Where to start," breathed Wendy, kicking off her shoes. "things have changed so much since your days. No one is safe to work the streets without protection. Everyone's got a pimp. They control the best spots for their girls" Wendy wriggled in her chair, took a sip of the wine and continued, "The kids are getting younger, too; the pimps send out gangs to find girls and boys. Picking them up from the stations and alleys. Just kids who've run away, they befriend them, then hand them over to the pimps. They either beat them within an inch of their lives or get the poor little sods out of their heads on drugs. Then force them onto the streets to earn the next fix."

Ruth interrupted, "That's terrible; why doesn't someone help them? If they're young, the police or charities should look out for them, don't you think?"

Wendy gave her a withering glare. "Don't make me laugh; a load of the top nobs are our best customers. The police, lawyers, magistrates, judges, and so-called respectable business people got no qualms shagging an underage boy or girl. Twisted, sick bastards, all of them."

Ruth poured out another drink, "What about the charities, though? They tried to help me in the old days."

Wendy waved her hand in dismissal. "Oh, sure they do, but these pimps have such a hold over the kids; very few get away and stay away. They might as well flog a dead horse."

"There must be others still able to work the streets for themselves like we used to." Ruth insisted.

"Well, if there are, they are taking a hell of a chance." She lit a cigarette and hissed out a plume of smoke through clenched teeth, "No love, I doubt that very much. I don't know any without some protection nowadays." Wendy squirmed at the thought, lifted herself from the chair, paced the room, and waved her arms in the air, agitated. "Even with all the dangers, some girls would be better off taking their chances alone. They're all cruel, greedy bastards. If they think a girl doesn't earn enough or holds money back, they bash her up. Too dangerous to work alone anyway; the cops harass away all the kerb-crawlers." Wendy sat back down with a deep sigh. "The safest way to work solo now is by putting cards in phone boxes and working from rented rooms or hotels. Some others use escort agencies for contacts." Wendy reached over to pour another glass of wine and passed the bottle to Ruth before continuing. "The hotel owners rip us off, and the agencies charge for contacts. The pimps are always chasing after them. Most girls give in after a few threats or beatings. I ask you, how's a girl to make a living? Everyone is on the make" She rubbed her stomach. "Got anything to eat, Ruth? I'm famished?"

Ruth got up to make a snack for them. Wendy followed her into the kitchen. "Remember poor little Alice?" she asked.

Ruth nodded. "How could I forget?" shuddering at the memory. "I'll never get over that night."

They returned to the living room and sat down.

Wendy sighed. "First of many, poor little cow. It happens all the time now. You got out at the best time. Things have changed so much nowadays; we girls have to buy protection, which means the bastard pimps get rich off our backs." Wendy flopped back down in her chair and smiled. "I'm so lucky I live with a bloke called Luke, massive build like a brick shit house and strong as a horse; no one messes with him. With me, he's gentle, so sweet, like a big teddy bear. He never hits me and doesn't care how much I make. Won't take a penny from me either. Imagine that a pimp who doesn't rob you must be a first," she laughed. "I don't love him, but he's a good man. The only person who ever cared for me despite what I am." She sighed in contentment. "If he had his way, I'd come off the game. But what else can I do? Can you imagine me slaving away in a factory?" Wendy screwed up her nose. "Still, it's never been a simple life, but it beats a nine-to-five job any day," she finished with a smirk, "and it pays better."

Ruth had the best night's sleep in a long time. Chatting far into the night with Wendy, who understood her past, was just the tonic she needed. Wendy left, promising to return soon. After that first evening, Ruth met Luke, a giant man with shoulders as broad as a door. Hands like shovels clasped Ruth's slender fingers in greeting. He had blond, long, thinning hair tied back in a ponytail and soft, kind, hazel eyes. A slow, shy smile always hovered on his lips as he spoke. With his awkward ways and stuttering speech, he reminded her of Eddie, and Ruth took to him right away and understood why Wendy felt safe with him.

"Come back in the game," Wendy persisted. "You still got your looks. You'll bring in a lot more money than that lousy factory job. You'd soon make yourself a pile."

The phone rang, Wendy got up to answer it. She came back to Ruth and picked up her handbag.

"I got to pop out, but I've got an idea. You're smart and talk all posh like. Go back on the game; you could buy a small business after a while. Set yourself up before Lucy's old enough to ask questions." Wendy threw on a coat and turned back to Ruth. "I'm off now, but think about what I said. Imagine the time you could spend with her instead of having a stranger enjoy her best years."

Ruth didn't want to resume her old life, so she resisted and carried on working at the factory. When the owners retired and lived abroad, they sold the business to an oversized dress manufacturer. They lay the legitimate casual workers with no employment details registered off, and Ruth is one of them. The urgent need to earn money to keep a roof over Lucy's head left Ruth with no alternative but to resume her past life. She found a young girl to look after Lucy in the evenings and worked from Wendy's flat but insisted on paying for Luke's protection. Only Wendy and Luke knew about Lucy; soon, her bank balance was back in the black.

While she passed an hour alone in Luke's company, he poured out his heart.

"One night, while on my way home from the club where I worked as a bouncer, I heard terrible screams coming from an alley. I ran up and saw this bloke bashing the hell out of Wendy. She told me later he didn't want to pay. He was a sort of scum that likes beating girls up after sex." He drew himself up, and his face tightened in anger at the memory. "Well! He won't beat another helpless girl again. I brought her here and nursed her. I hate being her pimp, but that's how Wendy wants it. She cares for me but doesn't love me. Still, I'm happy just to be with her."

Luke told her to be careful on the streets. He knew how others worked and treated their girls and avoided telling Ruth that other pimps offered to take her off his hands for a fair price. Luke refused, although aware of the personal risk he took.

The most persistent was an Italian named Rego, a man everyone feared. Four years earlier, he was arrested for the brutal murder of three wealthy Turkish men in Hatton Garden. The police found them stripped, mutilated, and strangled with dog leads but couldn't build a solid case to charge him.

Rego soon gained a reputation as the most sadistic gang member. Then he began working for the Frank brothers, the most ruthless mobsters in London. When the brothers disappeared without warning, Rego took over all their rackets. No one dared to challenge the undisputed boss of the most prominent organisation in the city. Casinos, money lending, protection, and prostitution, Rego had a hand in all forms of depravity. Vicious thugs took care of anyone who opposed his wishes. Whatever he wanted, Rego got. Now his greedy eyes were on Ruth. Luke begged her to avoid him at all costs. Thanking him for the warning, assured him she would be all right.

While enjoying a night out with Wendy at a nightclub, a man approached her. Ruth immediately recognised him as the defiant young boy called Çocuk from the casino many years ago. As his expert eyes appraised her, he murmured in a low, sensuous voice,

"Hello beautiful, we meet again. You certainly blossomed into a gorgeous woman. I'm sure you remember me; allow me to buy you a drink." As he placed his hand politely on her elbow, a shiver of delight shot through her body as he guided Ruth to the bar. "My name is Rego; I'm sure you heard of me."

Ruth had never forgotten how he roused her to such giddy heights. Rego fascinated her; he'd filled out and grown into a man who oozed sensuality. To the despair of Wendy and Luke, Ruth refused to believe the boy who held her with such tenderness could be as cruel as the reputation that followed him.

Over the following weeks, Rego plied her with expensive gifts. An attentive, perfect companion, he invited her to accompany him to prestigious events. Rego made no advances towards her, although Ruth longed and yearned for his touch. Each night she savoured his caress as he filled her delicious dreams. Ruth knew she would never love again but was irresistibly drawn to this sensual man.

CHAPTER TWENTY-FIVE

THE DARKEST HEART

Rego drove Ruth into the countryside. They travelled long before parking outside an imposing mansion converted into a nursing home. Rego explained,

"My youngest brother, Leon, is nursed here. When my mother died, I brought him here. this is the best home in England." His voice broke, allowing Ruth to view a rare chink in his armour. "He's got a terminal illness. While he lives, I'll make sure he has the best care and comfort my money can provide." Rego spoke with an undeniable affection for his bedbound brother, his voice so soft, loving, and tender.

Ruth's heart filled with compassion for the emaciated young boy gazing up at Rego, absolute devotion shining from his sunken eyes. Ruth reached out to hold a bony hand. Leon raised her fingers to his lips, gave a cheeky grin, and winked. She noticed a strong likeness to his elder brother.

"Oi! We'll have less of that." Rego scolded. "You want my girl now, do you?" He wagged his finger at his brother, who howled with laughter.

Ruth's heart melted as Rego spoon-fed his brother. They chatted on, enjoying each other's company. That evening, Rego took her back to his apartment. Ruth melted into his arms, remembering with pleasurable anticipation their first encounter. Sure, of himself, he swept her up and carried her to his bedroom. As they lay between the silken sheets, he leant upon his elbow and ran his free hand along the length of her body, stroking slow, tender circles with his fingertips. Tingles of excitement rushed through her as his fingers travelled until she shivered with delight.

"Come and work for me, Ruth," he pleaded, his voice as soft as silk. "I protect all my girls; no one dares to mistreat them. I have a unique plan for you away from the streets; you're above that." He touched every inch of her straining body, bringing her to a fever pitch. He rested his lips enticingly close to hers and whispered, "Just think of it, Ruth. You'll live in grand style, with a maid to see to all your needs. I'll buy you designer clothes and fabulous jewels. Nothing but the best for my special lady."

Half out of her mind with desire, Ruth pulled him to her, wanting no more talk. Breathless, she agreed to think about his offer. At last, he took her to the heights of passion.

After sending the child-minder off by a taxi, Ruth threw off her shoes and sank into a chair with a glass of wine to reflect on the day. It was impossible to miss the thinly disguised flashes of malice that Rego had shown to others while in her company. However, she had also seen a softer side, so gentle with his brother. He was capable of love.

Ruth gazed at her reflection in the mirror and pondered, "What if I'm special, and he means what he says?" Brushed her hair and muttered to her face, looking back at her. "How will he react to Lucy?" She shrugged her shoulders. "Haven't I earned the right to a better life, had my share of misery? I want security and material comforts for Lucy and to satisfy my sexual needs." She breathed, "I mustn't see him again until I find out the truth."

Ruth met an old prostitute called Linda; she had been one of the Frank brothers' first girls until she was taken over by Rego. He used her till she lost her looks and was no longer worth his investment. Ruth bought two large glasses of wine before moving to a corner table, out of sight of the others.

Lynda sucked in the smoke from her cigarette. "Right then, what you after?"

"Tell me about Rego; I need to find out everything. He wants me to work for him, but I've heard many disturbing rumours. I want you to tell me if they are true or gossip."

"Jesus Christ! Are you mad?" Linda gasped. "Work for Rego? Don't be a fool. Might as well sign a pact with the devil. Believe me, that is what he is." She glanced around and patted Ruth's hand with cigarette-stained fingers. "Take my advice and stay well away." In one gulp, she downed her drink. Screwing up her face, spat on the floor, "Just enough to wet my whistle. Jesus, Ruth, what's that muck? Tastes like shit! Can't stand wine; I'm off." As Linda rose to leave, Ruth held her arm to restrain her.

"No, don't go, Linda; I'll buy you another drink, whatever you want. I'm willing to pay you for any information about Rego. There's so much I don't know and so many rumours."

"You are kidding; split on that pig?" Linda shook off her arm. "Why should I? More than my life's worth. Find your answers somewhere else. I won't risk it."

Ruth took a roll of money from her purse. Linda's greedy eyes glazed over as she stared at it.

"I swear I won't tell anyone." Ruth pulled off two five-pound notes and offered them to Linda. "Look here, take this."

Linda snatched the notes and shoved them into her blouse. "Buy me a proper drink; a pint of stout will do," she grunted.

Ruth went back to the bar and brought the glass over. Sat down once more and waited for Linda to speak.

Between noisy slurps, Linda demanded, "You promise on your life you won't repeat anything I tell you. I'll be done for if you do."

"No, I said so dozens of times. Come on," Ruth, exasperated, passed over another note.

Linda reached out for the money, pursuing her bright, ruby red lips; she sneered, "I worked hard for that bastard. Before he decided I was too old and past my best." Pulling the short skirt over her stick-thin, blue-veined legs, raised her voice, she **complained**, "Day and night, I was at it. No matter what I earned, it never satisfied him. Had enough, been on the game since I was fourteen, first with those bastards, the Frank brothers, then him, an even bigger asshole."

She brushed her fingers through straw-like hair and declared, "Bet I could still earn a bob or two if I wanted to." She expected instant confirmation and stared into her companion's face.

"Yes, of course," Ruth lied. "Look, tell me about Rego. He's asked me to work for him. You've known him longer than most. I need you to tell me the truth." Ruth promised to pay generously for information. Linda looked around to make sure no one overheard.

"Take a tip from me, Ruth, that Rego can charm the birds out of the trees when he wants something. Stay away from him. Once he has you, he'll demand every penny you earn. You're his property, with no escape. Heaven help any girl who tries to sell him short or wants to jack it in before he decides to **be** rid of them. I could say more, but I've said too much already." Her eyes bored into Ruth's face. Linda smirked. "I can tell you're not convinced. I suppose he's got you hooked. I'm right, ain't I?" she fiddled around in her bag, retrieved her cigarettes, lit up and blew out a plume of smoke. "Think he loves you, huh? No chance. Swore, you were special, did he?" Linda mocked. "I'll bet he did, and you believed him. Well, more fool you. Money's all he cares about, nothing else. Go with him, and you'll learn the hard way."Linda shuffled in her chair. "How about a refill?" When Ruth returned to the table, she knocked back the drink and slid the glass forward expectantly. Ruth ignored the empty glass., Linda smacked her lips, convinced she could wheedle more cash out of Ruth. "Rego's a handsome devil. I'll give you that. Fancied him myself before I got my first hammering from his thugs for not earning enough." Crossing her arms, leant closer and whined, "I need a few bob more. Times are hard; I still got expenses, you know. You promised you'd pay."

Ruth brought out her purse again. "I understand, Linda," she coaxed, struggling to hide her impatience. "Take this to tide you over," offering a ten-pound note.

"Hum!" The old woman snatched the note. "Christ, I need another drink; buy me a short this time and make it a double."

Ruth returned with the glass and passed it to her.

Linda gulped it down and looked about furtively, "He's got ears all over, can't trust anyone. This place belongs to him. Pays me peanuts to sweep and clean the loo." Linda ran her tongue over thin lips and continued, "While Rego was still working with the brothers, I was always dumpy, even in my younger days. So, I hid it for six months when I fell pregnant, but Rego's no fool. As I gained weight, he got suspicious. Made me strip naked, so my condition was obvious. He slapped me around and ordered me to sort out a quick abortion. I never wanted a kid, but I didn't want to kill one, either. It would be about your age now." She paused briefly, starting at the walls with a faraway look in her eyes,

Ruth's heart went out to her, remembering her own abortion and how the heartache still lingered.

"I'm sorry, Linda, how terrible," Ruth said kindly.

Linda's eyes cleared. "Hang on, that's not the worst part. I told him I couldn't do that; it was too late anyway. I tried to reason with him and promised to work twice as hard afterwards. Rego went berserk and threatened to kick it out of me. Terrified, I had to agree. He sent me with these two thugs to an old woman's house. When I told her I was about four months gone, she refused point-bank, telling them an abortion so late would be too dangerous. The thugs threatened her with all sorts. She used a long wire with a hook on the end; the old bitch was so scared her hands didn't stop shaking. She kept missing and had to go in again and again. I can tell you it hurt like hell; I bled buckets and screamed my head off. It went badly wrong; the old girl went into hysterics and wanted me out of there. Rego's blokes just got her to fix old rags between my legs to stop the blood. Course, it kept running, and the rags soon became useless. They stuffed a gag in my mouth to keep me from yelling. Then drove me to the hospital and dumped me outside the gates. I had to hobble in by myself." Linda tossed back her head and sighed. "I could've died. If I had that bastard, Rego wouldn't have cared. Never made that mistake again, I can tell you. It was no sheath, no business from then on. When I came out, the swine put me straight back on the streets." She pointed a nicotine-stained finger. "I'm warning you, stay away. He was bad enough before he took over, but not a patch on what he'll do now. He's a cruel bastard. If you run off, believe me, he'll find you. There is no escape; he only cares about how much you earn." Holding up her hands, the wily old woman waved Ruth away. "I won't say more. That will have to do."

Ruth, exasperated, pulled out another note, and pressed it into her thin hand. "Linda, your manner tells me you know more. Tell me what you're not saying. It's important. Come on, I'll give you another one of these."

Grabbing the money, Linda took a deep breath, leant forward, and in hushed tones, mumbled, "Well, all right, but if you tell, I'll get my throat slit."

"I won't," Ruth assured her. "I promise this conversation will go no further." She had already decided to steer clear of Rego but wanted to be told everything.

"I heard that girls who run off are found cut up something awful; others just disappear. Word on the street says they got done on his orders. He never gets his hands dirty; I swear I won't cross him. Neither will you if you got any sense."

As she rose to leave, Linda held her back. "I got just one other thing you might like to hear. Worth a score, though this time, though."

Ruth groaned and sat back in the chair. "Go on then, greedy cow," she said, handing over the twenty-pound note to the woman. "What is it?"

"He's into child sex."

Shocked, Ruth stuttered, "What?! He sleeps with children. I don't believe you,"

"No stupid, course not, they're just stock, cash on the hoof, you might say." Linda curled her mouth as she delivered her final revelation. "He sells young kids to men for sex. Rego's speciality is porn films with boys and girls from four to thirteen, maybe a little older if they're small enough. He got a big studio up west and makes a mint selling the films to paedophile rings." Linda patted the money she had earned, tucked in her blouse, and smirked in satisfaction. The older woman hissed as Ruth snatched up her bag to leave, "Remember! This chat never happened!"

If Ruth had doubts, this last revelation convinced her to stay far away. She sent a message to Rego saying she preferred to remain under Luke's protection and wouldn't see him again.

The girls agreed to have one night off each week. They arrived back one evening to find Luke trussed to a chair, beaten near to death. "Oh! No," Wendy screamed, rushing to his side, "What have they done to you?"

As they untied his bonds and wrestled to lay his massive frame on the floor, Wendy caressed him in her arms as her tears flowed. A blood-coated mallet lay on the table; beside it was a brief note threatening the same treatment for Wendy unless Ruth was available the following night.

"What have I done?" Ruth wailed. "It's my fault. Oh! Luke, I'm so sorry. I'll ring for an ambulance,"

"No, Ruth." Luke, his strength fading, held up his huge hand. "No time for that. Clear out, both of you; they'll be back soon. Go as fast as you can; I'm finished."

"Don't talk like that," sobbed Wendy. "You can't leave me. What will I do without you?" Wendy bent to hear the last words of her dear friend. She nestled his head on her lap as his life drained away, her dress stained bright red with the blood oozing from his gaping wounds.

His speech laboured, gasping for breath, he said, "Do one last thing for me, girl. Leave me and clear out quick." He looked up at Ruth. "I never split about Lucy." The light faded from his eyes as he slipped away.

Wendy turned on Ruth, "I wish I'd never bumped into you. Why wouldn't you listen? We warned you, but no, you couldn't stay away from that bastard, now Luke's dead, and this is your fault."

Enraged, she flew at her Ruth sidestepped her blows, slapped the hysterical woman, and grabbed her thrashing arms.

"Wendy, get a hold of yourself; blaming me solves nothing. What's done is done; for God's sake, get a grip."

Wendy's rage spent; she desperately clung to Ruth and stuttered, "God! Ruth, he'll finish us; I know it."

Ruth pushed her away and demanded, "Come on, hurry up nothing we can do for Luke. We must get away." She dragged Wendy to the bathroom, "Clean yourself up," rushed to the wardrobe, and pulled out a clean dress. "For heaven's sake, move, come on, quick, change into this. We've got to go now."

In a daze, Wendy got dressed, then crossed the room to where Luke lay and kissed her protector goodbye. The girls fled, taking the time only to ring the police. Back at Ruth's flat, they passed the night jumping at every sound. Wendy decided to return to her hometown in the morning and begged Ruth to go with her. Tired of running from trouble, as no one knew her home address, Ruth was sure she'd be safe. "I can promise you one thing," she said. "I'm never going back on the streets."

CHAPTER TWENTY-SIX

TRAPPED

A few weeks later, she opened the door to Rego holding a giant toy cat in his arms. He smiled at Ruth's stunned expression. "Does a cute little girl called Lucy live here?" He called out, brushing past Ruth, frozen to the spot in shock. Lucy rushed to him with squeals of delight. He whisked her up in his arms and carried her into the main room. Ruth stood stunned as he played on the floor with Lucy and cursed herself for not moving away. Biting on her lower lip, every nerve in her body on a razor's edge, waiting for the storm to break.

After a while, he got up, saying, "Kitty's tired now, sweetheart; put him to bed for a while; I need to talk to Mummy. " Lucy picked up her new toy and ran off to the bedroom.

Rego took Ruth's trembling hand and led her to the settee, sighing in exasperation. "Well, now, Ruth. You cost me lots of time and money; I had to trace your friend Wendy to find you." He gave a smug smile. "Mind you, the slag sang her last song pretty quick."

267

"What did you do to her?" Ruth asked with trepidation, waiting for his reply, but she had already guessed.

"Me? Nothing, but I can tell you, the whore gave you away, dam fast. You should choose your friends with more care."

Ruth's eyes widened in horror. He grunted,

"She's keeping the fish fat in a river now. People don't run out or cross me. You should have realised that once I took care of that stubborn fool, Luke."

This was more than Ruth could bear and tried to move away, but he held her fast.

"There were arrangements made for you to entertain valuable clients. You disappeared, so I had to find a replacement. That's bad for business. You made me look a fool. I won't stand for that." He growled, his handsome face white with rage, "I've had scrubber's faces ripped apart for less." He exhaled and relaxed, leant forward, cupped her face, and kissed her tear stained cheek. He looked deep into her terror filled eyes.

"Relax, sweetheart. I'm sure we can put it all behind us now. No need for us to fall out, is there?" He held out his arms invitingly. "Come on now, Ruth, we can make a fresh start." Ruth backed away in despair that yet another death was her doing, unable to suppress a shudder of revulsion. Rego reached out and held her wrist, twisting the skin beneath his fingers until she screamed in pain. "No one does that to me," he snarled.

Ruth slapped him across the face. He shoved her away; she fell back into an armchair. Rego leaned over and placed both arms on either side of the chair, trapping her.

"No tart raises a hand to me either. You will work for me. I won't take no for an answer." He gripped her jaw in steely fingers that tightened until she cried out in pain. "Don't think about running off. You wouldn't want anything to happen to that little beauty you hid so well, would you? Think about my offer." He glanced around the dingy room with distaste. "I'll move you out of this dump to a place more fitting. We can be friends, Ruth. It will be as hard on you as you make it." Then he marched out and slammed the door behind him. Outside, a car remained parked with two men inside, watching her day and night. Soon, he would be back to demand payment. Rego gave nothing for nothing. Ruth had to find a way to leave the country, but where could she get a legal passport? Although some people supplied those, all were connected to Rego's organisations. Ruth dreaded contemplating what would happen if she approached these sources through the street girls or others. She racked her brains to devise an escape plan then, like a bolt of lightning, an idea came to her.

A wealthy peer Lord Rupert, one of her regular clients, came to mind. He visited her whenever he came to London. He owned a large estate in Wales and other properties in Portugal and France. He often begged her to be his mistress and live with him in France. With his connections in government, he might help her escape from Rego. It would be risky to ask him; he might not want to break the law for her. Also, he didn't know about Lucy. Ruth decided it was worth a try. She found his phone number and made the call. They met at the Claridges Hotel in Mayfair. He was one of her regulars, so there was nothing suspicious about her seeing him. Over a meal, Ruth told him of her plight and that she had a child.

Rupert stared at her for a while, deep in thought, and said nothing. Worried that because of her revelations, she might lose him, Ruth continued, "I will come with you if you still want me to."

"Will you, my dear? Could you?" He let out a long shuddering sigh; pale blue eyes searched her face. "I promise to keep you happy. A false passport and identity papers aren't a problem. Not much money can't buy if you have contacts in the right places." He smiled. "My son runs the estate; it's time I let go of the reins and retired. With a beautiful companion at my side to end my days with, what more could I ask?" Breathless with emotion, he clasped her fingers in his withered hands. "I fantasised and dreamt about this many, many times." He gazed at her across the table. "Are you sure you could ever learn to love an old fool like me? Balding seventy-eight, an overweight lump of lard." He laughed and lowered his voice to a whisper, then confided, "My health isn't good, and to spend what time is left with you is my idea of heaven. I'd die content in your arms." Rupert studied her face; tiny beads of perspiration gathered on his brow. His voice was thick as he strained to speak. "Ruth, never in my wildest dreams did I foresee this moment. I must tell you I will leave my estate and properties to my son as his birthright, but I promise to make provisions for you to be financially secure. You will have your own home and be safe always. If knowing my fortune won't come to you changes your mind, it will break my heart."

Ruth replied, "I don't want your money or care how old you are. Any kindness in my life has been from older men. I'm fond of you. If you help my child and me, with time, these emotions will grow into love," she lied. As they parted, Ruth swore she would never leave him. Ecstatic with happiness, Rupert kissed her cheek before the concierge called for his car. Watching him disappear, Ruth experienced a pang of guilt. Using him was cruel, and she would never love him. The arrangement would be brief and repay his kindness to make him happy. Living with him and sharing his bed to secure a haven out of Rego's reach was a small price to pay. When Rupert died, she'd be settled abroad, secure in her own place.

At last, she had her new identity papers and their departure date arranged. Rupert sent their passports and tickets. They'd soon be miles away from England, out of Rego's reach. Excited at the thought of a plane ride, Lucy raced like a whirlwind around the concourse. For a bit of peace, Ruth took her to the shops to look for a toy. Ruth picked up a newspaper and glanced at the headlines.

Lord Found Shot in Country Lane.

She bought a magazine, a comic, and a toy for Lucy, and then they sat in the concourse to wait for Rupert. Engrossed in a story, she felt someone standing in front of her. Looked up, and there was Rego, smiling down at her.

"Well, fancy seeing you here, precious. Going somewhere, are you?"

Ruth stammered, lost for words, "Just taking Lucy for a brief trip. She's never been on holiday."

Still smiling, he sat beside her. "How nice." He ripped up the tickets as the pieces fluttered to the floor. Mocked, "I'll hang on to these passports. I'm sure I can find a market for them. You won't need them anymore." Rego grabbed her bag. "Let's see what else you're hiding." Tipped out the contents on the seat beside him and picked up her false identity papers. "Sly bitch." He smirked as he read them. "How did you get these?" To Ruth's dismay, he ripped them up. "Well, Mrs Richardson, you don't need these anymore," he mocked, laughing at Ruth's discomfort, "instant divorce for you," he threw them in the bin."You've aimed high for a simple scrubber, don't you think? A decaying old git like that, how stupid are you?"

"What have you done?" Ruth gulped. A shiver ran down her spine; she felt a sense of dread.

He leant over his mouth close to her ear; and snarled. "Lying little slag, did you think I wouldn't discover your plans? Your decrepit old Lord isn't the only one with connections in high places. Thought you had better sense, devious bitch. I told you I have eyes everywhere."

"Oh! My God," Ruth moaned as the truth dawned. Her voice cracked with emotion. "It's him in the papers, isn't it? You arranged it, didn't you? Poor man, there was no need to hurt him."

"His blood is on your hands, my girl, not mine." He yanked her out of the seat.

Lucy tugged Rego's jacket. "Why's Mummy crying, Uncle Rego? We're going on a big plane today."

"Come on, sweetheart, we've got to go home; Mummy's not well today; we'll have a plane ride another time."

He rushed them out of the airport and bundled them into his car. Apart from an occasional smile at Lucy, he drove back to Ruth's flat in stony silence, saying he'll be back in a few days. Sure enough, he returned, telling her he'd arrange for her to entertain wealthy foreign men and give them a good time. They moved to an enormous luxury apartment, large enough for Lucy's bedroom to be far away from any sounds in the apartment. Rego engaged a live-in maid to handle all domestic

273

chores and a day nurse for Lucy. Ruth was aware he paid the maid to report everything back to him.

Rego took control of all her earnings, paid all the bills, and opened a clothing account in one of the top designer showrooms. He allowed Ruth a few pounds of her weekly earnings for personal essentials. To earn more, she had to secretly take on private clients. Susan, the maids' eyes and ears missed nothing. Ruth intended to leave London, move far away from Rego's clutches, buy a house in a small village, and revert to dressmaking and alterations at home. If Susan ran straight to Rego, the outcome was too terrible to think about. Ruth had to buy her silence somehow.

"Come on, rest, Susan, and sit down for a minute." Ruth offered, "Have a glass of wine with me" She passed her a bottle of her most expensive perfume, which Ruth knew she used behind her back anyway. Also, as small jewellery pieces went missing, the woman was far from honest. She might be open to bribery, given the right motive. Ruth was sure if she could, lure the maid in deep enough, she would have to keep quiet for her own sake.

Susan snatched the perfume, grumbled her thanks, and asked, "What you after?"

"Nothing; I thought we should get to know each other a little." She filled a glass. "Come on now, have a drink with me. Can't hurt for us to get along, can it?"

274

Ruth took the plunge and approached the woman with a proposition. Knowing full well what the outcome would be if things went wrong.

Susan snapped up her offer and agreed for a generous slice of the payments received; she would keep quiet about private clients. However, she insisted on an active part in bondage sessions.

"I don't do that sort of thing," Ruth gasped.

"That's fine start now; I fancy giving those bastard scum a good hiding," Only the blindfolded ones, though, don't want them seeing me." Susan rubbed her hands in glee. "I'll enjoy hearing them squeal like the pigs they are." Her voice, sharp and full of spite, confided to Ruth. "Be like getting back at my arsehole, Dad. Too free with his fists, he was. Every Friday wages night, we kids waited in terror for him to come home roaring drunk. Throw two pounds on the table and expect mum to provide a full dinner for him and us five kids all week. Then we'd listen to poor mum's screams when there wasn't enough food on his plate. He knocked her from pillar to post." She tossed her head to confirm and added: "We got our share of beatings most times just because he couldn't stand us being around and disturbing his sleep." She stopped talking for a moment; a vindictive expression crossed her face, bitter satisfaction edged in her voice. "I was the eldest, so I coped it for not keeping the kids out of his way. One night, blind drunk, he fell off the towpath. We were free of him and bloody good riddance too." She straightened up in her chair and sighed, "Then the poor cow got pregnant by another waster. Had two more kids with him, but the third got sick and died. The bloke buggered off, so we all finished up in the orphanage."

Ruth felt a twang of pity for her, but that soon passed as Susan continued, "But I ain't gonna do no fucking mind or dress up either. I'll leave that to you whores. I want more money too."

This arrangement worked well for a while, but sharing so much of her income meant Ruth needed more clients to fulfil her plans to escape Regos' clutches. She had to resort to offering extra services, including entertaining men with outlandish fetishes. With great enthusiasm, Susan used whips and sticks to beat the blindfolded and bound naked clients for the lion's share of the payment. Ruth salted away as much as possible. She knew how dangerous this was, but she had no other way to disappear forever with her precious child.

When Ruth told Rego, she knew about his films and wanted nothing to do with that line of work, no matter what. He roared with laughter.

"Gorgeous as you are, my girl, you're much too old. Maybe I will take cute little Lucy if you don't behave," he teased, pinching her cheeks.

An icy stab of fear penetrated her heart, and determination flashed from her wide green eyes. "Over my dead body. I'll kill you first!" she retorted.

Soft and charming again, he cajoled, "Just kidding, my beautiful tigress. I'm fond of Lucy; there's no evil, dark plans." He swept her into his arms. "Let's not fight, sweetheart. I can think of better ways to use our time." Once again, Ruth couldn't resist him.

CHAPTER TWENTY-SEVEN

BEHIND THE MASK

They'd only been in the new apartment for a few weeks when Rego walked in with a little girl. Her light brown hair was plaited and tied with ribbons. Violet-blue eyes framed by long, sweeping eyelashes looked out from her heart-shaped face. She wore a flowered dress and a short jacket. On dainty feet, lace-trimmed ankle socks, and sweet white flat buckled shoes. She looked so young and vulnerable.

"This is Julie," Rego informed Ruth. "I need you to act as her chaperone for a week or two. Her previous one had an accident, so she isn't up to work now. Julie has regular clients to satisfy."

"You can stop right there," Ruth declared, backing away, sick with revulsion. "I won't do it. She's a child; what's wrong with you, for God's sake?"

Rego glared, his dark eyes narrowed; he lashed out and slapped her hard. As the blood spurted from her lip, he barked, "You'll do as your told."

"No, Rego; I'll never be part of this," Ruth protested, "I don't care what you do. Get out," she gulped. "Go on and take her with you."

"Leave, shall I? Right then, I'll take a young one from that bedroom." He sneered.

"You won't!" Ruth screeched, placing herself against Lucy's bedroom door. Wiped away the blood that trickled down her face, growled. "I'll kill you before you touch Lucy."

"Don't be foolish, Ruth," Rego reassured her. "I won't touch Lucy. Come on, talk to my sweet little virgin slut." To her amazement, both laughed. "Enough of this look at her," he sighed impatiently and pushed the girl forward. "Show her, strip off," he commanded. Docile and without a moment's hesitation, she obeyed, stood naked and unabashed, and stared straight at Ruth. "How old do you think she is?" Rego asked.

Ruth looked at the slight, hairless, undeveloped form. "Around twelve, maybe fourteen," Ruth snapped, glaring at him as she bent down to retrieve the dress and handed it back to the girl. "Put this back on, pet."

Julie, smiling at Rego, took the dress from Ruth. "A proper caution, ain't she? I'm eighteen." As she dressed, Julie said, "I'm small 'cause my useless mother couldn't leave drugs and the drink alone when she was carrying me. Later, she was never sober long enough to earn any money. Sold me to any old bugger who'd pay since I was eight. The old bag taught me well; nothing I couldn't handle. Missus, there is no need to worry about me; the old bastards love a virgin. The younger, the better. I can't fail, can I, Rego? I'm gonna shag you one day; what do you say, handsome?" She sidled up to him. "He says I'm flighty and daft. What he means is I'm simple." Julie winked at Ruth as she poked a finger into his chest and grabbed his groin. "Ain't that right, mister?"

Agitated, Rego pushed her away and addressed Ruth. "All you do is wait and watch the time while she works. My brother has taken a turn for the worse; I'll be back in a few days."

The woman-child plopped herself in a chair, dangling her thin legs across the arms. "How about a drink? Got plenty, I hope?"

Ruth poured her out a glass of wine, sat down opposite her, and asked: "What happened to your usual chaperone?"

"Greedy old tart took in extras and pocketed all the money I earned," Julie told her. "I can't read or write because I had no schooling, but I can count, so I told Rego the old bag was cheating. He sent two of his blokes around. She won't do it again. You should see the state of the old cow." Julie laughed. "I expect she'll be out of action for good. Serves her right, too, the greedy bitch. Rego will find me a new chaperone when he comes back."

While they waited for the car to arrive, the girl chatted on, answering all Ruth's questions. "Rego heard about me and bought me from the old slag. Gave her enough money to buy her stuff for a while. Someone found her she'd taken an overdose, stupid cow. Stiff as a board in the gutter where she belonged. Rego takes care of me now."

"I'm sorry, pet. It must have been hard for you," Ruth interrupted. "What will you do when you age? You will in time."

"Won't happen," Julie said, noticed Ruth's frown, and smiled. "I got this thing growing in my head; nothing will fix it. I reckon that old shit gave it to me with her bashing me on the head so often."

Ruth laid her hand on Julie's arm. Julie brushed her away, jumped out of the chair and waved her small hands.

"No! None of that fussing stuff. I'll never be an old slag. Nothing wrong with that. Who wants a face full of wrinkles anyhow?" She tossed her head back, shrugged her shoulders and assured Ruth, "I'm fine. I don't want any bloody pity. Rego promised to look out for me. He knows a posh nursing home I can go to. Took me there once in an elegant place right out in the country. I saw a lake with swans swimming in it. There are huge green fields with horses, sheep, and cows. He's gonna pay, so I'll just enjoy myself while I can. Rego says a short life should be happy; that's what I believe too." She blew her nose into a tissue and pasted on a smile. "How about another glass of that plonk?"

The conversation ended, and they sat silently until the car came to collect them. Ruth had Julie with her for two weeks. However, she didn't dare to do private work while Julie stayed. Ruth missed her lively chatter after she had left; life went on much as before.

In the early hours of the morning, persistent hammering at the door awakened Ruth.

"Who's there?" she cried, trembling in alarm.

"It's me. Ruth, open the blasted door." Recognising Rego's voice, Ruth unlocked the door. He fell into her, arms dropping a small overnight case on the mat. Ruth couldn't hold him up; he slipped to the floor. This wasn't the Rego she knew and feared. On his knees at her feet, a quivering wreck of a man clung to her, sobbing his heart out.

"What's happened?" She coaxed him to the settee and cradled him in her arms.

He wailed. "I buried my Leon today, the sweetest boy in the entire world. Now I've got no one." He mumbled between heart-rending sobs.

Ruth struggled to understand his slurred speech, full of sorrow for the young boy's death and compassion for the desperate emotion unfolding before her. He had no swagger, no pretence, just a man grieving for the only person he loved in his shallow life. Ruth held him close and tried to pacify him. After an age,

282

the sobbing slowed, and he fell asleep. Ruth's mind was in turmoil while attempting to console the cruellest man in London, lying like a child in her arms. Every fibre of her being told her how much she despised all he stood for. Ruth's fascination with him had long since diminished, and he could no longer arouse her as they lay together; all she thought of was the murderous side of him. Still terrified for Lucy's well-being, Ruth acted out of unfelt desire. She didn't have the heart to push him away in this distressed state. This complex man was such a contradiction, so gentle with his brother. Willing to pay for a nursing home for Julie when the time came. Very confused, she dropped off to a night of restless sleep.

The following morning when she woke, Rego had washed, shaved and was busy preparing breakfast. "Morning, gorgeous," he hollered. "What's your poison, tea or coffee?"

Ruth stumbled into the kitchen, rubbing the sleep from her eyes. She stretched out her hand to him. He turned and moved away out of reach. He had let her find him vulnerable and now had regained his composure.

"I'm a coffee man myself." He grinned, passing Ruth a steaming cup. She couldn't believe her ears; the mask was back in place. As if the previous night had never happened.

CHAPTER TWENTY-EIGHT

LOVELY LUCY

Rego often joined them in the park, playing and chasing Lucy, scooping her up in his arms when her tiny, chubby legs were too tired to run. Ruth relaxed; Rego might not be all bad. He seemed fond of Lucy, who idolised him and always rushed to greet him. Rego brought an expensive professional camera. Lucy twirled and posed while Rego used up rolls of film. When developed, grumbled, they could be better. He begged Ruth to let him arrange for a formal studio portrait. With his constant persuading, Ruth had to give in but insisted she was present. In the studio, under the protective scrutiny of Rego, Ruth bursting with pride as Lucy poised and smiled for the photographer. The finished results were perfect; they reviewed the proofs together, selecting the best ones.

Lucy picked up each one, squealing in delight. "This one is best, Mummy," she claimed. "I had to dance and hold out my pretty fairy dress just like this." Lucy twirled around, her face bright with rapture.

Rego gathered her into his arms, hugging her close. "You look beautiful, like a Princess."

"I love you, Uncle Rego!" Lucy giggled in satisfaction and threw her arms around his neck. She planted a noisy kiss on his cheek.

Rego beamed with amusement and placed the child back on the carpet, "Run off now, sweetheart. Mummy and I have to pick out the very best one."

"God, I can't decide which is best," Ruth smiled.

"They are all perfect." Rego dashed around, holding upon print after another. "I told you Lucy was a natural model. You should have seen her pose like a professional. Follows the photographer's directions to a tea and tilts her head from side to side; so cute. She's a little star, one of a kind, Ruth, I tell you; she's perfect for this."

The portraits displayed her innocence and charm. Her porcelain complexion set off with rosy, chubby baby cheeks. Soft natural curls surrounded her face; bright honey brown, saucer-wide, sparkling eyes beamed from each frame. At last, they settled on the best choice. Rego ordered a dozen copies and insisted he registered Lucy with a reputable modelling agency.

"She'll leave the other kids standing," he boasted. "I'll open an account, put the money away, and build an excellent nest egg for her future."

Worn down by his constant pressure, Ruth gave way. Rego's face tightened in anger when she insisted he didn't use Lucy for his other films. Indignant, he retorted, "How can you say that? Lucy was a lovely child. Lucy's like my own child. You must know I love her and do nothing to harm her. Since my brother's death, there's no one left to look after. I think we should marry. A child needs two parents. I'd be a proper father to her."

Ruth couldn't help laughing and sputtered, "What! Don't be ridiculous married to you. Are you mad?" Her laughter turned to scorn. "Not a hope in hell. Never. Lucy's father was a better man than you'll ever be."

Infuriated, Rego gripped her and put his hands tight around her throat. He squeezed until, unable to breathe, Ruth fell to her knees.

"You will come to regret mocking me." He threw her across the room. "I'll be here as arranged tomorrow, be sure she is ready."

Ruth regretted her remarks; he appeared to be fond of Lucy, and she adored him. Maybe she should have been kinder. Rego secured Lucy several lucrative contracts. She loved the work and looked forward to each engagement. But in the back of her mind, Wendy's words lingered. Rego's films with young children and connections to paedophile rings. Ruth would be there; what harm could there be? Before long, Rego found more short notice use for Ruth, as the sessions were pre-booked, and Lucy was excited each time she had to let her go, accompanied by Rego.

Ruth felt pushed out and spent less time with Lucy as Rego took complete charge, chaperoning her from studio to studio. When they were alone, Ruth talked to Lucy about her day, and at first, she replied to her mother's questions in an excited, high-pitched voice.

"I love it, Mummy. I get delicious cakes and chocolate from Uncle Rego when I do what the photo man says."

"That is lovely, darling," Ruth responded. "I am glad you like having all these things, but what did you do today?"

"Well," Lucy mused, "first, I sit like this with the grown-ups." She jumped up on Ruth's lap to show her. "Then I give my best smile to the big camera, this one, look?" She beamed with perfect tiny teeth at Ruth. "Or, sometimes, a lady shows me how to dance like this. She scrambled down and waltzed around the room on her tiptoes. Gyrating her hips gracelessly, her plump, dimpled knees bent as she performed the steps. Ruth burst out laughing; it looked so comical. Lucy stopped dead, stamped her little foot and scowled, "Why are you laughing? I'm not funny. Uncle Rego says it's beautiful."

Ruth composed herself. "No, sweetheart, I'm laughing because I am so proud of you for being such a talented, clever little girl." Satisfied, Lucy rushed over and dragged Ruth from her chair. "Come on, Mummy, I'll teach you," Merriment shone in her eyes. Placed tiny hands on her hips in exasperation and sniggered as Ruth pretended to get the steps wrong.

"Sometimes," Lucy continued, "I must walk like this." She paraded around the room with exaggerated wriggles to show Ruth, placing chubby tiny hands on her hips. "I walk up and down and give a big smile; Uncle Rego says I'll be a real film star when I'm bigger" She Threw her arms around Ruth's neck and declared, "I still love you the bestest of all, Mummy!"

Over time Ruth noticed a slight reluctance to divulge the day's events; Lucy had grown up a lot since being in the limelight. Ruth thought perhaps Lucy, tired of all the glamour, was no longer so thrilled. As Ruth tucked her in bed one evening, she suggested to Lucy that perhaps she wanted to stop for a short while and return to the studio when she was a little older. Lucy's voice, full of alarm, cried,

"No, please, Mummy, I don't want to stop. I love wearing all the pretty things and having a fuss made of me." She lowered her voice to a whisper. "Guess what? If big people do things wrong, the film man gets cross and shouts bad words. Uncle Rego comes and takes me away until everyone is friends again." Later, after Lucy had her bath, Ruth peeked into her room and saw her in front of the dressing table mirror. She pursed her lips together in a pout and blew hard.

"What are you doing, pet?" Ruth asked.

"Oh, just practising how to whistle. My photo man says they will make pictures showing me whistling, but I can't make the noise. He says it won't matter; I can pretend to do it. What do you think? Can you do it?" She pursed up her tiny rosebud lips together again, blowing hard.

"No, afraid not, darling." Ruth laughed. "Stop now; get into bed."

Lucy hopped into her bed. As Ruth bent to kiss her, she said, "Uncle Rego says we can have our plane ride now you are better. So, can we?"

Ruth tucked her in and replied, "Perhaps go to sleep like a good girl. God bless, sweetheart." Their conversation troubled Ruth. Her instinct told her something wasn't right. She had to be sure nothing was wrong. Ruth had witnessed earlier modelling occasions with top respected catalogue and magazine agencies. However, to set her mind at ease, she insisted Rego give her the time off for the following modelling session and go with them.

Rego agreed. "Most of the sessions are closed. The photographers don't like distractions from parents. There is an open shot next Friday. I think I can arrange for you to attend. We'll make a day of it, have lunch, and then take our girl to the zoo, a proper family day out. I'll pick you up at ten."

They arrived at a fashion magazine photoshoot. Full of pride, Ruth watched as her baby paraded along with the set, showing off one outfit after the other, so poised. She followed instructions as if born to it. Unperturbed, Lucy mingled with ease around the adult models. Ruth relaxed, convinced Rego took proper care of Lucy and was convinced she was safe from harm. Then, as promised, they finished the day with a visit to the zoo.

CHAPTER TWENTY-NINE

EXPOSED LIES

A while later, Ruth passed the time with a friend at a bar when the conversation turned to one of Rego's runaways. One girl a short time ago was hideously mutilated. They discussed the hopelessness of their situation.

Pam, Ruth's companion, declared, "I wish the bastard would let us out when we've had enough. I worked as a kid in porn films for the Franks until Rego took over. At fifteen, I was too old for him, so he put me on the street. Sometimes he'll use me if he needs a dark-skinned adult."

Ruth agreed. "This life drains you. Men always prefer younger girls, anyway. What's the point in keeping girls once they lose their looks? He should let them go." Pondering on this, she stated, "I think he enjoys having power over their lives. That's his driving force, but using children is despicable."

"Yes, I suppose you're right. Poor little mites, Rego keeps them sweet by spoiling them something rotten." She raised her eyebrows and sighed, resigned. "Bless 'em' they love him to death. I suppose it couldn't work if they were afraid of him. He's using them even younger these days." Pam leant forward and muttered, "I did a shoot with a toddler about three. Besotted with him, she was. Such a dear little soul, never seen such a mass of mahogany curls and beautiful, big, deep brown eyes with eyelashes to kill for."

The description fitted Lucy in disbelief; Ruth grabbed Pam's arm and dug her nails into Pam's flesh until they drew blood.

"What?" Ruth screeched. "Where's his place? You'd better tell me."

She grumbled and rubbed her injured arm "Christ's sake, what the hell's wrong with you? What do you want it for?"

Ruth jumped to her feet, gripped Pam's shoulders and shook her violently. "You're talking about my child. Tell me the address."

The other girls gasped at this revelation.

Ruth shook Pam again until her teeth rattled and fiercely demanded, "Give me the address!"

"I never knew the address", yelled Pam, pulling away. "Leave off, mad bitch."

"Liar!" Ruth grabbed a fistful of the woman's hair and contumely banged her head on the tabletop. "You've been there; you must know." fear for Lucy increased her fury.

Onlookers tried to stop Ruth, but she was, determined to get the information.

"Bloody hell! Look, my head's split open. Fuck off, leave me be," Pam complained, holding her blood-soaked forehead. Pam ran for the door before she could open it; Ruth had barred her way.

"Oh no, you don't," Ruth held her against the wall and thundered, "Give me the address, or you'll be sorry."

Pam saw murder in her wild eyes. "OK, OK, just stay away from me! Mad cow, I'll find it." She dug into her handbag, threw over a slip of paper, mumbling, "Don't you dare say I gave this to you. He'll kill me. You too, if you go storming in there."

Snatching away the paper, Ruth rushed out, called a taxi, and directed it to the address. On arrival, she found herself outside a converted warehouse in the old docks area, pushed open the door and stepped inside. An old man sitting behind an enclosed counter looked up from his newspaper.

Staying as calm as possible, Ruth said: "I'm looking for the studio where Rego does his films."

"One of them, are you?" the man sniffed, looking at Ruth up and down and smirking through blackened teeth. "You're well late; they've been here hours," Staring at her flushed face, he leant closer, his breath foul from tobacco and alcohol. Ruth pulled back, nauseated by the rancid smell of his unwashed body. "Best take a minute to sort yourself out first. You're a right mess. Look like you've been dragged through a hedge backwards. Come in here, fix yourself," he invited, lifting the counter entrance flap. "You can give me a freebie blow-job if you like; it won't take long at my age," he sniggered. "Rego, lets me have one of his girls now and then with no charge, payment in lieu, you might say."

Ruth was in no mood to be polite; she slammed shut the flap and growled, "Just tell me where to go, you drunken old fool."

"Suit yourself," he retorted. "I ain't gonna pay for it." He picked up his paper, shook it in annoyance, and continued reading. Pointing to his left, he said: "Go through that door to the end of the corridor."

Rushing through the corridor, Ruth heaved open the heavy fire doors. The studio was a vast glass-roofed space comprising two levels. Above the lower level, huge floodlights and scaffold structures went across and around the open space. The second tier was a narrow mezzanine with a metal staircase for access.

Rego stood on an extended viewing platform attached to the top level, shouting directions to the main filming area. As she moved forward, Ruth realised her worst fears. In heavy stage makeup, Lucy sat on a flower-strewn chair swing, suspended mid-air, dressed as a ballerina in a pink tutu with dainty ballet shoes on her feet. As she dangled above a vast bed, she held a small bow and arrow in lace-gloved hands.

A scantily dressed woman with a hideous mask was slowly lowering the swing. She pointed at two young, semi-naked boys on the bed, performing exaggerated, bizarre body movements. Ruth rushed over, pushed the woman aside, and glared at the boys, who jumped off the bed and backed away. Sick to her stomach, Ruth lowered Lucy to the floor, lifted her out of the swing and wiped off the grotesque makeup.

Rego spotted Ruth and screamed. "Who let her in here? Clear out, useless lot!"

The film crew hesitated, unsure of what to do.

Rego roared again, "Work's finished for today. Go on, get out! Are you deaf? Out now!" he hollered. "I'll deal with this." Intimidated by his furious tone, the studio emptied.

Ruth removed the last traces of grease from Lucy's face. Spotting Lucy's clothes resting on a bench, Ruth dressed her. Buttoned up her coat, hugged Lucy and kissed the troubled little face. Ruth whispered, "Everything's all right, darling; we're going home. Mummy's taking you for a holiday."

Rego reached their side and bellowed, "Like hell you are. What's your game, busting in here? Stupid bitch, you wrecked a terrific piece of film. I'll have to reshoot the scene. A complete waste of time and money."

"Not with Lucy, you don't," Ruth yelled. "You promised me, like a fool, I took you at your word and believed you. Played an excellent game of deceit, didn't you, filthy pig?" Ruth sucked in a breath. "Even arranged that last fake modelling session, didn't you?"

"So, what?" he jeered. "Had to stick your nose in. That session cost me a pretty penny when I should have had her here earning."

Continuing to dress Lucy, Ruth, almost choked with rage, spluttered, "You've made your last penny with my child. I'm reporting you to the police; they should know what's happening here. You can do what you like; I'm taking Lucy well out of your reach."

"The hell you are, you're making the biggest mistake of your life," Rego bellowed. "The punters love her; these films are a goldmine. Lucy's a natural miniature whore. Like mother, like daughter," he mocked.

"Never!" Ruth screamed, "Before I let you ruin her life, I'll have her put in care."

He blocked her way as she tried to pass, his voice soft. "God's sake, Ruth. No need to make a big thing out of this. Let's go home and talk about it." Although he smiled, his eyes were full of venom. Rego cajoled, "It's just for a film, trailer sweetheart; no harm done. Nothing happens to Lucy; we just suggest it might."

All her illusions were stripped away, finally revealing Rego as the vile creature he was. Although fearful of what he might do, Ruth had to stand firm. She'd never find the courage to confront him again.

"Yes, I bet your perverts love it. Sick pigs, and you're the sickest of all. " Ruth proclaimed.

Rego jeered. "You had your chance. If you think you're getting out of here. You're a bigger fool than I thought." A stunning blow sent her crashing to the floor.

Lucy squealed, "Go away, Uncle Rego! You've made Mummy cry. You horrid nasty man; I really hate you! " Lucy flew at him with her tiny fists clenched in a fury. With little razor-sharp teeth, she bit his leg and kicked his shins as hard as she could.

He knocked her aside and snarled, "Think so, do you, brat? Well, your precious Mummy's a dirty whore. Go on, get over to her then." Lucy scurried to Ruth's side. "What a pair," he sneered. "Too much mouth, the both of you."

Ruth got to her feet. Holding on to Lucy, Ruth ordered, "Out of my way. We're finished."

Rego wrenched Lucy from her arms. "Is that right? Well then, here's what happens to scrubbers that cross me."

CHAPTER THIRTY

EMPTY ARMS

Rego spun around and ran up the stairs. Ruth chased behind him and clung to his jacket to prevent his escape. Lost her hold and fell on the rough steel staircase. Impervious to her bleeding knees, she scrambled to her feet and tore after him again. Rego sprinted to the top and leaned over the platform's edge. Out of breath, her heart pounding, Ruth caught up with him. With the weight of all three, the platform swayed. The studio floor was a long way below. Fearful of their safety, Ruth grabbed hold of him.

"Rego, don't hurt her; she's only a baby."

"She's a wildcat, like her mother." He sucked his knuckles. "Bit me, the little cow," he grumbled.

"She's only trying to protect me." Ruth cried, what are you going to do?" Her mouth was dry with fear.

"This's all down to you. Had to interfere, didn't you? Never lent to shut your stupid mouth," he thundered. "Not good enough for you, am I? As my wife, you would come off the game. Your precious Lucy would've done straight modelling as my daughter. You had your chance, I'm as good as any man, but you're too grand for that. I said you would come to regret mocking me."

Desperation engulfing her, Ruth stammered, "All right, Rego, I'll marry you. We can be a proper family if that's what you want." Frantic to find the right words, she wailed, "Lucy's a child. Buy her a few presents; she'll forget today and love you again."

He shoved Ruth aside. She crashed against the rails; they both had to cling on to stop the violent sway.

"Marriage now, is it? Empty words to save this bastard kid; she hates me, thanks to you. What kind of fool do you think I am? You'd both run off the first chance you get."

"Mummy, I want my Mummy. Let me go!" Lucy's nails tore at his face.

"If you think I want this wildcat now, you must be mad," he retorted. Lucy squirmed in his arms. He shook the child until her head rocked. "Be quiet; stay still."

Lucy fell silent, her tear-streaked face dwarfed by huge, terrified eyes. Defeated, there was nothing she could say to placate Rego; Ruth resorted to begging again.

"Please don't hurt my baby; give her to me." Arms outstretched, Ruth pleaded, "Let me have her. I'll do anything you want, I swear. Let her go; I'm begging you." As Ruth touched his arm, he snatched it away. Ruth swallowed hard, lowered her voice, and cajoled. "Rego, you don't want to harm a child. You want to hurt me, okay? Go ahead; I deserve it." She paused for a moment to catch her breath and continued. "I'm sorry I spoilt your film. We can start again. I can't exist without you. You know how much I need you and how good we are together. Imagine the perfect life, all three of us." Ruth eased back.

Rego's eyes flashed with pride. Ruth detected his manner softening as he accepted her acknowledgement of his sexual prowess. Ruth stretched out her hand, coaxing him. "Come away from here; this platform's not steady. We can talk on the studio floor."

Deep in thought, his brow furrowed as he mulled over her words. A sardonic smirk crossed his lips. Ruth knew he imagined himself as a respectable family man. To her immense relief, he followed her back off the platform. Rego hesitated at the top of the stairs. "You'll do anything?" he queried. "Even act in my films with the kids?" Ruth's brain was in turmoil; she struggled to find the right words. She would rather give her away to strangers than let him wreak his revenge on Lucy. Ruth backed down the steps; her trembling hand invited him to follow. Ruth held a frozen, encouraging smile on her lips as he did. Rego stopped again before he reached the second flight of stairs, running his free hand through his tousled hair. Still unconvinced, he questioned, " You'll work with young children?

Your kid, too?" He studied her intently. "No questions asked, and do anything I want?" A flame of defiance and loathing flared for a moment on her face. Far too late, replaced by a weak smile. "Bloody liar," he roared. "Do you take me for a fool?"

Ruth cried out. "No, never. I swear. I'll do anything you say." She moved towards him, holding out her arms to take Lucy, struggling to stay calm.

He smirked and insisted, "So I can keep using Lucy, then? With your blessing and no interference?"

Desperate to have Lucy back, Ruth's voice shook. "Yes, Rego, anything. We've known each other for so long. We can be friends again." She felt his temper subsiding, confident her words had softened him. "I've never forgotten; you told me as Çocuk that life's path is full of stepping stones to overcome." As she uttered this last phrase, his face tightened again. Ruth knew to remind him of his humble beginnings and his time with the Turks was a big mistake. Trying to reach him again, she attempted to erase her words by feeding his vanity. She stuttered, "Rego, everyone in London fears you. You've earned respect, position..." Her voice trailed off; the damage was done.

"Bastard liar," he howled. "I know what you're up to. Let you leave, and you'll run straight to the law. Take me for a fool, do you?"

"No, I won't. Just give me Lucy," Ruth spluttered. "I'm sorry, Rego, please let me have her," she begged, holding out her arms as Lucy, struggling to reach her mother, bit him again.

Rego flinched and secured his hold; Lucy squirmed and wriggled to be freed. He kicked out, sent Ruth tumbling back to the bottom, leapt onto the platform and raced up to the top landing. He waited until Ruth stood upright. Leaning over the rails, jeered, "Sorry now, are you? Love me again, will she? Huh! Like hell, she will. You ruined everything; got no use for her now."

Dazed and petrified, Ruth looked up as Rego lifted Lucy above his head and yelled, "What do you care about most, your looks or this squawking kid? I can't use her now, thanks to your interference. She's been a hindrance. I'm better off with you working free of her. I'll get rid of it for you. With nothing to give me grief over, perhaps then you'll behave." He threw the child across the studio.

In disbelief, Ruth watched Lucy's small body tumble as if in slow motion. The trailing cables and hanging drapes caught her in flight, bringing the enormous lights crashing to the floor and covering Lucy with broken glass and debris.

Rego bellowed, "Now look what you made me do! Hundreds of pounds worth of gear smashed to pieces! You'll pay for this, I promise you!"

Ruth, with stomach-churning dread, searched for Lucy among the rubble. Straining with the effort, she tried to lift aside the heavy equipment. Beads of cold sweat dripped down her face into her eyes, blinding her.

"Rego, help me!" she screamed. "All this broken glass must have cut her; she could bleed to death."

"Then you'll have the apartment to yourself. A much better arrangement, I'd say."

"Did you hear me?" Ruth screeched. "This equipment's too heavy. I can't lift it by myself." She looked up. He still hadn't moved. "For pity's sake, Rego, come here and help me."

Rego came bounding down the stairs and examined the damage. "What for? Don't waste your time. This mess is all your fault. Had to interfere, didn't you? You're better off with the blasted brat gone. Odds on, she's dead under that lot, anyway. Come on, help me sort this stuff out," he growled, dragging her away. "It's only a fucking bastard kid, for Christ's sake! You can have another, can't you? She's dead and worth nothing. Christ's sake, stop that blasted wailing." Frustrated, he hollered, "Make yourself useful and help me salvage what I can." He looked around at the rubble and picked up the arrow. Putting his hands to his head, mused, "Shame, she was so cute." Twisting and twirling the arrow between his fingers, he mumbled, "I suppose I could find a replacement for her part be a pity to lose the miniature ballerina image" Rego threw the arrow to one side and carried on sorting through the damaged props. He grunted, " other slags don't mind and won't give me trouble you did."

A raw, primal scream rose from her core. Ruth picked up the discarded arrow and rushed at Rego. She plunged the shaft deep into his chest with both hands as he looked towards the sound. His mouth twisted open in a scream, then collapsed to the floor, groaning in agony. Ruth heard nothing as if someone had pressed her life's "mute" button. She straddled his body, thrust the arrow in as deep as she could again, tearing through his intestines, and dragged the arrow through his blood-drenched body.

Exhausted, all strength and power diminished. Ruth snarled without a spark of regret, "There's plenty like you, Rego; more's the pity. Who will mourn your death or shed a single tear? I hope you burn in hell for eternity!"

Rego caught the hem of her dress and whimpered. "Ruth, help me. Please. I'm begging you. I never meant to harm Lucy. I just lost my temper; I'm sorry. For pity's sake, get me a doctor."

Ruth slapped his hand away. "You took a stepping stone too far, Rego; you're finished." Ruth scowled in disdain as he writhed. His strength fading, he could only plead from those dark, sensual eyes that had held her entranced for so long. Unmoved, she waited as his life slipped away.

Blinded by dust, Ruth screamed Lucy's name; her fingers bled as she tore away the debris with increasing hysteria. At last, found her child wedged under a girder, Ruth heaved it aside and pulled Lucy out. A dark bruise covered one half of her face, but there seemed to be no other injuries. Ruth placed her ear against Lucy's chest to find a heartbeat; there was none. She hooked the dust out of Lucy's mouth and covered it with her own, willing her to breathe. All her efforts were fruitless; she'd lost her precious baby. A long mournful earthy sound came out from the depths of Ruth's soul.

"Oh no, dear God, not my sweet baby." At that moment, her mind closed to all reality; something inside her died.

Removing her coat, Ruth covered the cold little body and carried her home. She washed off the dust, dressed Lucy in her favourite lace, trimmed nightgown, and finally brushed her soft, dark curls. All grasp of time and realism faded away. Ruth remained in a chair, rocking her baby.

The caretaker found Rego's body on his morning rounds and called the police. He informed them the film crew had rushed out the previous evening and told him the boss had gone mad with a prostitute from the club in a furious row. Ruth had been the last caller. It didn't take them long to track down her address.

With no response to their hammering on the door, the police broke it down and burst into the room. They found Ruth humming a lullaby of what appeared to be a lifeless infant in her arms. One officer reached down to take the child. Ruth's grip on Lucy stiffened. In a flash, conscious of the intrusion, she jolted back to the present and instinctively drew back. Ruth snarled, "No. No, leave her be. Lucy's mine; You can't have her."

The officer realised the woman was unstable, turned away and called for child welfare officials to attend. When they arrived, he made clear the situation to the attendants. One of them, a middle-aged woman, studied Ruth's distressed state and advised everybody to remain outside.

 She stepped forward and knelt beside Ruth, her tone low and calm. "Hello, pet, I'm Barbara. Can I have a look at your baby?"

"No! Go away!" Ruth snapped.

"What a sweet night dress and such lovely, dark hair." Barbara murmured, "You must be so proud."

Ruth scowled menacingly and held Lucy closer.

"I've two daughters myself, all grown up now. Barbara persevered; girls are such a comfort, aren't they? What's baby's name?"

"Lucy."

"What a charming name suits her." She smiled, "I called my daughters Anne and Alice." Barbara babbled on about when her girls were small but made no further attempt to take the toddler.

After a while, Barbara tugged Ruth's arm. "Come on, my love, let me see Lucy's little face."

Ruth leaned forward.

Barbara touched Lucy's cold face, grasped her tiny hand, and felt discretely for a pulse. There was none; she stroked the chubby legs and sighed. "Such delicate skin. I bet her Dad spoils her; they are rather good at that part, aren't they?" She glanced at the police officer standing in the doorway; her eyes conveyed the message they suspected. Then turned her attention once more to Ruth and, in a confiding manner, murmured, "Men, Huh! What do they know about all the sleepless nights, dirty nappies? A never-ending slog, but worth so much, isn't it?"

Ruth responded with a hesitant smile.

Barbara sat beside her, keeping her tone calm and even.

"They grow up so quick, don't they? One minute, babies, next before you know it, obstinate teenagers. I wish I had my time over again nursing a tiny scrap like yours." Barbara brushed her fingers against Ruth's hand, "She looks so cold, sweetheart. Why not let me wrap her in a warm blanket?"

Ruth **scowled**, "She's mine. I'll see to her."

"Of course, dear, just as you like," Barbara shivered. "This room is freezing; don't you think she needs something more than that night dress to cover her?"

Ruth felt Lucy's icy arms. "In her bed, she's got a thick quilt that will do."

"Shall I fetch it then?"

Ruth nodded.

Barbara got the quilt and passed it to Ruth.

Ruth tried to wrap it around Lucy without having to put her down.

Barbara held out her arms, "Here, let me help. I'll hold her while you lay the cover out. That way, it will be easier."

Although relaxed and comforted by the woman's gentle tone, Ruth hesitated, "She'll worry if she wakes up and sees a stranger. Best if you lay it down, and I'll wrap her in it myself."

As soon as she released Lucy, Barbara snatched her up and dashed towards the door. Horrified, she had been so readily deceived, rushed out of the chair after the departing woman. The police officers struggled to hold the frantic figure as Ruth screamed, kicked, and bit them. She'd held her precious child for the last time.

CHAPTER THIRTY-ONE

THE RECKONING

Arrested and formally charged with the murder of Rego and complicity in the death of Lucy. Due to the sensational press coverage that fuelled hostile public outrage, they considered granting her the right to attend Lucy's funeral unwise.

Time and time again, during the daylight hours, the memory of that dreadful day haunted her. The choking dust again filled her throat as she crawled through the rubble. Even then, her damaged mind wouldn't replay the worst of that day; instead, she recaptured the blissful moment when she carried her home. Safe in the rocking chair cradled her darling child. Willing against all sense for those soft brown eyes to open. Unable to accept the truth, her tortured soul refused to let go. At night in her dreams, she held her baby again, snuggled in loving arms.

Until morning at least, her heart and tormented mind felt comforted.

Ruth watched the dark grey clouds become edged with gold. As Dawn broke over the horizon, she reflected fleetingly on the lives cut short by her hand and the deaths of others she cared for. All the previous night's thoughts took her from the past to the present; she lay awake in the darkness. Ruth didn't have the strength or will to survive long years and lonely nights ahead. Resolved somehow to end her misery. A bell rang throughout the prison. Footsteps clattered along the corridors. Her door opened, and a warder rattling a bunch of keys ordered,

"On your feet, Page, you're returning to your cell before the others are let out for breakfast. Come on, move along." on reaching the fifth landing, Ruth hesitated. "Don't give me any trouble, Page, or it will be worse for you," snapped the warder, giving Ruth a rough push. "Get moving now." Dropping her keys, the woman bent to retrieve them. Taking advantage of the moment before her escort could intervene, Ruth heaved herself over the guardrail, intending to finally find peace on the marble floor below. Never again face another unending night.

When Ruth awoke, unable to focus, she struggled to make out her bearings or move. Shadowy figures flittered across her line of blurred vision. Low muttering voices echoed inside her head. She struggled to concentrate and bring all these sensations together but again slipped into oblivion. Slowly, the realisation dawned that she had failed to end all her wretchedness and was still alive.

"Back with us, are you Page?" sneered the officer assigned to guard her. She heaved herself from her chair, grumbling, "About time too. I'll be glad to return to prison instead of spending long boring days waiting for you to come around. I'll call for the nurse."

Desperately, Ruth tore out all the tubes and wires connecting her to the array of machines around her bed, screaming frantically, "NO! No! Not this, Oh God, I don't want this; let me die."

Pinning her flailing arms, the guard shouted. "Not yet, my girl. There's no easy way out. God willing, you'll recover and serve your time."

Reaching over, she pressed the bell for help. A nurse appeared, the tubes and wires reconnected, and a sedative injection to calm her.

A medical team visit told her a safety grill between the lower landing and the floor had broken the fall. She had a fractured skull, causing damage to the optical nerves in her eyes and other as-yet-unconfirmed injuries. Subjected to a battery of tests and scans over the next few days, Ruth waited for the results, knowing something was severely wrong. A grim-toned doctor told her the tests verified that the fall splintered her spine. The nerves were beyond repair, cumulating in total paralysis from the waist down. They expected her vision to improve, but she'd depended on others for all her medical and personal needs. Instead of ending her misery, she was destined to live in a wheelchair and live on with her memories. As a confirmed paraplegic with no possibility of escape, a constant guard was unnecessary. A subdued, unresponsive, and withdrawn Ruth ignored the medical panel

around her bed, discussing her future. The psychiatrist's reports confirmed she was not insane and deemed fit to return to court. Ruth sat motionless and silent in her wheelchair. Each hearing of the individual judgements against her trial resulted in a guilty verdict—her thoughts in a faraway place with a kaleidoscope of flashing, fleeting images of her past. At last, the daily drudge from hospital to court was over. Ruth began a fifteen-year custodial sentence.

CHAPTER THIRTY-TWO

OUT OF THE SHADOWS

Six years passed. Ruth received numerous specialists and prison visitors who tried to reach through her darkness to no avail. One woman, in particular, was the most persistent, calling every month to hold Ruth's hand and sit talking, despite receiving no response.

Somewhere deep inside her, Ruth recognised a familiar lilting voice. Lifting her head, she stared with vacant, empty eyes at the smiling face and small lily-white hands fluttering before her. As if a light switched on, her memory functioned. Ruth realised it was Sadie, much older but still the same dear friend. A slow smile curled her lips as recollection dawned.

"How are you today? Been coming for such a long time, hoping that one day you would respond; I can tell you how happy I am. "Sadie took Ruth's hands. "You still got nine years to serve, but the law has changed recently regarding people with your condition, providing you have somewhere suitable to go. You may be considered for alternative secure custody. I am responsible for a small, approved nursing home in Lanarkshire. We look after prisoners with problems just like yours. There's a vacancy coming up soon. I would love you to come to me." Her animated voice continued, "If you're willing, I can set the wheels in motion. Just think, Ruth, we will be together again, just like the old days."

In a rasping voice unused for so long, Ruth stammered Sadie. "Oh my God, it is you." She clasped Sadie's hand and brought it to her lips. "I never dreamt of finding you again." Hot salty tears filled Ruth's eyes and trickled down her cheeks.

Sadie wiped them away. "Aye, me all right, the proverbial bad penny returns. "She smiled. Dinna greets hen anymore; we will never lose each other again." Sadie dived into her bag. "Here, look what I brought for you," dangling from her fingers swung a small heart-shaped silver locket. Sadie opened it up, and inside was the old photo they had taken on her seventeenth birthday all those years ago.

"How did you find that?" Ruth asked, "I thought I lost it?"

I had a copy made when I found out you were here. Sadie grinned. Pulling back her blouse, showed Ruth she was wearing hers. Sadie slipped the locket around Ruth's neck. They sat, holding hands, savouring each other's company. Ruth's bitter heart warmed with an engulfing sense of contentment.

Ruth saw a future ahead when hardly able to believe her eyes. A tall man, supporting himself with a walking stick, hobbled towards her bed. Her father arrived. Ruth stared at him in disbelief as he eased himself down on a chair. His face, lined with age, was still handsome. The familiar red hair had now turned to silver, so thick and luxurious. "

Hello, my dear. How are you? I know it has been such a long time, but I had to come with sad news. Your poor mother died last month. I could have written, but I thought such bad news should face to face."

Ruth pressed her hands against her mouth to suppress laughter; he misread her reaction. "Oh, my dear, have I been too blunt? Please don't get upset; it was a peaceful end."

Ruth's laughter erupted. "Upset, Huh! What makes you think I'm upset," Ruth fixed him with a fearsome glare. "I'd like to dance on her grave with joy. Why on earth should I care what happens to either of you? Her voice rose in anger. I'm glad she's dead, can't wait for the day you're gone too. Go away. I never want to see you again."

He adjusted his tie, shuffled in his seat, cleared his throat, and spoke again. "Ruth, I have given your condition a lot of thought. After several inquiries, I learnt that the courts might consider realising you into my care if you had a suitable place with expert nursing at hand day and night." He reached out, touching her arm. "You'd like to be in better surroundings, wouldn't you, my dear? Back in your childhood home, safe and a free woman."

Ruth snatched it away, shuddering in revulsion. "Keep your dirty hands to yourself," she snapped, "I can guess how much you would enjoy having a helpless victim to maul at your pleasure." and turned her face to the wall, hoping he'd disappear.

Don't be like that, Ruth. People can change. I admit to my shame, not being the best of fathers, but I love you and would have forgiven you with God's guidance. As you must learn to forgive.

She turned back to face him. "Forgive? Are you mad? I will never forgive you," Ruth yelled. "You ruined my childhood and set me on a path I would never have chosen." gasping for breath, emotion overtook her. "Just go away. Go away, leave me alone," she sobbed.

"Please don't cry, Ruth; it breaks my heart. I'll go if you want me to. Another day, when you're calm, we will talk again. You know what I'm saying makes sense. You must come home to me in the end."

Ruth spat out her words, "What hearts that, Father? The one you keep with your belt. I would sooner die than be in the same house as you are again. Don't flatter yourself; my tears are not for you but for being born to a parent like you."

"Look here," he whined, "I would never hurt you again. What I did to you was unforgivable. I fell victim to unnatural lust and drink." he got up and limped to the end of her bed. With scorn etched on her face, Ruth watched unmoved as tears of remorse rolled down his cheeks like rivulets. "I'm so sorry and ashamed. I can make it up to you if you let me."

Ruth clapped slowly as she mocked, "Well done, Father, your tears are as false as your words. How long did you practice that flowery speech?" Seeing him acting so contrite was too much for her. "Just go away; I've heard enough!"

"Oh, Ruth, all that happened was so long ago." His voice was a husky murmur. "Can't we bury the past? Plans are being drawn up with extensive adaptions to the house. You're all I have left in the world." With a mournful sigh, he sat down and continued, "When I'm gone, you'll be my heir. You'll be a wealthy woman. If I can find it in my heart to forgive the terrible things you did, surely you can forgive a remorseful father. Let's forgive each other and start again."

"Forgive me," Ruth screamed, her voice full of loathing. "How dare you talk about forgiveness? You're not listening; it's because of you; I'm here. You robbed me of my childhood and wrecked my life. All the times I stole, each act of violence was down to your cruelty to me." Her eyes flashed with anger and resentment. "All the things I did were because your blood runs through my veins." The look of astonishment on his face gave her a warm sense of pleasure. "Well, I tell you this; you are evil through and through, and you made me the same. That's your inheritance. I will never forgive you if I live to be a thousand." He listened open-mouthed while his daughter continued her tirade. She could not resist twisting the knife of venom one turn further. "I pray you to rot in hell. The day I'm told of your death will be the best news ever."

His well-remembered temper flashed in his hard eyes as his face twisted and flushed bright red. Struggled to his feet and leered. "Is that right? Who else would look after you? I came here with an olive branch in good faith, and you throw it back at me. Well, you had your chance; I will not come again." He drew back his hand to hit her, but with a nurse in sight, he thought better of it and growled. "Go on, crawl back to the place you belong. I will leave my estate to a cat's home before a penny comes from me. You'll get nothing, do you hear, nothing! I'll go from here straight to my solicitor and make sure you don't profit from my death."

"Suits me fine," retorted Ruth. "Now get out," Calling for the nurse, she demanded they remove him.

He waved the nurse away. "Don't worry, I'm going." He leaned over the bed and sneered, "I'm glad you are in this condition. Your mother always said you'd come to a bad end; she was right. I should have known better; once trash, always trash. I'll never come again." With that, he threw the chair across the room and stormed out.

Later, Ruth learnt he had a severe stroke that rendered him unable to talk or move on the train home, leaving him bedbound and helpless until his death. As the only heir, Ruth discovered he gambled away the business and left a lot of debt behind. With Sadie's help, she sold the house to clear her father's obligations. To Ruth's delight, she had her long-awaited revenge as the estate's balance still a princely sum came to her.

Sadie began the lengthy, torturous procedure to remove Ruth from the unit. Within a year, her application was approved and granted permission to transfer Ruth to her nursing home.

Sadie saw to all Ruth's personal needs. As she manipulated her legs, she often remarked, "I wish I had your long legs. I always wanted to be taller instead of short and stumpy."

Ruth responded with a long, drawn-out sigh, "At least your stumpy legs work."

They'd listen to the news together to keep Ruth's mind active and discuss world events. Sadie redesigned Ruth's bedroom into an emporium full of smells, sounds, things to look at, and tactile objects to fuel creative thinking. Made it a riot of colour with fairy lights and beautiful feminine heart-shaped cushions. At the windows, she hung silk drapes. Soft music played to pacify and stimulate Ruth's senses. Sadie had a wicked sense of humour and often had Ruth crying with laughter. Sadie hadn't changed from her youth; still filled with energy, incessant chatter, and infectious laughter. The amount of positivity and drive that Sadie inspired was undeniable. She taught Ruth patience, tolerance, and acceptance of her condition. Worked to improve Ruth's life, teaching her how to cope with her disabilities. Showed her ways to keep a level of independence. Sadie created techniques to make each day enjoyable. It was a long hard road, often with emotional, frustrating lows and some unexpected highs.

With Sadie's patient care, guidance and encouragement, Ruth took an interest in her surroundings. Ruth's long lonely life imprisoned in her bubble of despair was over. Sadie's love, kindness, and understanding brought her back out of a bleak, black empty existence into the light. Sadie arranged all adaptations needed for Ruth. Managing with special aids to dress, take care of herself and have pride in her appearance.

Over the following two years, she pulled Ruth out of the shadows and back into the world. The authorities finally released Ruth on licence into Sadie's care. They bought a bungalow facing the sea near Brixham in Devon to start a new life together.

CHAPTER THIRTY-THREE

ENDURING LOVE

One morning, the postman brought a registered letter addressed to Ruth. Mr Robert Miller and his wife Lizzy had named Ruth the sole beneficiary of their life insurance and some shares they'd invested. The total amount was enough for her to be comfortable for the rest of her life.

"Who's this, then?" Sadie asked in delight as they read the letter. "You're an independent woman now." She pinched her arm and giggled, "What a dark horse you are."

"I used to live in the same flats as they did before they moved; such a lovely old couple, how kind of them to remember me in this way. Life is strange. Now I can repay you for all your kindness."

" Don't talk such rubbish; repay me as if I would take it," Sadie's face pinched with resentment. Folding the letter back into its envelope, advised," Tomorrow, you bank this windfall. You never know what's around the corner. "Sadie's voice took a different severe tone. "Ruthie, we spoke about almost everything except the time you disappeared from our lives."

Ruth held up her hands to silence her chattering friend. "Leave it now, Sadie; I don't want to think or talk about that day." Sadie came and sat on the floor beside Ruth.

"It was so terrible how Fay was attacked. Dad always blamed himself for not keeping an eye on that creep and a bad feeling about Eddie all along."

"Oh, Sadie ", Ruth implored." Don't spoil things now. We are fine as we are without raking up the past."

Although smiling, Sadie sighed and persisted, "Oh, Hen, sometimes the past needs to be told so we can bury it."

Ruth tried once more to silence her chattering friend. "Some things can never be buried. Trust me, best to leave sleeping dogs lie."

"No, I disagree; you must learn what followed." Realising Sadie wasn't giving way, Ruth lay back in her chair, so Sadie carried on. "We were all that grateful to you. Sam and Fay told us what happened and how brave you were. The police found your locket and the photo inside. They told us you had been on their wanted list for other terrible crimes, including murder. Although Sam refused to confirm their suspicions, the police were convinced you were responsible for Jerry's death. They questioned Mum and Dad for a long time because they suspected they knew where to find you." Sadie sighed. "Poor wee Fay was in a terrible state. It took ages for her to get over what that monster did. Sam was arrested for complicity in murder. The coroner's report said he was in no physical condition to do so much damage to Jerry's skull. The court sent him to prison for two years for his refusal to implicate you. Sweet man, he never once gave you away. He lived with us for a while and then moved back to his hometown when he came out. We had a letter a year to say he was getting married and moving abroad, and after that, we lost touch. Dad wanted to find you, but we had no idea where to start, so we always hoped somehow you would contact us."

"How selfish was I? I never thought he'd get into trouble. I wish I could have thanked him." Ruth cried in misery.

"Ruth, my poor wee hen, don't get upset," consoled Sadie. "Sam had no regrets, said so many times when we visited him, and even joked he was a hero to someone. Then we saw you all in the national papers and on the news. None of us believed you killed your own bairn. As for the other stuff, I am sure you had a good reason. There's no way I would think less of you." Sadie stroked her arm, "I haven't said before in case I upset you. I go to Lucy's grave each year with a bunch of flowers. The family arranged for a small headstone. Strange, though, I always find a tiny bunch of primroses tied up with a pink ribbon. Never a card through."

"Thank you. I often thought about my baby lying in an unmarked grave" Ruth's voice broke with emotion. "I can't tell how much that put my mind at ease." She explained, "The primroses are put there by a family who took me in. I had nowhere else to go."

"How sweet," breathed Sadie. "I wanted to see you, but no one would tell me where you were as I wasnae family. But fate took a hand and led me to you."

"I'm so glad it did," Ruth's voice cracked with emotion. "You were my salvation, Sadie. I was sinking into an endless deep black hole. I had long, empty years stretching before me with no escape. You drew me out and showed me I still had someone who cared and a reason to live and...."

"Och now, don't take on, so." Sadie stopped her mid-sentence, "this hasna been a one-way street, you bam pot. I needed you as much as you needed me." She told Ruth her father and mother moved out of the tenements into a modem house with a garden. The children had grown up families and led fulfilled lives. As if brushing away the past, Sadie dusted her hands together and kissed Ruth on the cheek. "Now all done, let's talk about lighter things."

"Good", retorted Ruth. "Now, how about you, Sadie? What happened in your life? Why did you never marry?" Ruth asked? "You were so popular with the boys."

"Well, that's true." Sadie grinned." I had loads of boyfriends, must be my Scottish charms, eh." She nudged Ruth. "I loved all the cuddles and that. I ran off like a scared rabbit when they got frisky or wanted to take things further. My favourite books and films are those ye ken a tall, dark, handsome hero sweeps the girl off her feet, and they live happily ever after. I dreamt about it many times but never found my hero." Glancing up beneath her lower lids, she said. "This will make you smile; I even wondered if maybe I was frigid. As women always seemed attracted to me, I thought, why not find out if it was the way for me? I enjoyed their company more than the boys. Even tried sleeping with some. I did experience arousal but felt only friendship, so nothing lasted. Got bored and moved on to the next affair. Searching for something or someone else, I suppose we're not different, except I was an unpaid lesbian whore." Sadie roared with laughter. "So, took to nursing and found I enjoyed working with disabled people. Because of that, I could help you. I never thought that life had passed me by. I stayed single by choice and never had a man. I'm still a virgin."

On fine evenings, Sadie wheeled Ruth along the sea wall walk, where they would watch the small fishing boats returning to the harbour with the day's catch. The setting was idyllic and so peaceful. Ruth mused this lovely place; all my troubles seemed to fly away on the sea breeze.

A smartly dressed woman walking her dog caught their eye as they approached the sea wall. Ruth gasped, recognising it was Viviane, the upper-class prostitute from the club. She glanced as she passed by, only to turn around and retraced her footsteps until she stood before Ruth.

"Well, I never! It is you after all these years, little Ruth. I can't believe it! Fancy running into you" Touching the wheelchair, bent down, her voice full of concern, Viviane asked: "Whatever happened to you, my dear."

"Just an accident," mumbled Ruth, wishing the pavement would swallow her up, and fixed her attention on the small dog struggling to climb onto her lap.

"Get down, Pippen, you little pest," Viviane ordered. "I can see he likes you. Not lost your way with the men, then."Clasping Ruth's hands, she continued. "I am so sorry, how terrible for you. You should have kept in contact. I called the club several times, but you disappeared. Last I heard, you were serving time for getting rid of that rat, Rego. That deserved a medal, not prison," standing upright, she smoothed down her skirt. "Time marches on and catches up with us all. I'm semi-retired, so I left London and bought myself a place around here." Turned her attention to Sadie and offered out her hand. "Hello, my name's Viviane. I worked with Ruth many years ago. Do you look after her? You have my utmost admiration, so dedicated. I could never do it. I could tell you a few things about this one." she laughed, wagging a manicured finger in Ruth's direction. "I'm late for an appointment with a gentleman friend." Viviane winked knowingly at Ruth, took out a notepad and scribbled down her phone number. "Call me soon; now, give him his walk," then she waved goodbye.

Gasping in awe, Sadie watched as Viviane glided away. "Wow! Who was that?" Sadie babbled, "Talk about oozing class. She's gorgeous and so elegant. A good friend of yours? She's so friendly and talks posh but not stuck up. What about that suit, pure silk? I bet it cost a packet."

"Just someone I used to know," grunted Ruth.

"What!" Sadie leaned over the chair. "Is that it? Tell me more; she's got something about her. Where did you meet her? Everything about her screams money by the bucket. I'd love to meet her again. Come on, Ruth, give me all the gossip."

"Not the gossip you want to hear, trust me." Ruth tore up the note and let the pieces flutter away.

"Why did you do that? She seemed so nice."

"Not now, Sadie; I'm tired. Let's go home," Ruth snapped.

Sadie clattered around in the kitchen, preparing supper. Confused by Ruth's strange mood thought it best to leave her alone when Ruth called out.

"That can wait, Sadie; I must talk to you." Ruth didn't want to leave Sadie ignorant of the truth; for it to come out later from Vivienne would be more than she could take.

"Be done in a minute," shouted Sadie.

"For God's sake, Sadie, leave it. Come here" Sadie, taken aback by her tone of voice, scurried to face her.

"Ruth, whatever is the matter? Are you angry with me? What have I done?"

"No, not angry, but I need to talk with you before I lose my nerve. I know you read my case notes, Sadie, and your kind heart didn't condemn me, but I want to tell you everything."

"No need to dwell on the past. We're fine as we are." Sadie interrupted.

"That is just it, Sadie; my past is part of who I am." Reaching out her hand, Ruth drew Sadie to her side. "This is important. I want you to know all the details, and then if you send me away, I'll understand." Drawing a deep breath, Ruth played out all her past from the beginning. Her eyes sparkled as she related her time with Violet and Eddie and the gipsy family that gave her so much love and affection. Continuing in a stilted tone, Ruth told of the abortion and her time on the streets.

"Stop now," Sadie implored, "I canna bear the pain in your voice."

"No, I must clear the way, so we will have no secrets. Sit quiet and listen now before I lose the courage to tell you what returns in my dreams and nightmares." Ruth told her all about Andrew, her only true love and how much she missed him. "There was never anyone else who could capture my heart, but there was my Lucy to remember him. I regret Mary dying in the washhouse, and I wish I could have explained what happened to Ted; he was kind to me. It was a pure accident; I bore her no malice." Her lips curled in rage," however, those who hurt me so much deserved to die. I lost no sleep for my actions. Fury blinded me; I planned nothing. For all those bad things, I may be destined for hell. Still, most of my life been hellish anyway; I'll dance with the devil when my time comes." Ruth hesitated, swallowed back a lump in her throat, and then related her time with Rego, Lucy's death, and all that led to that terrible act. "Until the day you came back into my life, I wanted to die and escape. You gave me a reason to live with your friendship, and I thank you." Emotionally drained, she shook uncontrollably; long, drawn out sobs racked her body, releasing all the pain and hurt long held inside.

Sadie gathered her in her arms, patting and stroking her. "There, now hen, all in the past. Now nothing you said changed my opinion of you. My dearest friend. Your life has been horrific, and your good times so few. It seems to me you've been a victim of circumstances. As for sending you away, no chance! What would I do without you? I'm afraid you're stuck with me until the end. We shan't speak of the past anymore." Sadie held her close, rocking her like a child. Ruth fell asleep, held in Sadie's loving arms. She woke, shocked to see tears streaming down her dear friend's face.

"What's the matter, Sadie?" Ruth asked, alarmed

"I'm fine; eyes are sore. I must get tested for new glasses." Sadie responded, but her voice broke as she turned away and walked towards the kitchen.

"Don't go, Sadie, come sit beside me. I've known for some time your feelings towards me went deeper than friendship. My first reaction was to dismiss the thought of reciprocating, but now I feel the same about you."

Sadie rushed to her side. "Ruth, do you mean it? You're not just kind". Sadie looked deep into Ruth's face, trying to read her expression. "When I saw you again, I realised it was you missing from my life. All those days when I sat by your bed, I told you many times about how much I loved you." Sadie held her hands. "It was only that you couldn't hear me that gave me the courage." Sadie struggled to speak. "Ruth, my heart always belonged to you." She gazed into Ruth's eyes. "Please don't just say these kind of things if you don't mean the words. I couldn't bear it."

Cupping the sweet tear-stained face in her hands, Ruth smiled. "No-no-no, Sadie, not kind. In fact, entirely selfish. What can I offer you this broken body?"

"Your love is all I ask for. I'm not looking for a full sexual relationship," replied Sadie, breathless, sheer delight radiating from her.

"Just as well, then"" responded Ruth. With a quiet sigh said, "I can never give you anything else. There can be no response or arousal from me. Can you cope with that?"

"You still have a heart to give, don't you?" said Sadie, "I won't rush you, Ruth. I want nothing to spoil what we have now." Sadie pushed back her hair and wiped the tears of joy away. "Ruth, tell me when I touch your upper body, you can feel my hands, right?"

Ruth nodded.

"Well, then, dopey, all's not lost. I'm sure I can stir something up. I might surprise you."

Sadie Ruth protested. "Hold on, I'm not sure. I am not ready."

"I'm not suggesting I leap on you now." Sadie sniggered, "Not saying the thought doesn't appeal." She walked towards the kitchen. "Don't worry, I won't rush you. Let's take one day at a time. We will know when the time is right. Not sure I have a sexual urge left in me. I don't see why I shouldn't die virgin pure; it's too late to change now."

Sadie brought the supper in. After they'd finished, she cleared away the dishes. Then Sadie pushed Ruth out to the veranda, and they sat together in the dimming light, relaxed and secure. Months later, as Ruth lay in bed watching the stars, silent tears fell as she returned to her past, remembering all lost. Sadie slipped into bed beside her.

"Dinna cry, Ruth, anymore, I will always be here to comfort you. We canna change our past, but we can look to a bright future together." Sadie began stroking and fondling her body. She snuggled her head between Ruth's breasts, running her tongue over each nipple, teasing them into firmness. Ruth's senses responded to Sadie's light touch. Being together and sharing this moment was right.

Sadie whispered. "It's time now. Are you ready?" Ruth sighed and nodded in response. Sadie raised her head and kissed the anxious face. Taking Ruth's hand showed her how to slide and caress, guiding her patiently as hesitant, inquisitive flickering fingers explored her dear friend's quivering body. Sadie moaned in exquisite delight. This was the love she had been waiting for. Uncomplicated, undemanding, and perfect. Ruth felt long-forgotten emotions rising with no regrets, succumbed to the growing waves of desire. It had taken forty-two helter-skelter years for her to find such peace. Ruth held Sadie to her and vowed to never let her go. They lay together that night, locked in each other's arms. Ruth's wandering life was over. At last, she'd found a home and crossed the final stepping stone.

THE END

Ingram Content Group UK Ltd.
Milton Keynes UK
UKHW010614280623
424142UK00001B/21